New York
State Facts

Nickname:	Empire State
Date Entered Union:	July 26, 1788 (the 11th state)
Motto:	*Excelsior* (Higher.)
New York Men:	Humphrey Bogart, *actor*
	George Gershwin, *composer*
	Edward Hopper, *painter*
	John D. Rockefeller, *industrialist*
	Theodore Roosevelt, *U.S. President*
	Walt Whiteman, *poet*
Bird:	Bluebird
Flower:	Rose
Fun Facts:	New York City has 722 miles of subway track. Niagara Reservation became the first state park in the United States.

"Don't," he said. **"Don't *understand*. Don't identify with me.**

"That's where we began *and* ended," Paolo continued. "I couldn't...live through it again. You stay on your side of the past, I'll stay on mine and we'll be fine."

"Will we?" Laura asked quietly. "I'm not fine. I look at you, and I'm not okay. I think of you, and I come apart inside. You reach for me, and I remember the times we touched and the times we didn't and it's like seeing some hope I had dumped into the ocean, and I'm *not fine*, Paolo. Not fine at all."

"You think I am?"

"Aren't you?"

"No."

"No?" she asked, daring him like a grown-up child to be honest.

"No," he stated. "I'm not."

Paolo remembered vividly how it felt to be skin-to-skin with her. Remembered the many times she'd opened her heart and taken him in. Remembered how strangely peaceful it had been to simply love her.

And wanted to again.

American
HEROES
AGAINST ALL ODDS

Winter Beach

Terese
RAMIN

Silhouette Books

Published by Silhouette Books

America's Publisher of Contemporary Romance

To Jeanne Savery Casstevens and Joan Shapiro—otherwise known as
cattle prod and bullwhip—for living up to their aka's;

To Joyce A. Flaherty, agent, and Leslie Wainger, editor, with love and
gratitude for their patience and their willingness to beat me about the
head and ears whenever I forgot to believe in the possibilities;

And to Melissa Senate, editor, for trusting me:
My inadequate thanks for a gift without measure.

For Laura

SILHOUETTE BOOKS
300 East 42nd St.,
New York, N. Y. 10017

ISBN 0-373-82230-8

WINTER BEACH

Copyright © 1993 by Terese Daly Ramin

Printed in U.S.A.

About the Author

Terese Ramin lives in Michigan with her husband, two children, two dogs, two cats and an assortment of strays. When not writing romance novels, she writes chancel dramas, sings alto in the church choir, plays the guitar, yells at her children to pick up their rooms (even though she keeps telling herself that she won't) and responds with silence when they ask her where they should put their rooms after they've picked them up.

A full-fledged believer in dreams, the only thing she's ever wanted to do is write. After years of dreaming without doing anything about it, she finally wrote her first romance novel, *Water from the Moon*, which won a Romance Writers of America Golden Heart Award in 1987 and was published by Silhouette in 1989. Her subsequent books have appeared on the Waldenbooks romance bestseller list. She is also the recipient of a 1991 *Romantic Times Magazine* Reviewer's Choice Award. She hasn't dreamed without acting for a long time.

Books by Terese Ramin

Silhouette Intimate Moments

Water from the Moon #279
Winter Beach #477
A Certain Slant of Light #634
Five Kids, One Christmas #680
An Unexpected Addition #793
Mary's Child #881
Instant Wife #965
A Drive-By Wedding #981

Silhouette Special Edition

Accompanying Alice #656

Dear Reader,

When Paolo Gianini first took shape in my head I told him "Look, buddy, you're a secondary character, no way will I write a book just for you, it's way too hard." Fortunately, Paolo didn't listen. He introduced me to Laura, the woman of his dreams, then began to tell me not only their story, but also *his* story. Sucker that I am for dark, intense guys whose hearts are in the right place, but who have trouble showing that heart to their women, I listened.

Winter Beach is unlike any book I've ever written. It tore my heart out, but the experience was one of the most rewarding of my life. In the writing I met two characters who made me dig deep inside myself before I could understand them—and then they trusted me with all of themselves, both good and not so, something even the best of characters won't always do. They shared with me their possibilities and taught me a lot about myself in the process.

I also got to spend a lot of time "visiting" New York state, one of my favorite places. I love the Atlantic coastline, especially in winter, love to prowl the beaches, feel the power in the cold and the wind. I also love Manhattan. The island teems with life, sights, sounds, smells, languages, foods, people—it's incredibly different from where I live in the Midwest!

Anyway…here's *Winter Beach*. I hope it touches you as much as it touched me. And may you find a way to reach your dreams the way Paolo and Laura helped me to achieve one of mine.

Cheerfully,

Terese Ramin

Chapter 1

The cloud cover was heavy, unbroken to the horizon.

Paolo Gianini stepped out of the salt-browned stand of scrub pines along the side of Laura's house and into the chill wind sweeping the Long Island coastline. The unbuttoned jacket of his gray silk suit whipped about his back, and the cuffs of his trousers flapped around his ankles when he paused to get his bearings. His attention focused on the activity on the beach. Below him, plainclothes and uniformed police spread along the rocky shoreline, searching for the body. A coast guard helicopter, buffeted by the breeze, hovered a few yards offshore; below it, a pair of divers surfaced in the slate-colored waves.

On the beach just above the wave line, a uniformed officer slid a pair of men's leather boat moccasins into a white paper evidence bag, while a second did the same with a pile of neatly folded clothes. The clothing was part of a classic beachfront suicide scenario, a testament to the state of calmness that frequently succeeded the decision and preceded the act.

Kill yourself, but be tidy about it, Paolo thought. Contain the mess. Like going on vacation.

His mouth twisted. The folded clothes, the straightened home, the highlighted clauses in an insurance policy, were the only part of a suicide that was ever neat. The true disasters lay where they always had, underneath the pristine surface, lurking in depths. Left to the survivors to find and take care of. Even now, twenty years after his sister Lisetta's suicide, he was still unraveling threads, sifting through the emotional mess—

Paolo blinked himself back to the here and now. The officer with the clothes was having trouble juggling them into the evidence bag one-handed. They see-sawed a bit on her arm, and then the white sweater at the top of the pile slipped, partially unfolding as it fell to the sand.

At the sight of it, something inside Paolo twisted in involuntary revulsion. Even at this distance, the fisherman-knit pattern was visible. Laura had made him a sweater just like it for Christmas the year before their marriage had gone to hell.

The rancid taste of bitterness rose like bile in his throat. Sand-and-salt-misted wind burned his face, and he blinked, finding her face where it too often was, lurking behind his eyelids. Laura. The second of his two ex-wives, the one he'd loved most. Or maybe he'd only thought so at the time. His memory had a bad habit of romanticizing the past, so it was hard to remember the truth about these things anymore.

He rubbed a hand across his mouth in a useless effort to massage away the sudden stiffness in his jaw. Being bitter about the past wasn't healthy, but it was something he did well. Why couldn't he simply accept the fact that everyone made mistakes, that what she'd done, what he'd done—what *they'd* done, or not done, to each other—shouldn't matter anymore?

But it did. After five years, he still reached for her sometimes in the night, felt her beside him like phantom pain in an amputated limb. God, *Laura.*

Damn, Paolo thought, he didn't need this. Why had he come?

Because Laura needed, and unforgotten love died hard.

Cursing the inexplicable vagaries of his heart, he turned at the sound of iron scraping on patio tile, automatically taking in the white-painted wrought-iron table and chairs left out for use on the few remaining nice mornings of November. The patio furniture was one of the pettier things he and Laura had fought about: Winter came early here, and he'd hated having to wrestle the heavy stuff out of hurricane winds and sheeting ice merely because Laura liked to greet the changing seasons with espresso on the terrace.

He eyed the huge sun umbrella, closed and sheathed against the elements, as though it were to blame for everything, then noted the reflections of the furniture in the curtained glass door-wall behind it and the unwelcome ripple of human disturbance across the scene. The balding, going-to-paunch Treasury agent who'd wakened him at Laura's insistence two hours before with the news of Gus's apparent suicide tamped a cigarette against the glass tabletop and stuck it in his mouth without lighting it. Paolo regarded Talon's presence with suspicion. The man was hard, smart and abrasive, moved beyond the need for explanation by access to power. No matter which direction the preliminary evidence pointed, no matter what he'd told Paolo on the phone, if Talon was involved, nobody suspected that Laura's partner, Angus Abernathy, had killed himself.

"Little early for the IRS, isn't it?" he observed.

"Early worms," Talon suggested laconically, then skipped the rest of the amenities. "She's inside. Get her to talk."

"What makes you think she'll talk to me?" Paolo was stalling, and he knew it. "We're not exactly close."

"Trust. She asked for you. You came."

Talon waved insight like a flag, challenging response. Paolo's jaw tightened, the joint clicked in recognition of the truth. His professional path had crossed the government employee's off and on for well over ten years now, but Talon's uncanny intelligence and ability to size up a situation never ceased to irritate. Talon was a man who used his facts-on-file government intelligence—and his contacts—well. Paolo's marital history with Laura was a matter of public record. His leftover feelings for her were not. The cost of civility rose to a premium. "What do you want her to say?" he asked.

Talon shrugged. "We want to know about her partner's activities over the past few weeks. You know the drill—who he saw, who he talked to, what he did—with whom...." Innuendo trailed away when he looked at Paolo for reaction and got none. Dismissing his failure to find a target in the dark, he continued, "We also want a client list, including records. And we want to know about her involvement in Abernathy's activities."

Paolo glanced at the beach, covering sharpened interest. Was that a threat he heard? "Why?"

"We were about to bring Abernathy in as a material witness in a mob investigation. The suicide note she found taped to the computer inside apologized for leaving her to deal with his mess, but said he couldn't face what he'd done. I can believe that, but the rest of this suicide bull is too convenient. I don't like conveniences. Tell her that."

Paolo studied him. It was an old routine: when the FBI, ATF, DEA or any of the numerous other specialized federal agencies that investigated suspected criminal activities couldn't find enough evidence to produce arrests, they tossed the bone to the IRS. A top-notch, if somewhat cutthroat, criminal investigator, Talon was, as Paolo had reason to know, late of both Alcohol, Tobacco and Firearms, and the Drug Enforcement Administration, and had served time with Customs and Immigration. In his three years as a special investigator for Internal Revenue, Talon had made an art of uncovering tax evasion scams and jailing drug dealers and mobsters who'd covered their tracks everywhere else. He had a mean personal conviction record, and far more enemies in the world than friends. And now he was after Gus.

And that meant Laura was under investigation, too.

The instinct to protect her rose uninvited. "In other words," Paolo said curtly, "Internal Revenue doesn't have enough evidence for probable cause, so you couldn't arrest Abernathy and you couldn't get a warrant to search and seize, am I right? And now that he's gone, you want me to see if I can get enough out of her cause to give you cause to use her, instead of him."

Talon shrugged a negligent assent without apology. Paolo turned on his heel and headed back the way he'd come, Talon in step with him. No matter how he felt toward Laura personally, he wouldn't help anyone bury her in Talon's version of the legal system.

"Do your own dirty work, Talon."

"I did. She told me to get a warrant and talk to her attorney."

Paolo stopped at the edge of the terrace and swallowed an involuntary smile. That sounded like the Laura he knew, quick-witted and sharp-tongued if anyone tried to step on her toes. "Smart woman."

Talon nodded. "Maybe too smart. Abernathy wasn't playing with gentlemen. They won't care whether she knows anything or not. Where they live, everybody's got a price, and what they *think* is all that counts. Proof means nothing, and gender means squat. The way they think, all women are whores one way or another anyway. They want something from her, they won't ask nice."

There was something in the Treasury agent's voice that made Paolo's stock response to grim federal predictions die unspoken. He studied Talon. "Give me a name," he said softly.

Talon eyed him for a minute, then wasted silent seconds looking at the beach before speaking a single word. "Dunne."

Adrenaline beat a sudden response in Paolo's veins; his attention keened. "William Dunne?"

"In one."

Paolo stared. He'd met Dunne once at a reception in Scarsdale. The reputed crime don had impressed him as intelligent, sane, and stone-cold dangerous. He reassessed the federal agent. "How sure are you Dunne's involved?"

"Can't prove a damned thing. Yet."

"That's not what I asked."

"I know." Talon's odd eyes—one hazel, the other mud brown—measured Paolo. "You gonna deal with me?"

"You gonna lie to me?"

Talon conceded the possibility with a one-shoulder shrug. "Whatever it takes to get the bad guys."

"You're a real sweetheart, Talon."

"Ain't trust grand?"

Paolo felt the muscles along his neck and shoulders tighten. Even when it could be used to his advantage, he hated this game of intimidate, outfox and control; he played it too often, with too many different opponents. "You're wasting my time, Talon."

"Gotten precious, has it?" Talon began, but then he seemed to catch the danger signals that warned him he was about to lose his fish, and he changed his tack. "You tell anyone this came from me, I'll deny it."

Paolo nodded impatiently. That was a given. Always.

Talon sucked air between his teeth, worked it around his gums for an instant. "We got an undercover in tight with Dunne. Two years we get nothing back on the investment but static. Five months ago we hear a whisper with Abernathy's name on it. With a little luck, we'll seize your ex-wife's office and Abernathy's apartment in the Village in about an hour. Ought to get a warrant for this place within two. I'd put my pension on this one.''

"You think she's involved." The idea shocked Paolo; he hadn't felt shock for years.

"Probable cause, babe." Talon dismissed suspicion as academic. "She's living off the proceeds."

Realization dawned. Paolo viewed Talon with contempt. "You self-aggrandizing bastard. You want to retire on this."

Talon didn't deny it. "I want Dunne. Whatever it takes. And it'd sure beat a gold watch all to hell."

"Popular means, emotional ends, and what's a few casualties or ruined reputations along the way when they're justified by a big payoff, right?" There was menace in the statement, and Talon heard it.

He moved to the terrace railing, glanced back at Paolo. "Your emotion's showing, Gianini. Better watch that. Besides—" He rolled his still-unlit cigarette between his fingers, then flicked it over the railing toward the beach. "Your lady's got a smart attorney, and there's always court. Let the shysters figure it out."

Paolo felt the blood pound in his temples, imprisoned fury like a physical substance in his fist. Gratifying as beating Talon to a pulp might be, soothing his baser instincts at the moment would hardly do either him or Laura any good. He drew air through his nose, blew anger out of his system by expelling it through his mouth. He'd deal with Talon later. Voice flat, he asked, "Does she know about the warrants?"

Talon smiled. He enjoyed jerking hotshot civilians like Gianini around. It relieved the boredom. "We told her, but she's pretty shook up. Whether it went in or not..." He let speculation hang.

"Hell," Paolo said.

Talon nodded. "It will be. For her."

Without another word, Paolo stepped across the terrace and slid open the door in the glass wall behind them. The drapes that prevented the house's interior from being viewed from the beach belled outward at the release of pressure. With one last glance at the ocean below, Paolo shoved the drapes aside and stepped into Laura's house.

Laura started and clutched her grandmother's favorite dulcimer hard at the sound of voices on the terrace, trying to school the panic hammering in her lungs. Oh, God, this was getting out of hand. Every sound, every breath, spooked her—had for months. She couldn't live like this anymore.

But, as the hooded man who'd broken into her office last night had assured her before he'd stuck her in the windowless bathroom and locked the door, she had no place to run, nowhere to hide that they wouldn't find her.

"Don't worry, pretty lady, you'll be all right." She could still hear the scratchy whisper in her ear. *"I'm just here to let your partner know we mean business—shake him up, if you see what I mean. Tell him that. Then tell him that I left without hurting you—this time."*

He'd scared the hell out of her, trashed the office, and gone without saying exactly what he wanted from Gus. She didn't like being scared. Fright had a tendency to enervate rather than adrenalize her.

She'd been scared a lot lately, listening for whispers in the dark, full of some persistent dread from a source she couldn't name. Been too frightened to name, maybe, Laura admitted with shame.

Tiny tongues of anger licked suddenly at her bloodstream; her hand tightened until the dulcimer's strings grooved her fingers. She wished to hell she knew what *they* wanted so that she could stick it to the frightening bastards by giving the information to someone who'd use it to take them down. She also wished to hell she knew who *they* were.

Her stomach cramped swiftly in sickening fear. Well, no, not really, she didn't.

Better the devil you know, the perverse little demon who lived inside her head argued. Fingers kneading the dulcimer's neck, Laura shook the voice off. Not always it wasn't. Sometimes not knowing was infinitely better. Healthier. Happier.

Safer, she thought bleakly.

Oh, God, it has been a long twenty-four hours.

Early yesterday her partner, Angus "Gus" Abernathy, had come into the office on top of the world, pulled her out of her chair and waltzed her around, telling her he was about to pull off the financial coup that would give Abernathy and Associates the world by the tail. Then he'd left, still laughing, gaily urging her to close the office, cruise the Caribbean, he'd be gone a few days, too.

Two hours later, Special Agent Talon of the United States Treasury Department, Income Tax Division, had shown up at the office to cast suspicion on an Angus Abernathy she didn't know, suggesting things she couldn't believe. Things, she was shocked to discover later, she hadn't been surprised to hear. Then Talon had left, too, handing her his card with clipped instructions to call immediately if she heard from Gus. Promising her—or had it been a threat, perhaps?—that they'd talk again.

She'd spent the rest of yesterday trying to locate Gus, following a crisscrossing computerized trail of stripped agency bank accounts that led to hidden agency bank accounts that wound through a maze of agency acquisitions and assets she hadn't known existed—all of them in her name, his mother's name, or the name of a lover Laura thought Gus had discarded three years before. By the time she'd gotten to the confused string of airline, train and bus tickets he'd bought, refunded, reserved again, then left unused, she was exhausted and soul sick, wondering exactly who this man was that she'd thought she'd known.

It wasn't the first time she'd thought she knew a man and found she didn't.

Paolo...

She scrubbed a fist across her aching eyes, rubbed tired fingers through the salt tracks dried on her cheeks. But that was history; better not to think about it now. History was about who you'd been, and it ordained the future by whatever lessons you took from it. Her granddad used to say the future should be best friends with the past—which was true as far as it went, except that she and this part of her past weren't on speaking terms.

She'd have to face Paolo—have to face herself, and how badly she wanted him here—soon enough. Right now she had other things to distract her, deeds to face, mistakes to sort out. Reasons to understand...

Can't find logic where there isn't any. More homespun grand-father wisdom.

She stroked the smooth oiled cherrywood of the mountain instrument in her hand, comforting herself with its familiarity. Back home in the shelter of the Adirondacks, in northern Essex County, nasty things had happened, but never without explanation. Motives were always up front, never hidden; everybody always knew why bad things happened: Eli was drunk and got careless with his knife; Jerome provoked Gary's rage by stealing his wife; Marge Hancock's baby was born too early and the doctor came too late. People died for a reason. Not necessarily a good reason, but a reason nonetheless. Not like this. Not like Gus, on a beach by himself, by his own choice.

She particularly couldn't understand that. Not over something he supposedly couldn't face.

Laura bowed her head. She'd known Gus for twenty-three years, since her family moved from the mountains to Buffalo when she was eleven and he was fourteen. Suicide wasn't his style. No matter what he'd ever done—and once or twice in twenty-three years he'd done some incredibly stupid things, God, who hadn't?—he'd always faced up to his mistakes in the end. Hemmed and hawed a bit sometimes, occasionally tried pretty hard to squirm away, but in the end he'd fess up and pay the piper, despite the cost to himself. That was why, if he was dead, she couldn't believe he'd killed himself.

That and something the man who'd accosted her last night had said—something she couldn't quite remember, that made her think Gus wasn't really dead at all, that this was all a sham, a show produced by someone she couldn't see and put on for whose benefit she didn't know—which didn't make it better or less frightening or anything.

A great stuffy sob of ironic bravado found its way out of her lungs. In fact, if he wasn't already dead, she'd kill Gus herself when she found him. If she found him.

Damn it, where was Paolo?

Shoulders shaking, she slumped forward, elbow on the dining room table in front of her, face in her hand, and let the tears slide through her fingers. Damn him anyway, damn him to hell.

Who? Gus—or Paolo?

Both, she thought wearily. Hiccuping a bleary sigh, she

smeared moist emotion across her face. God help her, for different reasons she needed them both.

Loved them both as much as they'd hated one another.

Never did have the sense God gave a flea to love what's good for ya, was her mother's favorite gripe.

Learned it from somewhere, Ma. Learned it from you.

She hadn't talked to her mother in three years.

Silence closed around her in the sudden *thud-thud-thud* of a departing helicopter.

Laura jerked erect, breath caught, heart stopped, listening…for footsteps on the terrace, for the triumphant mechanical crackle announcing the operation's success. For voices professionally hushed out of respect for the living.

Hope and dread burned deep, scarring swaths inside her. Hope to have it over, dread that it was over. Had they found Gus? In the waves, on the rocks, washed ashore… Had they? Every breath she took seared her lungs with waiting.

She wished for numbness, but her wish went unheard.

The voices on the terrace changed. She recognized Talon's lazy gravel-pit imitation, canted her head to catch the other voice, daring to overhear what she couldn't bring herself to get up and ask. The murmur rose and fell, almost indecipherable. Then she recognized him.

He'd worked hard to lose the accent, but, faint as it was through the triple panes of heavy glass and thick curtains, she heard it underneath the careful American: Italian tinged with the British inflections of his boarding school English instructor.

When he'd first decided to stay in the States, Paolo had taken classes to Americanize himself, homogenize himself and his voice so that he could better blend in with his surroundings— go unnoticed, he said, be discreet—and deliberately schooled himself not to resort to Italian excla-mations, endearments, gestures. He'd become a creature of his own creation, the original self-made man.

The effort had been largely successful, but Paolo was sometimes, Laura knew, uncomfortable in his adopted image. The natural inclinations of his culture and heritage, trying to sneak underneath his vigilance, often caught him unawares and unprepared. Passion and impatience, pride and honor, the will to dominate and the ability to compromise, were a volatile mix in the person of an Italian Catholic man taught from the cradle that family honor was paramount and to dishonor the family was a crime above all else; that, no matter what misery was involved, marriage vows were sacred and divorce a mortal sin; that lying was justified when used to protect the uninformed; that women were icons to be cosseted and kept home where they could care for a man and his children, left in the dark about his business dealings—no matter what they were.

That is, all women except his partners, Acasia Jones and Julianna Burrows.

Envy, old and crabby, rose from deep hibernation inside her. Damn, she'd hated his double standards—hated his partners for the kind of fraternity they shared with him that she could not. He'd never talked about "Casie" and "Jules" much, but they'd been there, always there, residing in the background of her marriage, where they didn't belong; the first people he called when there was trouble, the last people he checked in with at night. His damned partners, not his wife.

"Come to bed, Paolo."

"I've just got to check in with the office, I'll be there in a minute."

In an instant, all the reasons she'd loved Paolo—the same reasons that she'd divorced him—flashed through Laura, burning away the fog of the morning's events. Relief was a dizzying, galling sensation fizzing through her bloodstream, into her limbs. At the same time that her heart sang with elation—*"He's here, he'll take care of it!"*—her spirit recoiled in chagrin because she wanted him to "take care of it." Needed him to take care of her.

Badly.

She shut her eyes, covered her mouth with a hand, breathing...breathing. Deep calming breaths, struggling for control. God, she couldn't let him see how badly she needed him here—couldn't let him see the toll five years without him had taken. The whole thing would start all over again if she did; he'd burrow his way back into her heart, take possession of her soul, and she wouldn't let that happen. She needed his help—his *professional* help—to sort out this thing with Gus and the federal government, to find her friend and partner and prove Talon's suspicions wrong.

That was all.

Yeah, right, the sarcastic voice inside her said. Laura ignored it. With a swiftness born of years of practice, she clamped a lid on her emotions and rose from the table to cross the living room and hang the dulcimer in its customary spot on the wall. The voices on the terrace rose and fell; she flinched from the sound of animosity in them, turned to flee, then caught herself and recrossed the room at a graceful pace, not running from what threatened her. She headed for the bathroom to throw up, wash her face and put on the cool, unfeeling mask her sanity demanded she wear to face Paolo.

Chapter 2

The room was dark and close, smelled clean. Smelled of Laura.

Paolo stood in the cloistered dimness, letting his eyes adjust, lungs trapped within the claustrophobic confines of his rib cage. He couldn't breathe without tasting her. Her fragrance, warmer but more intangible than perfume, clung to the air, sent little shock waves of heat skirling toward the small of his back, splaying into his belly. Intoxicating. Blood shimmied excitedly through his veins, and his lungs contracted.

He shut his eyes. Seven years ago in Atlanta, she'd stood behind him during a reception the first night of a business security conference. Divorced that day, he'd been emotionally ripe for trouble. Before he'd ever seen her, he'd known her by her scent. Within two hours they'd been in her bed. Within three weeks he'd married her. Two years later they'd divorced.

The scent of her always made it impossible to think.

Damn, he thought again. Get off it, Gianini. Think with your brains around her for a change, would you? Thinking with anything else buys trouble.

He blinked, struggling to inhibit his instinctive desire for her by looking at her home. She'd redecorated since he'd been here last. The carpet under his feet was light-colored, deep and springy and sound-swallowing. The furniture, too, was light and plush, furthering the impression of being caught in a soundless white vacuum.

But it wasn't *white,* of course, Paolo knew. The colors Laura chose were lacy and elusive: "champagne," "Chantilly," ... colors that absorbed mood and atmosphere from subtle accents. He felt his nerves tighten, his muscles bunch. Colors that would sterilize her memories of him so that she could share the house with someone else.

You didn't have to come, he reminded himself harshly. You could have said no; you could have sent Burrows—

"Paolo?"

Laura's voice was low and tentative; his shocked response to it was immediate. He turned and found her dark figure on the threshold of the bedroom hallway. Cast in shadow, she looked the way he remembered her, sleek and unruffled, in control. Her fine dark hair was swept up, away from her face; her skin would be clear, almost translucent, he knew, a gift from her Norwegian ancestors.

Again his body responded to better memories of her, indifferent to his unruly thoughts. *Damn,* he thought. He should have sent Burrows. No one got to him like Laura.

He shook himself, adjusting his emotions by force while he watched her straighten and sway—tiredly, cautiously—toward him. Where Laura was concerned, appearances often lied, suggested things that were patently untrue: that she was serene, collected, havenlike—

Safe...

He shook his head, annoyed with the Madonna image, and looked for another word to describe what he first remembered about her, telling himself as he did so that it was one of the most ridiculous exercises he'd ever engaged in. He'd used up too much of the past five years looking for adjectives to describe bits and pieces of their relationship that evaded him. Somehow their entire marriage had become nothing more than a confusion of smoke and mirrors, a lie of appearances that hid the facts. A sham of things he'd wanted to see.

He blinked. He'd wanted to see so many things in her that would make his life better than it had ever been before. First love, he thought dully, should be experienced by teenagers who were young enough to recover from it, not by adults whose emotions had lost their elasticity.

Behind Laura, the house seemed to brighten as she came, as though somehow her presence caused the illumination. She stopped in front of him, toying with the dark glasses she carried, and the pale glow seemed to move around and encompass her. Seeing that illusion now, even though he knew it was caused by nothing more than his imagination and a break in the clouds outside, cut at him still....

Somewhere deep inside him, where it had no business living, he felt hope stir and say her name. *Laura...*

"I need help, Paolo," she said.

She looked at him, and suddenly hope and illusion faded and all he could see were the shadows that pain and self-doubt had left around her eyes. Pain caused by Gus.

Sentiment became bitterness in a snap.

In an instant, he forgot everything that had brought him here, forgot about remaining professional, forgot Dunne. A long time ago he'd warned her about her partner. She'd ignored him then, undoubtedly would resist him now. He turned his back on her. "What have the police told you?"

"That Gus must have committed suicide. But there's no body. He's not dead." She said it again to convince herself. "I know it."

"How do you know it, Laura? Gus always was a coward. Those half-baked deals he bragged about—one of 'em probably backfired on him harder than the rest and he didn't have the guts to face the results." He eyed her over his shoulder. "'Course, I don't know where he got the guts to drown himself, either. I figured him for the ninety-miles-an-hour-into-a-bridge-pylon type. Harder to back out at the last minute."

"You never knew him, Paolo." Emotion, passion—either or both—left tears in the corners of her eyes. She blinked and looked away, compressing her mouth into a line, tightening her control. "You hated him the first time you met him, but he was always there for me. He helped me through some rough times— took care of me when I needed him."

"Yeah, he took care of you." Paolo's voice was scornful. It wasn't the most admirable attitude, he knew, but bitterness played havoc with admirable emotions, and it seemed somehow better to feel contempt for Laura for depending on someone like Gus than to despise himself for not being there when she'd counted on him. "But that's what you wanted, wasn't it? Someone to watch over you, take care of you, bail you out when the going got tough, no matter what he wanted from you in return. When I wouldn't fall for that, you—"

"Go to hell, you bastard. When I needed help, I asked for it, period. Just because you didn't—" Anger was an all-consuming push-away feeling covering up pain, sadness, grief. Laura caught hers, put it aside with an effort; temporary states of mind had gotten the better of her all too often where Paolo was concerned. She wouldn't let this one sidetrack her now. No matter how much his accusation hurt. She swallowed. "Look, Paolo. I hurt you, you hurt me, but we're done, we're past—get over it. This isn't about either of us. This is…this is…different. Please."

Bitterness arrested by something in her voice, Paolo steepled his fingers in front of him and watched her struggle with herself. She was not a woman who begged for anything. She was a woman who hoped, expected brighter days, understanding, expected to find the best in people. She'd looked for the best in both him and Gus; they'd both failed her, but she still hoped. Still trusted them to live up to her expectations.

Paolo's hands knotted into fists, seemingly of their own volition, and his heart twisted. He'd buried love under an avalanche of lesser emotions a long time ago, but Laura's vulnerability touched him, made him hurt for her. He knew better than to see a china-like fragility in her features; she was neither made of china nor particularly fragile, was tougher than most of the big-wheel sharks he dealt with everyday—as tough, in her own way, as Dunne's reputation. He knew that.

He saw the china anyway. And cursed himself for seeing it. The hollow place she'd left inside him ached. Perception winked against his thoughts like blinking neon lights, spelling it out: *Too little, too late, stupid.* The road to self-awareness was paved with so damned many failures, mistakes he shouldn't have made—but had. And correctly diagnosing the illness didn't always ensure finding the cure. Not where Laura was concerned, anyway.

"Who's William Dunne to you, Laura?" he asked shortly, looking for a way not to feel what he felt.

"What?" Again she was bewildered, not Laura at all.

"Dunne. William. Real estate shark, owns a couple of casinos, couple of warehouses, three or four apartment buildings—"

"What are you talking—? I don't—"

"Rumored to be connected to half the crime on the East Coast—"

"What are you telling me this for? What do you want from me?" Her voice was shaky, pleading. He steeled himself to it.

"Is he a client?"

"I don't—I don't know. I don't live in Gus's pocket. We share an office, that's all. Sometimes business overlaps, but generally we have separate accounts, separate clients. He could be on Gus's private—" She stopped herself from revealing something she wasn't sure he needed to know. Trapped in ambiguous ethics, conflicting loyalties—who to talk to, who to trust, who to believe. For an intelligent woman, she felt awfully stupid.

She bit her tongue, stared at Paolo, looking for answers she knew she wouldn't find written on his face. Half hoping to find them anyway. But she didn't.

Her shoulders slumped. She knew better than to frame a question in the negative, couldn't care enough not to do it. "You're not going to help me, are you?"

Knuckles tight, Paolo looked away from her again; exhaustion, defeat and hopelessness slackened her features, tormenting him. It was their last day all over again. She'd looked like this outside the courthouse after the divorce, like she couldn't believe what they'd done, said, accused one another of. Like she wished...

He shut his eyes and felt the ghosts gathering in the darkness, knew they'd haunt him forever if he didn't face them soon: Laura, the truth, the reasons...

But not yet. He wasn't ready yet.

He swallowed. God, he thought, he couldn't be here anymore. He couldn't trust himself around her. She undid him. He craved her from the darkest, most terrifying reaches of himself, but he couldn't trust his cravings. Cravings were impatient liars in search of instant gratification. He had history to work from, and history proved Laura was bad for him—and he was bad for her.

The past ordained the future, wasn't that what she'd always said?

He should pay attention. This woman had taken him apart from his soul out once, left him hanging by thumbs in a void he'd found no way to fill. He couldn't give her the opportunity to do it again, wouldn't resurrect either his feelings for her or the bald truth about himself by getting involved with her again. Survival depended on it.

Someone else should handle this, he thought. He'd known it when Talon called, but, insensitive fool that he was, he'd come anyway. Let her hope. Cursed himself for it.

The swift cut would be kinder, heal cleaner. Abruptly he moved back to the sliding glass door. "No. I can't help you, Laura."

"No?" Despite their years of differences, she'd never expected him to say anything but yes. "Just like that, you're leaving? But I thought— You *came.*" Laura eyed him, bewildered, shivering slightly inside the high-necked sweater dress she'd worn for the past twenty-four hours. She was so cold, couldn't get warm.

She shrugged her arms tight against her sides, trying anyway. It seemed like an incredibly long time since she'd had any rest, any peace. Any warmth. This morning...last night...

Her fingers clenched suddenly, bruising her arms. Had she told the police about last night?

She swallowed convulsively, turning to hide from Paolo, her hand to her mouth. She couldn't remember, couldn't think. The world as she knew it was snowballing out of control, filling with unfamiliar things whose origins she couldn't grasp. Fear blurred everything. She didn't handle fear well, wasn't used to being afraid. Wasn't used to feeling like going to pieces and crawling to anyone—especially her ex-husband—on her belly like some abject puppy begging for protection and table scraps. Begging him to hide her inside his coat, where she could feel warm and safe against the ticking of his heart. No matter what he thought.

A tiny whimper pressed the back of her throat. Oh, God, please, she thought, not again. Don't let me fall apart in front of him.

This was a mistake.

A moan rose inside her, became a hard, silent ache somewhere between her chest and her throat. Dear God, she didn't want to need Paolo.

Too late.

"I didn't know what else to do," she said honestly, speaking more to herself than to him. "I didn't know who to call. When the police asked me who I wanted to call, I couldn't think. There isn't anyone else. Just you." She viewed Paolo with despair. "I couldn't think of anyone but you."

Paolo took a step away from the door, eyes on Laura. Despite what he'd accused her of wanting from him and Gus, he didn't really remember ever seeing her broken, fearful, unsure. Tentative sometimes, yes, who wasn't? But not this coming apart at the seams.

All at once the guilty urge to explain himself to her rose in him like a reflex. The reflex made him angry. Anger made him snap. "No. I can't help you, Laura. Not with this. Not for Gus."

Nonplussed, she stared at him; emotion flickered on her face—confusion, doubt, resignation. Then it was gone and she was Laura once again, as apparently self-contained as any woman he'd ever known. "I see," she said, and Paolo had no doubt that she did. Clearly.

Without another word she turned and went into the kitchen. Over the half-wall pass-through, Paolo watched her gather herself together as she collected a bag of coffee from the refrigerator and set up the pot. She moved as neatly as she dressed, with swift, compact self-assurance, cool and businesslike, but always, always feminine, so that you knew that beneath the efficient exterior lay the frills—and the fire.

It was that sense of things unseen that had attracted him from the start; the sense that nothing with her was ever as it appeared, that she knew the value of intimacy, that anything shared with her remained private. Not like Maria, who'd had the unpardonable tendency to violate the sanctity of their marriage by sharing every unholy detail with her parents.

Paolo swallowed, hating the vague surge of shame that thinking about Maria, comparing her to Laura, made him feel. They were nothing alike, the two women he'd married; there was nothing to compare. The only emotion his honor-bound family-arranged marriage to Maria had elicited from him was indifference; the emotion that came most readily to mind with Laura was a kaleidoscope of pure, obsessive, savage need. And he was a man who had no business needing anyone.

A sudden thud and the sound of shattering china startled him. Laura stood in the kitchen doorway, no longer pale and accepting, but vibrantly angry. "Why?"

"What?" Her stance, her beauty, threatened him; he felt defensive.

"Why did you come?"

"I don't know. I don't remember. But I'm not going to find that bastard for you, Laura. Gus is dangerous. You're better off without him. You always were."

"In your estimation."

"What else have you got? He'd sell his soul to the devil to get what he wanted—if he had one."

"And you haven't?"

They stared at one another, chests rising and falling, breath coming hard and fast. History stood between them, a whip with lashing tails: accusing, condemning, revealing. They'd never cut corners or pulled punches when they were angry. They'd held nothing back, kept no reserves. Confront-and-fix equaled resolution. Paolo remembered the sheer adrenaline high of their combat, the extraordinary pleasure of making up. And hated himself for remembering. Hated her for reminding him of his weaknesses and that no one was exempt from temptation. Especially him.

He sucked air, held it until the tightness in his chest eased. "That was different."

"How? You lied to me, Paolie."

"I loved you, Laura."

"My mistake, forgive me. I wasn't aware that loving me meant leaving me out of everything that mattered to you, or running off to God-knows-where for weeks at a time without a word."

"That was business." Paolo looked away from her, at the wall where her dulcimer hung, the only evidence that she'd ever had a childhood, a family. "And family. Responsibilities and obligations. Nothing you were part of."

"Bull." Laura made a stiff-handed motion at her chest. "*I* was your family. Your wife—part of *you*. You were responsible to me."

"I had another family. An ex-wife. Sons, parents, a business. I was responsible *for* them. Obligated."

"You could have talked to me about them—shared a little bit. I would have listened."

Paolo's mouth quirked sadly. "There was nothing to say." He lifted a shoulder, let it drop. "You didn't listen."

Guilt flickered momentarily among the emotions on Laura's face, then died. "I was a different person then," she said softly. "Young. Immature. So were you."

He shook his head and shrugged it off. A bad habit. "It's old, it doesn't matter anymore, Laura."

"Everything matters, Paolo, especially the things we try to pretend don't count. When you left—"

He swung on her harshly. "Let it lie, damn you. I didn't come here to do this."

Laura straightened her shoulders, raised her chin to gaze levelly at him, dark eyes to dark eyes. "Maybe not, but it has to be done. I have to tell you—"

"Believe me, I'd rather not know," he said quickly.

She'd tell him anyway, he knew. She'd always been stubborn as hell—except the one time it had counted most. Wanted the last word and usually got it. Until the end, when she'd given it to him.

He blinked. That was what hurt most, perverse fool that he was, the fact that she'd let him go.

He watched her lips tremble for an instant, then firm. Touchable lips. Kissable. He remembered them well. *Get off it, Gianini....*

"There was always a piece of you I couldn't have," she said. "Something dark, something—" she hesitated "—outside the boundaries. You had all of me, everything. I wanted—I needed—the same from you. Then. No excuse, but it was...hard. There was always something else you had to do. Someone—" She paused, regrouped and went on, "I wanted you to know how I felt, always coming second to your guilt over Maria, second to whatever else you had to do at the time, wondering every time you went out if you'd come home...." Her voice trailed away, and she swallowed.

Paolo studied her, glanced away. Love unfulfilled was the bitterest emotion, left the bearer adrift, a castaway—made even the gentlest and most forgiving soul blind to every emotion but rage.

They'd come together so fast, so impatiently, that there had been neither time nor room for many honest emotions between them; that had been their problem from the start. He'd tried to warn her about himself, about his obsession with responsibility, his sense of duty and honor, his lack of visible emotion. About why a woman as emphatically Catholic as Maria had finally agreed to their divorce.

But Laura had loved him and hadn't listened.

But he had...to her love-husky voice, to her laughter, her plans...all the things that deafened him to the "slow down" warning in his head.

They'd lied to each other and to themselves, pretended a lot of things after that—that everything was *fine*, that simply being in love would be enough to see them through. Now that single precipitous lie stood between him and Laura forever, denying happiness and even the pretense of honesty. Denying love.

"There was never anyone but you, Laura," he said quietly, offering the truth in place of apology. "No one before, no one after. You sapped me. You spoiled me. I've never wanted—never needed—anyone but you."

"Don't." Laura put a hand to her mouth, covering a sound of pain. "There are other ways to be unfaithful, other mistresses than women."

Again Paolo looked at her hard, looked away. He'd told her that himself once. Warned her. "That's my line."

"I borrowed it. Sue me."

His laughter wore an edge. "I did that already, remember? Divorce court. You countered."

"I didn't want to."

The hurt invaded him again, unforgotten and unforgiving, stinging. Pride, his conscience reminded him. In the end, love had become just another victim of pride. "I forced the issue."

She nodded. "Yes."

Silence slipped between them with an almost audible sense of time clicking slowly by, lengthening rather than shortening as the seconds passed. Paolo blinked, eyes like camera shutters memorizing every detail of the moment: the position of the light feeding through the three little windows in the door in the front hall; the unexpectedly delicate beauty of the hand-carved dulcimer against the living room wall; the defeated, vacant look about Laura's eyes as she stood opposite him, twisting her sunglasses in her fingers.

And very suddenly, without wanting to understand why, he reached for her.

It was a small, sad movement, more an unspoken, open-palmed bridge across the years than an effort to touch. Too little, too late, and they both knew it. Laura turned from the gesture as though in pain, a tiny moan caught in the back of her throat. "Help me, Paolie," she whispered.

"I can't." Paolo's hand dropped to his side, became a fist. "I'm too close to this. I might not—" He stopped and drew a breath; the admission was painful. "I might not be able to get past...the past. I might hurt more than I help." He shook his head. "I'll send someone else from the office, but not me, Laura. I'm not big enough to deal with this, you—*us*—myself."

In the front entryway, the phone rang. Laura twisted toward it, slumping for an instant. "I wish," she said softly, to no one, and her fists clenched. Then she straightened and, regally erect, went to answer the phone.

Paolo wheeled to face the draped doorwall, cursing himself. He hadn't come to grind his heel in the past. Hell, he'd divorced Laura, he should be able to divorce his emotions, too. He was a professional, after all, he had a degree in indifference.

But knowing what should be didn't always make it so.

The clang of the phone disrupted his rationalizing. He turned to see why Laura hadn't answered it, starting forward almost in the same instant at the sight of her crumpled against the wall, her hand to her mouth.

"What—" he began, then stopped. A dead pigeon with a black ribbon tied neatly around its beak lay on the memo pad beside the phone, the single word Remember written in rusty red on a piece of paper pinned to its chest.

Remember what?

Or who?

The next questions were automatic, too: who had left the bird, and for whom? Gus or...

The protective hackles rose on the back of Paolo's neck, and a sense of urgency beat in his veins. With all the police who'd been through the house in the past couple of hours, someone had undoubtedly used, or at least passed, this phone. No way the pigeon had been here long.

It had to have been left for Laura.

Why?

Because it was dead, and dead pigeons couldn't talk.

Beside him, Laura drew a thick breath and stared at the dead bird. He glanced at her, feeling suddenly cold, then to the floor-to-ceiling window facing the beach, where police and emergency teams were still searching for Gus. The realization that she was responding to this with the kind of dull acceptance that suggested something of this nature had happened before—and she hadn't called him—shook him to his socks. He might not have wanted to face her, but he'd always assumed if she needed help she'd call.

But she hadn't. Good old I'll-handle-it-myself Laura, he thought bitterly. She'd never shrunk from asking Gus for help, but she'd never been able to ask him. Until now.

His conversation with Talon took on sudden weight. Talon had been about to bring Gus in as a witness, to talk; Gus was gone, possibly dead.

No proof without the body.

The tumblers churned in Paolo's brain, sorting through the maze of intricacies at lightning speed. After more than twenty years spent daily dealing with people who hid more than they shared, of sorting motives, believing guilt before innocence, his mind performed with cynical agility, leaving nothing to his imagination—except proof.

Talon was here with Laura, pushing her ex-husband to get her to talk.

Talon, who wanted Dunne any way he could get him, regardless of the cost. Talon who needed someone to bait his trap now that Gus was gone.

Smart money—Talon's—said Gus was involved with William Dunne. The same money—also Talon's—suggested that by association, guilty or not, Laura was also involved. With Dunne.

Dunne the elusive, Dunne the wealthy, Dunne the well-informed, who had his fingers everywhere, in every pie, taking what he wanted. Buying a cop, a rescue worker or a disgruntled government employee was an everyday business expense, nothing more, low cost for high return—and, eventually, the purchase was disposable.

Acceptable losses, he thought cynically. The price of organized warfare.

Then, staggering on the heels of that observation, came another, far more damaging one: Talon thought Laura was disposable. Dunne knew it.

The knowledge nauseated Paolo.

"Talk to me, Laura," he muttered fiercely. "Damn you, talk!"

Breath shuddered in Laura's throat. She pressed her face to the wall. "Oh, God, Paolie, please," she whispered, "Help me. Make it stop. Make it *stop*."

Chapter 3

Laura clamped her arms tightly around herself and huddled deeper into her shoulders, hanging onto the pieces of herself that seemed to want to fly away at any moment.

"I'm cold," she whispered.

"Laura—"

"I'm so cold, Paolo. I think I've been cold for years."

"Laura." He was being gentle, Paolo realized, surprised. Gentleness was uncharacteristic of him. Impatience was far more up his alley when he wanted information from someone—no matter who he was talking to, but perhaps particularly when he was talking to Laura.

He glanced at the single word Remember printed on the slip of paper in front of him, then studied Laura across the kitchen table. The note hadn't been left for him, but it struck chords inside him nevertheless. He *did* remember—many things about Laura, some good things and a myriad of bad things, but he had no memory of this; for the second time in less than an hour, he saw a side of her she'd never shown him during the two years of their marriage. Laura didn't "do" fear, didn't show it under any circumstances—at least not that he could remember. No matter what had passed between them, no matter what pieces of his pride still hurt, he'd married this woman once, and the urge to protect her was undeniably strong.

With a sense of crossing unfamiliar terrain in unfriendly territory, he ignored the urgings of impatience and kept his voice soft. Mild. "Laura, talk to me." He picked up the note, let it drop in front of her. "This isn't the first threat you've gotten, is it?" Her eyes flickered, but there was no other indication that she'd heard him. He wanted to shake her; he wanted to help her. "I can't do anything if you don't tell me what's going on." She eyed him blankly, almost as if she wondered who he was. His jaw tightened; he studied the weather through the slats in the venetian blind-covered window beside him. Only a few minutes ago he'd decided he couldn't stay with her to save his life, and now...

You could toss the baby out with the bathwater, he thought, but doing so didn't rid you of the complications. The ensuing confusion. "Laura, you have to do this. Look, let me get someone it'd be easier for you to talk to...another woman, maybe Acasia or—"

Her head came up. "Not them," she said violently, then hunched herself tighter, ducking away from his scrutiny. She'd never told him how she felt about his partners, and she wouldn't now. Pride, she guessed. Same song, same verse. "No, please. Just give me a minute. I can't think. Let me...let me... It doesn't make sense. I have to put it in order."

Noise filtered through the house from points beyond the kitchen. Outside, the weather fulfilled the promise of the clouds; pellets of rain rattled the window, bounced off to hit the ground like hail. In the foyer, the local crime scene unit packed up their equipment and departed. Talon said a few words to their backs, made a comment to Paolo about the coming warrants that Laura didn't catch. Then he, too, was gone, and the only sounds left were made by the coffee-maker, her anxious lungs, and the rain.

Remember...

Remember what? Laura wondered numbly. Remember who? Gus, you bastard, where are you?

Dunne, Paolo had said before. William Dunne. Why could she almost, but not quite, place that name?

Coffee steamed, hot and fragrant, in front of her, but she didn't see it. All she seemed able to do was taste the powdery rubber flavor of the surgical glove that had covered her mouth last night, hear the calm threat from the voice in her ear, feel the scratch of acrylic fibers against her cheek—see Gus's clothes on the beach, the dead bird beside the phone....

Mustn't fall apart, she thought, folding her hand into a fist on the table and squaring off against her instincts. *Mustn't even look like it. First rule of business: Keep reality to yourself.* But the truth was, she felt like a stuffed doll coming apart at the seams, losing her ticking in dribs and drabs. Every time she thought she was about to get a handle on things, another incident came up requiring instant response. She needed time to repair the rips in her emotions before she went out and lost them all in public, but the best she could do for the moment was a little temporary mental patchwork and hope nothing would burst, leaving her naked and vulnerable in front of...Paolo.

She swallowed and watched him lift the coffeepot off its burner, then straightened with an effort and folded her hands on the table, a picture of calmness and serenity that her voice belied. "Last night, when that man came to the office...and he said...then he made me...and—"

Paolo put down the cup of coffee he'd just poured himself, twisted to find her face. "What man?" The question was abrupt—sharp, tense and uncalculated. Concerned. He covered the space between them in two strides, and then he was standing over her. Something in his face, in his voice, seemed to reach out and physically shake her, even though he kept his hands to himself. Talon had said nothing. "What man, Laura?" he repeated.

"He came to the office last night. After I closed. He—"

"Did he hurt you?" Another thought occurred to him. "Did you tell Talon or the police about this?"

"No, not—I don't remember." She shook her head. "I meant to, but he..." She swallowed and tried to make herself smaller inside her own arms. "He did something to the office systems. When I got out of the bathroom they wouldn't respond—just static. I got in the car and drove until I got here...."

And by the time she'd gotten here, Paolo thought, hell had been and gone. She forgot. "What did he look like?"

"He wore a stocking cap—the kind with the holes in it for eyes and mouth. He wanted to know about Gus. Where he was, where he kept his private files. He...made threats...locked me in the bathroom...wrecked the office...promised...'' Her voice trailed away. She was doing this badly, she knew; she hadn't been this woman for a long time. Edgy, desperate, weak. Vague. She hated this side of herself.

"Who called Talon?" Paolo switched directions, giving her a moment to collect herself.

Laura sent him a grateful glance. "I did. He came in yesterday morning and gave me a card, asked me to call if—'' She rubbed her cheek, wiping away the *if*. "It was handy."

Paolo nodded. That was Talon: set up his pins and knock 'em down. "Tell me about the note, Laura. What are you afraid of?"

"It's not me— It's, I don't know, I think—''

She stopped, once again trying to contain fear, to organize and gather herself, plaiting her fingers about one another, looking at Paolo. Time hadn't changed him much: at forty-two he had even more of the arrogance and power to command with a glance than she remembered, his carriage was still firm and straight, his hair short, dark and curly, his physique health-club sexy. And he still managed to keep his distance from people without appearing to.

Forty-five minutes ago, in his coolest professional manner, he'd steered her out of the hallway and into the kitchen, set a mug of coffee in front of her and gotten Talon and the police in to take charge of the bird and the note without seeming to notice what kind of fall-apart shape she was in. Without once touching her.

Cold seeped around her from the inside of her soul. Old memories ached, new ones seared. Retrospect was painful, hindsight full of guilt. His inability to touch, to accept being touched, had been a major sore point between them. She'd been too emotionally inexperienced and immature when she first met Paolo at twenty-seven to know how to tell him what she wanted and needed from him, been too much of a novice at the art of intimacy to know how to teach him to accept everything she had to give him in return. To understand that the lessons and habits of a lifetime could not be discarded overnight just because love had stepped into the picture. To learn the differences between want and jealous need, how to balance reality against the fantasy passion wove around them.

Been too naive to understand how the passion that had pre-
cipitated their relationship could later get in the way of it. Could
wither without fertile ground to help it grow.

She pressed her lips over her teeth, felt them shake with both
new and old regrets. No matter what experience had taught her
about Paolo, when push came to terror and she'd sat shaking
and whimpering in the darkness of the office bathroom last night
thinking over the past five months, the horrible suspicions she'd
entertained about Gus—sweet, loving, adopted-her-as-his-baby-
sister-when-she-was-eleven-and-fought-all-her-battles-since
Gus—the only person she'd wanted to call was Paolo, the only
refuge she could imagine was Paolo. And God knew she wanted
refuge, wanted to feel safe, protected. Taken care of. Reassured.

To be told that Gus hadn't run away, run out on her, left her
to account and atone for his sins. Whatever they might be. To
be reassured that she hadn't made the wrong decision when
she'd chosen to blindly trust Gus.

Her hands tightened on her shoulders. She'd never begged for
anything in her life—particularly not from Paolo—but she was
ready to beg for assurance now.

All alliances are temporary. Gus's credo beat a constant ca-
dence against her thoughts the way the winter waves beat her
beach. *Get what you can out of the relationship while it lasts,
cut it loose when it's run the course,* he'd advised her after her
divorce. *The faster you do what you have to do under the circumstances, the sooner you get past it. Whatever you have to
do, just do it and get on. Don't lose yourself trying to hang on
to an empty package.*

Easy for Gus to say; the world was littered with the baggage
Gus had left behind. But Laura was a collector of emotional
mementos, mental images, the half-whispered promises of
dreams.

She wrapped her hands about her elbows, collecting herself
physically and emotionally. The silence had gone on long
enough. She saw Paolo open his mouth to start to speak, and
she beat him to it.

"Paolo, I don't know where else to go. I don't know what to
do." She paused. Admitting her suspicions about Gus was difficult. She felt disloyal. She also felt culpable, compromised by
her own inability to see what must have gone on beneath her

nose. But come what may, it had to be said. "I think Gus was laundering money."

Paolo glanced sharply at her. Money laundering would certainly mesh with Talon's suspicions about Dunne, would mesh with Paolo's own long-held personal animosity toward Gus—enhance his perception that Gus was always just a tad too good, too slick, too philanthropic, to be true. Vindicate his dislike for a man who'd played such an important role in Laura's life. "How long have you known?"

Laura made nervous circles on the table with her mug. "It's not exactly knowing, Paolo. It's... I *think*, that's all. I don't have any proof, just..." She kneaded the mug in her hands. "Things have...happened lately, the past few months. Little things. You know, odd phone calls, weird messages, tiny, penny-type inconsistencies in a couple of the accounts. Nothing, really—unless you put them together, and even then... I—I didn't want to believe—"

"I need specifics, Laura."

Her laugh was hollow. Bleak. "You mean something besides the IRS showing up at the office just before his suicide and threatening to take the business and the house and everything?"

He nodded. "Try."

Laura compressed her lips, struggled to isolate the doubts and unease of the past five months into unambiguous pointers. It was as difficult to do as she'd thought it would be. "Gus was nervous," she said finally. "He'd get phone calls and leave the office and when he'd come back he'd look like—" she hesitated "—like maybe somebody scared him. He started looking out the windows before he'd leave the office, checking around, you know? I started to feel like someone was always watching us, following us around. Got a funny sensation when the line would click after I'd pick up the phones—a sort of paranoia that the lines were tapped."

She paused, and the dread of the past many weeks slunk around the edges of her control. It was a dirty, sleazy kind of dread, the kind that had crawled inside her conscience and told her that something very wrong was going on with some of the

investment accounts she and Gus handled and that, whatever
wasn't right, Gus was behind it.

Again that sense of disloyalty raised its head inside her, made
her uncomfortable. She'd never felt anything more for Gus than
the kind of comfortable love that came from growing up around
someone, sharing much of the same history and experiences. For
more than twenty years he'd championed her, made her life a
little easier to manage—which wasn't to say he hadn't had his
weaknesses, everybody did, but he'd recognized his susceptibil-
ity to wanting to do things the easy way, and he'd done what
he could to avoid it.

Easy was so damned seductive. All it took to make life *easy*
was a truth shaved here, a blind eye turned there....

Again that spiritual sickness invaded her soul. God, Laura
realized with something akin to revulsion, he'd really done it.

Despite what she'd told Paolo, she hadn't actually believed it
possible before. Now she had to. Gus had finally crossed the
line; he was really guilty. She should have seen it coming. But,
hard as she'd tried, she couldn't be Gus's conscience forever.

No one to blame if she lost the house she'd wanted for so
long but herself, she thought. No one.

She flicked a quick glance at Paolo, gulped a guilty breath
and plunged into deeper water. "A couple of weeks ago, Gus
came back from lunch limping. His clothes were torn and his
face was all cut and bruised—he said he'd been mugged, but he
had his wallet with him, and he wouldn't talk to the police when
I called them. Said it was just a misunderstanding, he didn't
want any trouble."

She stopped, sorting the rest of it out, putting it back together,
hating what she saw.

"After that, he started asking to use the house a lot. We'd do
that sometimes, trade places. Especially in the summer. You
know—" her mouth formed a sad *moue* "—mutual convenience
kind of things. I'd want to see a show or whatnot, he'd want to
entertain in private." She paused, made an ironic offhand gesture at Paolo. "No big deal, we were friends. Right?" Again
she made a grim *moue* of self-contempt. "Last week he stopped
coming in to the office altogether. And he told me to stay in the
city. Said he'd finally found someone he wanted to be with and
they needed some time out here, away from everybody. Alone."

"You believed him?"

"I've trusted him for a long time. I wanted to believe him."

Paolo stared at her, measuring disgust against disappointment at her refusal to accept what had gone on in front of her. At her deliberate naiveté. Laura stared back, unblinking, without apology. She'd believed in him once, too, Paolo recalled with pain, counted on him blindly and without apology. And, like Gus, he'd managed to disillusion her, too.

Eyes on her face, he said harshly, "Finish it."

Laura ran her tongue along the ridge of her teeth, studied the table hard. "I didn't see Gus for four or five days. Yesterday he was in the office when I got there, going through some of the accounts. He looked high—really up. Said he had a couple things to take care of, then everything would be all right, he'd be back. Talon showed up after he left, talking about doing an audit, about things the IRS suspected Gus was doing—about me being an accomplice to everything under the sun, but if I cooperated…"

She shrugged. "After that, I went through some of his stuff, looked at the bank accounts, trying to figure it out. But it doesn't make sense. It looks like he's hacked into somebody's system, moved all the money around, opened new accounts, but I don't understand why. The old ledgers match the new accounts to the penny. Except that he moved the money around to begin with, there's nothing for anyone to find. But then, last night, after I locked up, that man came in and—"

"Why didn't you call sooner?"

"What?" Flabbergasted, she looked at him. Didn't he ever pay attention to the things he said? "Why didn't I *what?*"

"Why didn't you call? Why did you leave it go so long?"

The coffee in her mug tasted flat and muddy. Laura swallowed it the way she swallowed almost everything life pitched her way—without letting anyone see how she felt about it. Then she took a deep breath, expelled it, watching Paolo. All the fear and anxiety she'd experienced in the past twenty-four hours faded into the background in the face of emotions she'd spent three years in therapy learning how to handle. "Who was I supposed to call with my suspicions, Paolo?" she asked neutrally. Pointedly. "You?"

He avoided her eyes. He'd answered that question himself

almost as soon as he'd stepped through her door. They could hardly stand in the same room without animosity rising to tidal proportions. "The office. The police. Someone with the background to help you sort it out. Someone you trust."

"I trust you." Her voice was soft. "You don't want to be here. I trusted Gus." Her lips worked over her teeth. "He's gone. Or dead. Or lying. Doesn't say much for my instincts, does it?"

"Don't try to manipulate me with guilt the way you used to, Laura," Paolo said harshly. "I stopped worrying about what people think of me a long time ago. Easier to live with some of the things I have to do that way."

"What do you have to do now, Paolo?" Laura's soft question was quick, analytic, raw.... She had a bad habit, Paolo thought, of pushing him to the brink of emotion, then toppling him off the edge. She opened her left hand, palm up, on the table, almost but not quite reaching toward him. Her fingers were long and slim, bare where his ring had once been. "Will you help me?"

Paolo ignored the plea in the half-offered hand; his eyes were black and hard. A little fresh air right now would be a blessing, clear his head. Instead, all the air he had to breathe was filled with Laura. "How often was Gus out here alone?"

"We were hardly ever here together." Laura rose, prowled the kitchen restlessly. Paolo watched her move: Laura visibly unsettled was worthy of note. "I told you. Gus had his apartment in the Village, but we traded back and forth a lot."

"So when he told you he wanted you to stay in the city while he was here, that wasn't particularly unusual."

"Well, he didn't usually tell me not to come out at all—it usually wasn't that important. And it's my house, not his."

Was that defiance he heard, or a note of warning? Paolo wondered. "Who did Gus entertain?"

"Friends. Clients during the summer—he thought bringing some of our bigger accounts out here was good PR. You know the ploy—relax, show off, and do more business."

Paolo shifted in his chair, his attention caught by the nuance of censure in Laura's voice. "You didn't like the idea?"

Laura avoided his eyes. "It's sound business."

"But you didn't like him bringing clients here."

"No."

"Why?"

"I don't know." She struggled with an answer that eluded her, gave it up. "I'm not sure."

Paolo regarded her thoughtfully. "Did he introduce you to any of the people he brought out here?"

"Some." She hesitated an instant, hovering over the decision to add something to her answer. Decided against it. "One or two."

He pounced on her indecision. "You didn't like them?"

"I didn't know them."

"Laura."

She eyed him directly. "No."

"Ah." Paolo sat back, weighing her response, choosing his next question. "Did he bring clients out here often?"

"Most weekends and some weeks during the summer." Laura made a motion of frustration. "We've been over this. What are you looking for, Paolo? A backhanded way to say you believe me, you'll look for Gus?"

Again he ignored her question, feeling the relentless rhythm of his pulse, breathing in her perfume. "Who did he bring—I want names. Was William Dunne on that list? *Did* they do business while they were here, did he invite some clients here more often than others?"

Laura blinked, containing irritation, animosity...mis-trust. Not mistrust of him, not entirely, but of herself around him. The urge to run to Paolo, to let him handle all her problems—to become just another dependent on his list of obligations—was incessant, damaging. She hated his questions, hated the feeling deep inside her that he had a right to know everything about her, all the secrets she hid so carefully, the truth behind all the lies she'd ever told him. *I don't care what you do, Paolo, I don't love you anymore....*

Liar, her heart mocked her. *Liar.*

"I don't know," she said aloud, "Sometimes, I suppose, yes—sure. I told you I don't know about Dunne. I don't. Yes, I'm sure there were clients Gus got along with better than others, clients he had more in common with that would make him want to invite them out more often—that's human, isn't it?"

"When Gus was out here by himself, did he work?"

"I don't see—"

"Did he?" Paolo repeated quietly.

"Yes, of course, that's easy. We handle investments. Equipment-wise, all it takes is a phone, a computer, a modem—"

"Show me."

The office was down the back hall, across from the closed door of the guest room Gus often used.

Originally the master bedroom, it was a corner room, open and airy, banded by windows along two sides and halfway up the banked ceiling. The view of the Atlantic was immense and breathtaking. Austere. On a clear night, one got the sense of sitting in the vast field of the sky, harvesting stars. In a storm, when the ocean burst its seams and climbed high up the beach, the room became part of the tempest, drew moody exhilaration out of the fury. The ocean and sky were the only decorations, besides their bed, that the room really needed, Laura had once said.

Blindly Paolo took in the office, the Spartan line of the L-shaped desk in the center where the bed had been, the shelves in the recessed area in the closet wall where Laura's vanity had stood, the filing cabinets partially hidden behind half-open closet doors that had once fairly dripped with Laura's clothes.

The inevitable image of the last time he'd been in this room rose mercilessly to his mind. He slammed the door of the nostalgia vault shut on it before the ghosts of other ages had time to do further damage to his present. Why the hell couldn't a man discard memories the way he discarded the other reminders of a relationship? Paolo wondered.

He crossed the room, poked among the few papers and colored diskettes left on the desk, then riffled the neat stack of spreadsheets beside the computer. "Has anyone—the police, the IRS, Talon—been through here yet?"

"No." Laura moved around the desk and flattened a hand on the pile of computer printouts, preventing Paolo from opening the pages and reading them. "I'll tell you the same thing I told them—wait for the warrant. Client files are privileged."

"Who left the bird in the hall, Laura?" The question was quick, calculated, unforgivable. Paolo forgave himself for asking it the moment Laura sucked in a breath of realization, eyes wide, and pulled her hand off the files. He didn't bother to justify driving the point home. He did that because he had to. "*You* called me, I'm here for *you*. If you don't plan to cooperate, we've both wasted a lot of energy on emotions we'd rather not remember, and I might as well pack it in right now. Talon will take this place apart as soon as he's got paper, so if you want my help, don't stonewall me. Nothing's sacred. You think Gus was playing dirty games, I think you're probably right. Don't protect him from me, and don't use loyalty to hide the truth about him from yourself."

He sucked air between his teeth, calming himself. Above them, rain ran down the ceiling glass in rivers, wind pounded the eaves. Laura stood still, examining him, emotions naked on her face. The ache she felt looking at him was only fear, exhaustion and frustration, maybe a touch of loneliness—physical cravings, nothing more. She told herself. She had no response to his assessment of the situation before them; it was, as ever, accurate. He'd always been good at telling her the truth about herself; she'd been equally good at revealing his weaknesses to him. She held Paolo's gaze steadily, heart sinking, nerves wilting, defenses tumbling, and cursed Gus with silent fluency.

"What do you want from me, Paolo?" she asked. "I didn't expect this to be easy, but I didn't expect to have to stand here and listen to you judge me for my sins, either."

"It's not judgment, Laura, it's my opinion."

"Your judgment always did masquerade as opinion, Paolo."

Paolo swung around the desk, toe-to-toe with her in the heart of the late-November storm. "Did you want to fight? Is that why you called, to find someplace else to shift the responsibility? If you did, you'd better start looking for another scapegoat, Laura, because I won't take the blame for what Gus has done, and I damn sure don't intend to let either of us use him as an excuse anymore. For anything."

"That'll be a change," Laura began, but then the fire died, as quickly as it had risen. She shut her eyes and stepped away from Paolo to stare out the window, wrapping her arms about herself for warmth once more. "I'm sorry," she whispered. "I don't want to do this, either. It's just...hard. He made things easier for me most of my life, especially after you..." She hesitated, stumbled on. "I don't want to have been wrong about him, Paolo. I want you to find out he's really the good guy in all this.'' She looked at him sadly over her shoulder. ''But I don't think you will. I think you're going to find he's used me to front for his real business, that I've been playing his fool for years. It's not a pretty image. I don't look forward to facing it.''

''I can understand that.'' Her honesty tugged him across the room; the caution of years kept him beyond arm's reach. ''There are things about myself I never want to know, either.'' He paused, choosing words and tone carefully. ''I can also understand you wanting to protect client interests—you have to, to keep faith. But, Laura, dead or alive, Gus is gone. Whoever left the note, whoever broke into your office last night—if they don't know it yet, they will soon. If they didn't find what they were looking for, either here or at the office, they'll assume what Talon assumes—that you and Gus shared more than a business, and therefore all his private interests are yours, too. That you were in on, and part of, everything Gus did. Fact or fiction won't be the issue—making a statement is all that counts.''

He huffed a short, unamused laugh, made an inadequate gesture. ''Believe me, I never thought I'd hear myself say this, but for your own safety, you've got to cooperate with Talon. I've known him a long time—he wants this. He wants to retire as the guy who took out the unreachable William Dunne. He thinks Gus can help him do that. If he can't use Gus, he'll opt for the next best witness, and from his standpoint, that's you, too. I'll do what I can, but if you don't play straight with me...'' He shrugged and let the threat hang unfinished between them. ''At any rate, we need to find a place to start unraveling this. You don't want me in Gus's files, fine. You look—if you can't trust anyone else, trust yourself at least. Someone's got to.''

Someone's got to what? Laura wondered numbly. Trust me? Or look at the files?

Stillness coated the office between bursts of storm; dark gazes held—hers questioning, wondering where she stood, his offering no quarter. As usual, Laura thought.

She turned her back on Paolo to confront the less intimidating view from the windows, using her tongue to work moisture into the dryness of her mouth. At the back of her mind, she wondered who Paolo turned to in the rain. If he turned to anyone.

Probably not, she assured herself. *He's too much like you to let himself need anyone.*

A moody lisp of air escaped her. A few years ago she'd known Paolo as well as he'd let her know him. He sprawled in his sleep, treated the bed like a life raft in a heavy sea, spreading himself evenly over it as though to maintain balance, clinging to the edges to keep himself from falling in and drowning. He never relaxed; even when he slept, part of him was alert, on guard against changes in the atmosphere. He was a generous lover, but not a cuddler. Even during the first bloom of their meeting and marriage, when passion was the focus that drew them together, often and repeatedly, he'd never snuggled up to her afterward, never drawn her into his arms simply to hold and be near her, never touched just to touch. Never shared all of himself. Never lost control.

Never forgot himself for an instant.

What do you believe about me, Paolo? The question beat a tattoo against the plummeting sensation in her stomach, against her unwilling desire to court his approval—their past stepping insistently on the heels of her present. *Do you think I'm part of Gus's business? Would you be here if you did? I don't care what anyone else thinks about me, but what do you assume? Tell me. Just talk to me. What do you feel? Even if it hurts, share it with me. God, don't do this, don't make me guess where I stand with you! Don't keep it to yourself...again.*

She pressed her face against the glass, looking for solace in the window's cool plane. Emotion was sharp, hovering somewhere between love's memory and love's limits. Being with Paolo had made her feel safer than she'd ever felt in her life. Being with him had left her feeling lonelier than she'd thought it possible to be. She remembered that about him with anger and frustration.

And regret.

The glass panes reflected her image, the image of Paolo behind her, casting reality in illusion. On the other side of the his-and-hers reflections the rain distorted her view of the ocean and the beach, cast deeper illusions over the scene. Her time with Paolo always seemed cast in something that wasn't quite real. And, as she'd learned, living outside reality was risky at any time, but wandering the fringes of reality with Paolo could be deadly.

Protect Gus, the business, or myself? she thought. Trust Paolo, the IRS, or me?

When it came down to it, honor told her that to protect Gus was to safeguard the business; common sense told her that if she didn't look after herself first, there was no way she'd be able to defend either of the above. Common sense also told her that although she should never again trust Paolo with her heart, entrusting him with her business and her life was something else. Security, protection, finding things that were lost, that was *his* business, and he'd been married to his trade longer and more successfully than to either of his wives. Acceptance was bittersweet.

"How do we start—" she began, but the dramatic sound of a lock bursting and feet pounding quickly through the house interrupted her.

She caught a quick breath filled with fright and turned her face to the office door. Paolo made an automatic pass at the desk, gathering the scattered diskettes and tucking them into the inside pocket of his jacket. Then Talon was there.

"That was fun," he said to Paolo. "I've always wanted to break in a door." Face alight, he waved a sheaf of papers at Laura and indicated the man in the sport coat and slacks beside him, the assortment of men and women already moving quickly through the house. "These people are U. S. marshals, ma'am. They're here to execute a court order to search and seize these premises. You'll have to vacate immediately. Marshal Marconi here will help you pack a few personal items to take with you. If you choose..."

Numb, Laura stared at Talon, hearing but not absorbing what he said. She'd known this was coming, but she still couldn't believe it was happening. It didn't make sense. If they took her house, where would she go?

As though from a long way off, she felt the brush of fabric against her shoulder, the warmth of Paolo's breath near her ear. "Call your attorney, Laura, then get your things. You'll stay with me."

Chapter 4

Paolo pushed open the door to his apartment and gestured Laura in ahead of him.

There was a certain awkwardness in the motion that made Laura think he didn't invite people in often, didn't grant access to his life outside the office to anyone. Even while they were married he'd only sublet the place, on a month-to-month basis; she'd never been here before, and she'd never set foot inside his office. Almost as though he'd instinctively hedged his bets.

From the start they'd taken up housekeeping in her hotel room, her bed, her house, her life—never his. The illusion created suggested he'd had no life where she wasn't. A lovely and romantic thought, but hardly true, and certainly not real. The more cynical side of that thought hinted that Paolo had never trusted her enough to share his private sanctums with her. The sad niggle underneath said that they'd simply never really taken the time to get to know each other well enough to be comfortable sharing their souls. Or much of anything else, for that matter. Except their bodies.

But maybe that was just her; maybe she'd been too sensitive about his constant need for secrecy. Maybe, as he'd once indicated, it *was* all to do with his work. Maybe she wasn't the only one he didn't let come near. Maybe he always hedged bets that involved trusting other people. No matter who they were.

Three sides to every story, Laura thought irritably: yours, mine and the point-blank truth.

Picking up her dulcimer case and her dress bag, she stepped into the unlived-in-looking fifty-third-floor suite and looked around. Two steps down in front of her, a sunken living room faced a black marble fireplace that had never been used; two steps back up and behind it, a nearly wall-length tinted window framed Manhattan. A broad counter-with-breakfast-nook separated the kitchen from the formal dining area, where a glass-topped table looked permanently set with black candles, black linen napkins and black-and-silver-rimmed dishes. Done in ultramodern sterile, the suite was wide open, with everything visible at a glance, professionally spotless and gray, Paolo's favorite uncommitted color.

Laura almost smiled. She might have guessed. Gray—dove gray, French gray, pearl gray and charcoal gray—textured, silvered and hued every visible surface: carpeting, drapes, furniture and walls. Subdued but not somber, conservative without being right-wing. Not quite colorless, but completely unrevealing; the world was never black-and-white, but always shades of gray—Paolo to a T, Laura decided. By cloudy afternoon light, the apartment was the color of a brewing storm.

Which would not, she prayed, be a portent of things to come.

She turned when Paolo switched on the wall lights, warming the atmosphere marginally, and brushed past with her suitcase and overnight bag.

"I'll put these in the bedroom," he said.

"I don't want to put you out."

"There are two, and I'm not here much anyway."

Polite noise. Strangers would do better. Except that was what they were, she realized: strangers who'd met briefly, once upon the past.

All at once, she wished they hadn't. Wished they'd saved themselves for today.

Suddenly indefinably weary, Laura followed Paolo down the hall beside the apartment's entryway and into a bedroom. The colors of the wintry autumn sky permeated this atmosphere, too, coupled with an undercurrent of blue. She set down the dulcimer and laid her dress bag out on the slate-and-blue quilt covering the bed, then stood, not quite sure what to do next, waiting for Paolo to leave. Wishing she knew what to say so that the ice would break and he would stay.

In that instant their glances crossed, made circumspect observations and fled. Nerves sang with awareness, but acknowledgment was bleak. They were afraid of each other, afraid of being alone together. Afraid of themselves.

Reticence and caution tripped the air between them.

Carefully Paolo placed Laura's bags side by side near the high dresser and opened a door in the corner of the back wall, leaning in to flick on a light.

"Privacy," he said tersely, indicating the bathroom with a nod. "Closet's there—" he pointed to the folding doors opposite the bed "—extra towels, blankets, tissue...whatever you need, it's on the shelf. Housekeeper comes Mondays and Thursdays, sees to the apartment. Professional shopper comes Tuesdays and Fridays to take care of the errands. She also drops off and picks up the dry cleaning, stocks the larder and sees to the rest of the supplies. You want anything, let me know and I'll add it to her list."

Laura watched him, disturbed by an emotion she didn't intend to feel. He'd set up his life so that he needed nothing, no one. No sympathy, no empathy, no contact. No Laura.

Damn, she thought. *Damn.* Time moved forward, but nothing really changed. *He divorced you, you idiot, what the hell do you want?*

Oh, not much, she assured herself wryly. Just the moon, sun, stars...Paolo.

Shut up!

"I'll be fine," she said shortly, swinging away from Paolo. "You said yourself Talon doesn't have reasonable cause to seize my house or my accounts—freeze my assets—that he's just buying time to snoop. My attorney should have me home by Friday."

Paolo snorted. "Maybe in Oz, but this is the federal legal system you're dealing with. Everything always takes longer than you think. And you're not going home—at least not alone—in any case."

Laura stiffened, looked over her shoulder at him. Her natural inclination was to go on the defensive and ask him who the hell he thought he was to tell her what she could and couldn't do, by herself or otherwise. But there was something in Paolo's tone—some half-forgotten knowledge she possessed that reminded her that, no matter how few explanations he gave, he never did anything without a reason. Ever.

Blood leapt and shied nervously in her veins, air skittered in her lungs. "Why?"

Paolo's eyes were dark on her face, liquid, direct. "Because I've never seen you afraid of anything before. Insecure, but not frightened. That says something to me." He paused, but before Laura could decide how his statement made her feel he threw in the kicker. "And also because Talon's after Dunne, and you're the bait."

Uncomprehending, Laura stared at him. He spelled it out.

"Talon was putting pressure on Gus to testify against Dunne. One way or another, Gus is out of sight, and Talon can't make his case, so he turns to you, the partner and longtime friend. He's pretty sure you know nothing, but you share Abernathy and Associates' business profits—some of which may be part of Gus's ill-gotten gains. That gives Talon enough of a thread of probable cause to pursue a court order to seize your stuff and make it stick long enough so Dunne thinks you know what Gus knew, or at least have access to the information that will bring him down. When Dunne comes after you, Talon's got him."

Laura felt her stomach twist and heave queasily. *Oh, God, Gus. What have you done?* "But I haven't—I don't—That's— He can't— Can't we just—"

"Make a complaint?" Paolo shrugged. "No proof. And while it may not be ethical, it's also not illegal—and, if that pigeon is any indication, it's getting results. For what it'll buy us, I'll talk to your lawyer and we'll file a grievance tomorrow, anyway. In the meantime, Talon's smart and he's thrown away the book. That makes him dangerous. Dunne's smarter, never had a book, and he's got more to lose. You're not going anywhere without a baby-sitter."

He paused, mentally reviewing his list of things to tell her, then continued. "Doorman, guard and elevator operator were trained by Futures & Securities. They know who to let in, accept no substitutes for any reason. Phone's unlisted—it's on the answering service when I'm not here. You won't have to see or talk to anyone, no one sees or talks to you. It's safe, private—nothing to think about. No worries."

"Very neat." Laura felt bitter saliva run beneath her tongue. As usual, without consulting her, he'd wrapped her in cotton and packed her away with the other breakables. *You asked for this,* she told herself. Then, faintly, wistfully came the doubt: *Did I? Really? Did I?* "Very sterile. Secure as Mama's womb."

The muscle beneath Paolo's left eye ticked. "Be grateful," he suggested softly. "That's three men downstairs, the two bodyguards who'll be here shortly to stay with you at all times, and me, who'd die before anyone got to you here."

"I don't want anyone to die." Laura shut her eyes, swallowed against the sudden tightness in her throat, the tangled emotions crushing her lungs. "I wanted to go to a hotel by myself."

Paolo adjusted the vertical blinds covering the window. "Believe me, if I thought I could forgive myself if anything happened to you, I'd make the reservation for you. Things would be a hell of a lot easier on both of us if I could."

"All I asked you for was help. I don't need your protection."

"Right now that may be true," Paolo agreed. "But you know...an ounce of prevention." He shrugged. "Just think of my help as insurance to maintain the status quo." He crossed the room, started to shut the door on his way out.

"Paolo."

He pushed the door halfway open again, waiting. Laura moistened her mouth, looking for words. "Do you—do you really think there's any danger?"

"No." Paolo shook his head. "Not yet. But there will be. That's enough for me." He turned away, hesitated, then faced her once more. "We were never good at communicating, Laura, and I want this clear—if Gus really has crossed Dunne, the things that have happened to you lately are only the beginning. They're nothing to what will be."

"And whatever *might* happen, you've stuck yourself between me and it."

"That's the job."

"Not *your* job. *Your* job, if I remember correctly, is to sit at a desk, make nice with the clients and direct interoffice traffic."

An odd sensation curled inside Paolo. Was that worry he heard? "Not this time."

"Because it's me?" Laura took a step toward him. "Because that damned guilt-plex of honor you live by still has you protecting what used to be at the expense of what is?"

"I'm not married to you anymore, Laura. I don't have to justify myself to you."

Laura snatched her overnight bag onto the bed with a caustic laugh. "As if you ever did."

"Don't—" Paolo began sharply, but Laura did an abrupt about-face, and the moisture glistening on her cheeks silenced him. "Laura?"

"Don't you ever die for me," she said fiercely. "Not for any reason. I couldn't live with that."

Something indefinable entered Paolo's expression, darkened his eyes. "Better me than you," he assured her with unexpected passion, and left. The door clicked tight behind him.

Strangling the knob in his fist, Paolo sagged against the door, breathing...breathing. Take in air, expel it, repeat the reflex. Simple, he thought, use oxygen to clear your head. Only it wouldn't clear. He couldn't get Laura out of his mind; she wouldn't leave.

He wasn't sure he wanted her to.

He shut his eyes, and her face was there, more vivid than usual; he knew every detail of it, saw every nuance through the former lover's eyes—the slight widow's peak where the wispy line of her hair brushed her forehead, the heart-shaped face with its serene, wide-set eyes, small, straight nose, full mouth and flawless skin—the granite jaw, iron will and stubborn chin beneath.

And it was what lay beneath that flawless skin that got to him every time.

He recognized something in her, some pieces of himself, some kinship of experience that somehow joined them. She was a survivor, as he was. She knew what temptation meant, took responsibility for her choices and her life, and made neither excuse nor apology for either. And, as with him, her greatest strengths were also her most stubborn flaws.

She was monogamous by nature, too, a person who loved once and well, if not wisely, one who found it difficult enough to forgive her own sins, let alone her lover's.

Take out *she,* insert *he,* and therein lay their problem, Paolo observed. They were cut from the same cloth.

His heart stung, his chest cramped for an instant. Every nerve and pulse inside him, every nebulous instinct he possessed, assured him that he and Laura belonged together, but they couldn't be together. They'd had to divorce, yet they'd been wrong to divorce. The contradictions were all true.

One hand stiff and flat, he felt the smooth plane of the door at his back; with the other, he twisted and held the metal knob beneath his fingers. All he had to do was open his hand and let go and the door would open. Simple. They'd stare at one another an instant, then emotions—or libidos—would rule and, without consciously choosing to act, they'd be together on the bed and—

And back where they'd started from, he thought dully, caught in the same undertow that had trapped and drowned them before. God, nothing was worth that; no amount of loneliness or lust, anger or remorse, sentiment or nostalgia, was worth reliving that misery.

Don't die for me, Paolo, she'd said. *Don't die...* And, *When they asked me who to call...I couldn't think of anyone but you.*

Maybe, he thought, if we tried...

"Don't try, do," Futures & Securities' hostage-retrieval expert, Acasia Jones, too often told him. "Thinking will only mess you up."

A muscle jerked in his hand, and his fingers clenched. As far as Paolo was concerned, Acasia Jones spent far too much time doing and not enough thinking. But she was also right—to a point: he was much too old, too cynical and too mindful of what stood between him and Laura to speculate on their future in terms of *try* or *maybe.* But he wanted to, wanted to get back a right that was no longer his—a right he'd thrown away, would have to earn.

He wanted to touch Laura—just to touch, nothing more, to feel the beat of the pulse in her wrist beneath his fingers, the warmth of her flesh, the living color of her. He wanted to reach for her, wanted to comfort and console—himself as much as her. To hold her—hold on to her—for dear life.

But he wouldn't. He couldn't. She wasn't his. Had never felt enough like his to allow him to "just touch."

If it doesn't belong to you, keep your hands to yourself, his priestly teachers had scolded, then "thwacked" him a good one to drive the point home. Most of the time he didn't bother to remember priestly platitudes anymore. Except around Laura.

Nothing easy ever is, he reminded himself mockingly. He should know. This woman who'd seemed to become part of him so easily in the beginning had not been "easy" at all, had been harder to get close to than Maria ever dreamed of being. He and Laura were both guilty of a certain amount of restraint in their relationship, of a lack of emotional generosity and depth. It was an old song; stinginess cost them both.

Walking wounded, his other senior partner, Julianna Burrows, called them. People who found it difficult to accept and cope with the reality of failure, the vagaries of life. Who made love an insurmountable obstacle instead of a lantern to light a dark path.

To a certain extent, he agreed with her—five years was a long time to harbor sentiment for a woman he'd only been married to for two. But the heart didn't adhere to a timetable. At least not in his family. His family gripped the past like a weapon, carried honor like a shield, wielded both with the precision of a precious-gem craftsman. Every cut exposed brilliant facets, irreparable flaws. His sister, Lisetta, had been a family facet; he was a flaw. His family blamed him for her death, for not seeing the signals of suicide that the family cop was supposed to be aware of and that retrospect made obvious; they had disowned him for dishonoring them when he'd finally divorced Maria, then compounded the sin by immediately marrying Laura.

Yet, despite their best efforts to pretend otherwise, he was still a product of his family.

He'd left Italy, left family, history, behind when he'd moved, first to London, then to New York, only to discover that experience and history bound him no matter where he went or who he became. Paolo Gianini, founder of the private security company Futures & Securities, Inc., American citizen, epitome of the American dream, was still confined by the tenets of his Italian Catholic upbringing. No matter what he did, he couldn't forget who he'd been or what he'd been taught: loyalty, honor, pride, unyielding judgment, one-wife-for-life, no matter who got hurt....

Can't find logic where there isn't any, his conscience smugly reminded him.

With a soft curse, Paolo untwisted Laura's doorknob and shoved himself toward the kitchen. His numbed palm tingled with the return of feeling; he rubbed it, wanting to bring more than its sleeping nerves back to life. This thing with Laura was getting out of hand; he had to stop it. It was time to take the cure, to forgive. To heal. And maybe he was finally ready to do that, to recover himself by facing Laura; to get well by letting go. Except that she was here, now, where he'd never invited anyone before, invading his place at his insistence. And he'd certainly never intended to let her do that. Ever.

He opened the refrigerator for something to do, found the plate of sandwiches the housekeeper had left for him, and selected one.

At the beginning of their relationship, he'd found serenity in Laura, a peace that he'd never experienced anywhere before in his life. He'd buried himself in that repose, clung to it, married it. But even a hurricane had a calm eye that belied its intent.

In the long run, Laura had had the unmitigated nerve to be more of a person than he'd wanted to see—wanted her to be—in those first days and months: happy, angry, insecure, "together," desperate...in need of reassurances and explanations he wasn't in the habit of giving. And in the most honest reaches of himself, where *I didn't know* couldn't hide, he suspected that he'd never quite forgiven her for that.

The phone at one end of the counter chirruped. He picked up the handset, glad of the excuse to suspend thought.

"Gianini... Right." The front door guard telling him Laura's baby-sitters were here. Not much time, he thought. For what? he wondered. "Send— No, have Kyle escort 'em up."

Lips pursed, Paolo replaced the handset, then withdrew a tiny key from a nearly invisible crack between the counter and the wall and crossed to the small secretary against the side wall of the living room. The key fit the drawer on the far side of the desk; the nine-millimeter automatic inside the drawer fit snugly in his hand. Code of survival: The only person you could trust was yourself. Better paranoid than sorry. In all things, with all people, all ways.

Again he felt the tightness through his neck, along his jaw. It was a hell of a way to live, especially around Laura, but Dunne had hired somebody to intimidate her with that bird. Somebody paid by Laura's taxes to be trustworthy, straight and true.

Suddenly weary, he turned to the huge picture window beside the desk, peeked through the blinds at Manhattan. He loved this view, especially after dark, when the lights came on, draped against the night like stars, and the city came alive. Most of the time, from this vantage point, fifty-three stories removed from the earth, he could see everything this city was supposed to be, see the hope that brought thousands of immigrants, refugees and small town wannabes to its doors every year. Remember the hope and the beliefs that had brought him here.

Most of the time.

Just now, however, wherever he looked, buildings and shadows limited his view, maimed his perspective; opinion shortened his sight.

What he saw from his window now was the dirt of human corruption, the squall of human survival—the limits, not the opportunities, of life. Gus taking advantage of a childhood friend to cover for his sins, putting her in jeopardy, betraying her trust. Talon exploiting the letter of the law, instead of the intent, to legally foster his role of court bully, and, like Gus, placing Laura at risk for his own gain, without her knowledge or consent. Dunne manipulating everyone and everything, the judicial system in particular, to meet his own grimy ends. The whole thing exhausted him.

His mouth twisted with disgust. Yeah, right, he thought. Like you're completely blameless. What's your motive, pal?

Laura, always Laura.

Clouds moved, shadows shifted. The view changed. Retrospect grew too painful.

Sightless, Paolo let the blind fall back in place and moved to watch the television security monitor on its stand beside the door. Nostalgia wouldn't help him do this job, he told himself. He'd avoided memory for a long time, he'd put it off a little longer. Better for Laura that way. Better, too, for him. He told himself.

Yeah, right.

Movement stirred on the screen in front of him; his attention keened gratefully on it. The security camera in the hall showed the elevator light flash on, the doors open. The computer diskettes rattled in his pocket when he bent to scrutinize the screen more closely, and his jacket swung wide, hitting the stand. Momentarily distracted, he straightened and pulled the disks out of his pocket, tossing the red, yellow, blue and green plastic bits of technology onto the stained oak surface, wondering again why Talon had let him out of Laura's house without patting him down. He knew Talon too well to think the lapse in procedure an oversight. Nothing slipped by Talon without a reason.

Waiting, Paolo tapped the monitor thoughtfully. Although they'd probably lead nowhere, he'd have the guys in the computer lab fine-tooth the disks before they made him a hard copy of the contents. It didn't happen often, but every now and again a blind alley led to a secret passage. Couldn't afford to miss a hiding place just because it was obvious.

He smiled grimly, acknowledging the humor without appreciating it. He'd also put someone on Talon. Talon undoubtedly had someone on him. One played their game with fear and arrogance, a drop of judicious diplomacy. On the job paranoia was a simple fact of the business Paolo conducted and the company he kept. A matter of survival. Not only his and Laura's, but also Futures & Securities'. And the well-being of his business was something he took seriously.

The sudden taste of self-loathing caught him unawares. More memories, costly and bitter, reached for the surface of his mind.

He and Laura had argued about the business a lot. She'd wanted children, but he'd already been that route; he had three, ages twenty, seventeen and... He thought about it a minute. Giani, the baby, must be all of, what, fifteen and a half by now. They resided on the other side of the Atlantic, in Milan, where their mother had sole custody and kept a tight rein on his visitation rights because the courts agreed with her estimation of Paolo—however much he wanted and loved his sons, he wasn't a fit example for them. He made a lousy father.

He'd fought that judgment for years, but children learned to express the attitudes they were taught. His had been taught corrosive lessons about their father that he couldn't be around them enough to counter; on his last visit, seven months ago, Edouardo, the oldest, had told him not to come anymore. At Christmas and Easter, as usual, he'd go anyway.

However much they might all want to drift apart from each other—however easy a solution that might be—there could be no easy outs for any of them. He'd take no more regrets with him to his grave. In the end, he and his sons would face what they had to face: each other.

Now if only he'd been able to explain that to Laura.

If only he'd tried.

His jaw stiffened, drew hard lines around his mouth. The curse and the blessing of age was how much history it gave you to review so that you wouldn't make the same mistakes twice. He had to live with what he'd done and the way he'd done it. Still it seemed he should have more to show for forty-two years than a Ph.D. in bitter lessons learned.

Again he was saved from confronting further history by the present.

There was a knock on the door. Paolo studied the monitor, then opened the door to admit Laura's bodyguards. Nodding at him, they entered silently and made a swift, professional appraisal of the premises before finding discreet niches that allowed them to keep watch without thoroughly disrupting Paolo's routine.

Used to having them around, Paolo still appreciated the courtesy trained into them. He wondered briefly if Laura would.

Thinking about her made him look toward her door. She'd been in there a long time. Maybe he should check on her....

Once more his body made traitorous comments on his desire, his need for her. He shut his eyes. Then again, maybe he should just leave well enough alone. She was a big girl; if she wanted or needed anything...him...

Oh, hell, shut up, Gianini. You're in over your head. Deep and drowning.

"Thought you should know—" Terry Kyle, the "elevator operator," who'd trained with Britain's Special Air Service and served with the U.S. Navy's SEALS and now did what were referred to as "odd jobs" for Futures & Securities, appeared in front of Paolo. "Couple of cars across the street with guys in 'em, been there a while."

"Check them out?"

Kyle nodded. "One of the cars has dealer plates, the other's a rental. We're running pictures of the guys through the computer, see what shakes loose. If you don't mind me sayin'—" he glanced at Paolo, who shrugged a go-ahead "—they're pretty obvious, sitting out there. Like they don't care who notices—or they want someone to."

"Mmm." Paolo tucked his tongue behind his teeth, made a pensive clicking sound against the roof of his mouth. "I expected something of the sort. Let me know what the computer says, and keep 'em covered. Oh, and, ah...check around, will you, Terry? Make sure no one's out there who's not so obvious."

"Will do," Kyle said, and was gone.

Thoughtful, Paolo retreated to the kitchen. The sharks were gathering as predicted, so now what? Talon's deal, he thought. Wait and see.

He looked at the counter. His sandwich sat untouched where he'd left it. Not hungry, but aware that he should eat, he collected a linen napkin from the drawer beside the refrigerator, automatically pausing to run the fine weave back and forth between appreciative fingers. His tastes were expensive, no doubt about it. He'd learned the differences between good, better, best and superior quality early in life, at the hands of a master, his mother. Quality, she'd taught him, told in the feel of the cloth and the care of the craftsman, not always in the price tag.

Laura to a T.

Again he touched the napkin lightly with his fingertips, and, without consciously making the choice, he shut his eyes and conjured the texture of living cloth, of skin warm and vibrant, pulsing with awareness. Laura's skin, Laura's warmth. Laura flowing beneath his hands.

Lungs working, he opened his eyes. God, what was he doing to himself? They didn't even like each other; the distaste between them had weight, substance, tangibility. Years ago, in a moment of weakness, they'd walked away from each other, split up for a reason—many reasons, *good* reasons. Or so he'd chosen to console himself at the time.

But all the rationalizing and righteous anger in the world couldn't stop him from needing Laura.

Can't find logic...

He turned at the soft swish of fabric to find Laura poised uncertainly at the edge of the living room. Her gaze found the bodyguards, flinched to Paolo.

...where there isn't any. Paolo's mind repeated the expression uneasily. Something in Laura's stance made the dictum read like an epithet.

"I don't like this," she said without preamble. "I feel like I'm paralyzed and living in the middle of an avalanche. I don't know what to do. I feel like I should do something, call someone, make some arrangements, but I don't know what. I mean, I don't think—I can't believe he's dead, but if he is..."

She ran her tongue around the inside of her lips, and her face crumpled. "What do I tell my clients, Paolo? What'll I tell Gus's mother? Somebody should tell her something, try to soften it, make some sense—"

"Laura, don't."

He was halfway across the room before he realized he'd moved, but that instant of awareness was all it took to stop him. He wanted to reach out, to comfort, but the ability wasn't in him. He didn't know how. He was inadequate that way. It was a genetic flaw: Gianinis didn't coddle.

"The police will handle it."

"I should be there. They won't be kind. They'll tell her, then they'll question her and try to make her feel like she raised Jack the Ripper's cousin." She looked at him. "And what about this William Dunne you mentioned? What if he decides to—"

"They'll do round-the-clock drive-by's, put a man on the house, offer her protective custody—"

"But they won't *care*," Laura said bleakly. "It's a job, that's all."

"I can send someone to tell her, stay with her...."

"No. I-It's not enough. *I* have to do something, do you understand? I *need* to." She turned a hand over, made a little shrugging motion in the air with it. "For a lot of reasons. I owe it to her, maybe—to myself. To—" She hesitated, searching for the word. "To my history with her—if for no other reason than I care about her, Paolo. I care what they say to her, how they treat her."

She grimaced. "I didn't like her very much as a kid, she was kind of mean, but at least I know her. I cared about Gus. It may not be the smartest thing I've ever done, but there we are. And I can't just not care anymore because the circumstances aren't kosher. I just...can't.''

Paolo glanced at the bodyguards struggling to maintain neutrality in their discreet corners. He knew what was coming, but some things had to be asked anyway. ''What do you want to do?''

Laura didn't hesitate. ''Go to Buffalo and see her.''

''You can't call?''

''I tried. No answer. And I have to do this in person.''

''We'll be followed.'' There was no sense arguing, but he tried anyway. The bodyguards expected it. ''Talon will think Gus sent something to his mother for safekeeping and you're going to pick it up. Dunne's bound to be out there thinking the same thing.''

Laura looked at him, and all at once, where he thought he'd see more of the shocked fear and inadequacy that had plagued her off and on all day, he saw something else; something about her seemed to straighten and stiffen—not in defiance, but in determination. Something so subtly reckless that it made him unaccountably afraid.

''Well,'' she said softly, ''if they think we've picked up what they want, then they'll leave her alone and come after us, won't they.''

Stunned, Paolo stared at her. ''Do you know what you're suggesting?''

''Gus is my partner. Whatever he might have done, I'm guilty, too, of not seeing it. I can't sit here and wish it away anymore. I need my house back. I want my self-respect. Right now I can't have either. I've got to do something, Paolo, make things right somewhere along the line.''

''You don't know what you could get into.''

''No.'' She made a broad motion that encompassed the bodyguards. ''But you do.''

Paolo ran a tired hand across his face and through his hair. The smartest thing would be to say no. The second-smartest thing would be to send someone better trained and less involved with her in his place. Unfortunately, he'd never once done the smart thing where Laura was concerned. "Let me make some arrangements, and we'll go in the morning," he said.

Laura eyed him directly. "I hoped," she said, "we could leave tonight."

Chapter 5

Being shut up in a car together for eight hours was not exactly on their top-ten list of things to do, but Paolo and Laura didn't even consider flying. Laura flew when necessity dictated, but never when ground transportation was available and the traveling distance could be covered in less than a day. Paolo, on the other hand, flew someplace several times a week and never went by ground when he didn't have to. Every minute of his time wore a premium that flying minimized.

But, oddly enough, modes of travel was never something they'd fought about, was one of the few places in their relationship where one of them unconditionally accommodated the other. Without discussion, Paolo automatically adjusted himself to indulge Laura's unspoken preferences now. Her day had been long enough and stressful enough without adding air travel to it.

Instead he turned over the computer disks with instructions on what to do with them to the Futures & Securities operatives, who knew better than to verbalize their disapproval of the new plan. Then he called for a car, declined a driver, and made some arrangements with his office that Laura couldn't hear. By the height of rush hour, they were off.

Except for the phone that rang almost as soon as they opened the door, the Lincoln Town Car was plush and silent. Paolo drove, listening to someone on the phone and occasionally nodding, committed to the task at hand, blocking out everything else. Laura sat beside him, pale and distant, trapped in a self-imposed exile she no longer fought to breach.

They weaved through traffic, west, crosstown, flowing into the bumper-to-bumper of early rush hour. Outside Yonkers, the traffic diminished; they picked up speed, crossing the Hudson at Tarrytown, sliding through the dusk in Nyack, and on.

As Paolo predicted, a veritable caravan of nondescript late-model cars followed them. When he pointed them out, Laura watched them in the sideview mirror, unable to tear her eyes away. At least three cars rolled steadily behind them without attempting to disguise their presence. The sense of intimidation was all the more frightening for its overtness. God, what did it mean? What had she done?

Bait, Paolo had called her. Something to thrash around and lure, then hook, the sharks.

What she'd felt earlier in the day paled beside what cramped her stomach now. That fear had been simple horror, numbed disbelief; this one left a taste, harsh and metallic, in the back of her mouth. This was real, inescapable, unknown. Her throat seemed to squeeze shut, robbing her lungs of air. She'd never felt so awake.

With an effort, she canted her head away from the sideview. The only way to deal with the unknown is to bull your way through it, ignore it, notice anything else, but don't let 'em see how scared you are, Gus had told her when, in high school, she'd been nervous about a face-to-face interview with the college scholarship committee. He'd been right. Even digging into the past, her mistakes with Paolo, would be better than scaring herself silly by dwelling on things that might go bump in the night—or might not.

Images reflected at her off the windshield, almost registered, then were lost in the glare of lights in the dusk. Buildings, underpasses, windows, became figments of a life, recollections of another age. Paolo bent over the desk on the other side of their bedroom in the middle of the night. Paolo moving the desk into the guest room across the hall and installing a computer-modem-fax machine command post, then a daybed where he could rest when he waited for calls so that he wouldn't "disturb" her at night. Paolo fighting a losing long-distance custody battle with Maria, refusing to share his frustrations with Laura because "the outcome had nothing to do with her."

Paolo pulling in all his emotional drawbridges and throwing himself more into his work by the day, until he once again spent most nights at his apartment in the city, rare weekends with her. No explanations, no apologies, not even a simple "Bear with me, I've got to work some stuff out." The silence had been deafening.

It had gotten to the point where she knew she was married by the ring on her finger, the surname they shared, but she no longer remembered why she was married. With no Paolo to talk to, no reassurance to guide her, she'd brooded. It hadn't taken long for anger to hatch.

When she'd finally decided to confront him, he was gone— dealing with an emergency at the office in London, the receptionist said. Back in a few weeks. Surely, as his wife, she must know?

No, Laura had responded, she didn't. As usual.

She stared out the window into the present, watching the lights in the buildings go on as they passed. Later—too late, and not from him—she'd learned that the London emergency had to do with one of Paolo's sons faking his own kidnapping to get attention, panicking the family. Crude, but effective. To her embarrassment, she remembered that, at the time, she'd wondered along similar juvenile lines herself. If she was gone, would he miss her, would he notice? Would he drop everything to find her?

She glanced at him, still concentrated on the phone, engrossed in driving. His ability to concentrate so completely on an aim, to block out all distractions, was what made Paolo exceptional at what he did—was, in fact, the very ability that had allowed Laura to conveniently side-step her morals and forget the self-protective instincts that had kept her a virgin until the night they met.

She'd never before felt the peculiar rush that Paolo's eyes on her made her feel. His intensity, easily a match for her own, had left her breathless; his desire, unspoken but naked in his expression, had made her giddy. His gaze had never left her face, but her entire body had tingled with an awareness as physical as touch.

He'd wanted her.

And, more fantastic than that, she'd wanted him.

He hadn't approached her until a laughing group, making its way across the crowded room where the cocktail party was held, bumped her into him. His hands, steadying her, had been surprisingly tentative; his breath had gone shallow, his eyes uncertain.

Her hands, braced against his chest, seemed to burn him through the layers of his silk jacket, vest, shirt; she felt the recoil of his muscles beneath her fingers, saw him flinch. A warning sign that read *He's walking wounded and you're not a social worker* had flashed inside her head, and she'd instantly withdrawn from him, turning to slip away. He'd caught her hand with shaking fingers, drawn her back.

She'd craved him badly then. She'd never craved—or even wanted—any man before.

Recognition had been a link between them, something that allowed normal barriers to be crossed before they should. Emotion had been a nebulous shape on the horizon, a seed of hope flung wild to a storm on a prayer that it would find fertile ground and take root—whether someone tended it or not.

At the time, no price had been too high to hold the moment. Even if it meant losing something of herself to be with him.

Hunger had been an emotion visible in his eyes; heat had traveled through his hand and into hers, melting everything in its path. Need had been evident, overpowered want, pleaded with her—not for sex, but for something far more elemental. *Don't leave me alone*, his eyes seemed to say. *I don't want to be alone anymore.*

And she, who knew everything that *alone* meant, had drawn him away from the party, back to her room and into her bed without a word passing between them.

Completely romantic, but, given the day and age, unforgivably stupid to lose herself so thoroughly in the moment. Even now the possible consequences of her irresponsibility didn't bear thinking about. Smart women, foolish choices, she thought. Wasn't that the title of a book?

But that was the way she was with Paolo. He got to her heart, her instincts; he inflamed her soul, invaded her spirit. Where he was concerned, she couldn't depend on herself to make the wise choice. And that scared her to death.

Under the guise of mercy, she'd offered him herself and gotten back something without measure: for a single, breathtaking instant, he'd given her all of himself without conditions or restraints.

Even then she'd known the gift was rare, known he didn't share himself easily, or often, with anyone. Now she knew the gift was priceless.

Everything Paolo did had boundaries, everything he was had limits.

Forever after that evening, even the desire she'd seen in his eyes was guarded, even his lovemaking had perimeters beyond which he could not go—no matter how hard he tried. Before that first night with her, he'd never shared himself with anyone, never asked for anything, never accepted—or expected—anything in return. Only with her had he demanded everything she had to give and replenished it with himself.

Only with her.

And only once.

She regarded Paolo moodily from the corner of her eye. Such a waste, she thought, as she'd thought too often toward the end of their marriage. What a crying waste. Sexy to look at, challenging to be with, financially secure, incredible to love—Paolo was everything she'd thought she wanted in a man.

Until she'd gotten him.

A small sound escaped her throat. He had so much to offer, and he spent so little of it on himself and those he loved. Or perhaps, she thought suddenly, he spent too much, gave more than he had to give. Whichever, when he'd been too young to understand, someone had taught him to equate love with constraint, and constraint with self-denial—to forgo joy in favor of duty, to deny passion for the sake of sense. Had destroyed the child to create the man.

As though on cue, a full-blown, adult-size bangeroo hit her forcefully between the eyes. Remembering Paolo always seemed to do this to her—produce physical pain to express the emotional imbalance. No matter what course she'd pursued at the time, she'd never really wanted their divorce; he'd been the one to file. She'd wanted time to make the difference.

But, as impatiently as he'd come to her, he'd gone. Impatience was his trademark, instant decisions were his way of life, and forgiveness was alien to his creed. Absolution was something to be sought in the confessional, not granted by Paolo—even to himself. Or, if he was anything like her, especially to himself.

Even after three years of monthly confessional-type therapy, she was still having difficulty dealing with her failures where Paolo was concerned. Bottom line was that, in order to move on, forgiveness was what she needed—to give, as well as get. No way on earth would she go back.

However, she would really have preferred to face Paolo under altogether different circumstances. By choice, rather than by Gus.

Suppressing a rueful laugh, Laura jammed her thumbs into the slight depression where eye sockets met brow and leaned over her knees, willing the pain in her head to dissolve. Glancing at her, Paolo covered the handset with his fingers and lifted his chin.

"You all right?" he asked.

Angling her body slightly toward him for comfort, Laura nodded. "Just a headache. Today's catching up with me."

"Need anything?"

"A time warp out of this?"

Paolo grinned at her, a flash of white in the shadow-strewn light. "Sorry, fresh out. How about some aspirin?"

Laura sighed. "If that's the best you've got."

This time a chuckle accompanied the grin. "It's extra-strength."

"Oh, well, in that case, by all means, bring it on!"

"It's in the glove box." Paolo turned his head, spoke a few quiet words into the phone and put it down. Then he reached over the back of the seat, retrieved a thermos and offered it to her. "Tea," he said.

"Thanks," she returned.

Again the silence plunged between them, seemed to drip from the atmosphere like rain. Which would be appropriate, Laura thought. Rain to complete the haunting, close them in with the gathering ghosts.

Smiling slightly at that flight of fancy, she opened the thermos and poured herself a jot of tea, then downed the sweetened heat with a pair of painkillers. Poured another capful and offered it to Paolo. He glanced at her sideways and shook his head.

"Thanks, too sweet. That one's yours. There's another one back there for me." Laura tilted her head and eyed him oddly; he shrugged, embarrassed. "I remembered."

Laura's stomach seemed to drop, then fill with the tickly euphoric sensation she used to get when her father drove through the hills of northeastern New York State at roller-coaster speeds designed to make her and her younger brother giggle. Her lips twitched involuntarily, but all she said was "Mmm."

She settled her cup in the holder on the hump between the seats, then leaned over the seatback, feeling around for the other thermos. She held Paolo's filled cup to her face and let memory waft into her nose: harsh black tea, stronger than Turkish coffee. He used to make it at night and let it stew forever in an insulated pot that kept it hot till morning. Enjoyment was a matter of what you got used to, she supposed, shuddering. But, afraid the brew would eat away the lining of his stomach and aggravate his tendency toward ulcers, she'd frequently tried to get Paolo not to steep it so long, make it so strong—to add sugar, at least.

His stock response had been to inform her that her nagging him about his tea aggravated his potential ulcers far more than anything he actually put into his stomach. To which she'd most often pointed out that since, as his wife, she had a stake in whatever he did to himself, she was entitled to some loving concern. It was the word *loving* that usually made him smile and shut up. But he drank the tea anyway.

She passed him the brew, commenting, "This stuff'll kill you."

He accepted the offering with a grin. "Hasn't yet."

The silence eased, losing some of its animosity; the northbound Thruway rolled soundlessly beneath their tires, absorbed by the Lincoln's suspension.

Winter darkness, somehow deeper and more insistent than any summer's night, closed in, isolating them in breath-drenched stillness. Laura watched her window, seeing nothing. The last time she and Paolo had been in a car together they'd driven to the mountains and made love in her old bedroom in the shadows of the moon. They'd been married about eighteen months then, give or take, and known they were on the downslide, though they hadn't acknowledged it yet. Desperate to find a means to hang on to each other, they'd climbed into the car and fled— away from Futures & Securities, away from their disagreements about Gus, about Paolo's other family. Away from everything they couldn't discuss rationally, everything they couldn't find a way to work through.

But there had been no magic in the mountains that night. Or maybe they were simply too desperate, too far apart, too close to the end. They'd made love, but felt empty; slept together, but been cold; driven home to the beach knowing they'd lost the way back before they'd really begun. She didn't tell Paolo that the deserted cabin they'd stopped at was where she'd grown up; she'd never told him anything about her childhood at all. Maybe if she had...

Maybe he wasn't the only one who didn't know how to share.

Laura leaned back, trying to relax the stiffness in her shoulders and neck, trying to keep track of anything but Paolo. Oncoming lights seemed to prick her eyes and flee; trailing lights grew bright and blinding in the rearview, dropped back or passed on. The Town Car hurtled forward.

Her eyes wandered to the sideview, and the cramp of fear in her belly returned. The glint of chrome and headlights remained constant in the darkness, making it difficult to tell which cars were following them, which were simply traveling the same road.

She kneaded her jacket over her stomach, wishing she knew where to pick up the conversation with Paolo, then switched on her seat light and reached into the soft bag between her feet to withdraw her knitting. The wool felt warm and scratchy against her sweaty palms. The needles clicked together, already lulling; counting the stitches in the repetitious pattern would eventually numb. The activity had gotten her through hundreds of nights waiting for Paolo. It would get her through the trials of this night, too.

Paolo glanced across the car at the determined *snick-snick* of her needles, the soughing of wool pulled from its skein. Watching her hands had always fascinated him; using yarn, wood or fabric, her hands created with the same ease with which his could pull a trigger to destroy. She'd eternally had some project or other going, he remembered. Something that occupied her far into the nights, barely allowed her to acknowledge his homecomings.

That had irritated him, sometimes, the fact that she kept working even after he got home—as though her projects were either more important to her than he was, or some sort of shield against the unimagined. Against him.

The old feelings poked him, gnawed at the mental field dressings he'd used for five years to keep the wounds she'd given him covered and dry. He ignored the momentary pain in favor of the nudge of some new insight trying to kick its way out from underneath the rubble in his mind. Watching her concentrate now, the tightness in her face, the tension in the creating hands, the way her teeth worried her lower lip, it occurred to him that that was exactly what the projects were: protection, a means to get her through, a way to prove to both him and herself that everything was fine, no need to be concerned, nothing to worry about. *Oh, you're home? Good, just let me finish this row, I'll be in. Rough day at the office? No, everything here's fine. Just fine...* Lies she'd worked into the patterns of their lives to protect herself, soothe him, pretend she didn't worry, wasn't afraid of anything. Wasn't afraid for him.

Courageous lies, a woman's lies, told for centuries to wayfaring men on their way out the door. Deceptions she'd lived in order to stay with him as long as she had.

God, why hadn't he seen it before? Why hadn't he known?

Because he was stupid and blind. Because he hadn't realized that by trying so hard to keep his pair of personal lives separate, separate from his business, he denied Laura and himself the most elemental precepts of their wedding vows: to have and to hold, no matter what. To claim each other's concerns, through sickness, health, and spiritual disability—the retroactive hellfire of a former marriage, and the damnation of a family torn apart by terrorism, suicide and guilt.

Because he'd never bothered to come out of his self-involved concerns, his self-righteous attempts to create a more perfect world for somebody else, long enough to understand that he was letting his own erode. Letting Laura slip away.

He looked at her again. Her profile, her movements, were

intimately familiar; the way he saw her was new. "How you doin'?" he asked quietly.

Laura kept her eyes on her knitting. "Fine."

"Laura..."

Her fingers crimped tight around the needles. "I said I'm fine, damn it, now let it lie."

"Like you used to when I'd say it?"

A puff of air escaped her. Her hands dropped forcefully to her lap and she turned to him, pupils wide, eyes gleaming in the dim reading light on her side of the car. "Okay, fine, what do you want me to say? That I'm scared? You already know that. That I can't stop thinking about who might be in the cars you said are following us? Or why they are, or what they might do? I'm the one who dragged you on this trip, what right have I got to suddenly get hysterical thinking about possible consequences you already tried to warn me about? That I—" Her voice quavered. She lifted her chin and looked away from him, biting her tongue and tightening the muscles in her neck and jaw, regaining control. "That I can't stop wondering 'what if' about us? Thinking maybe ... remembering ... rehashing ... going over every damned fight we ever had, every instant where we might have gone a different way, if only..."

"Laura."

Something immediate in the way he said her name demanded her whole attention. Laura quieted. In the underlying shadows of her mind, the part of her that unconsciously kept track of such things noted that this was the second time today he'd deliberately reached for her in some fashion. She had no idea what to make of that, but she was aware of a sharpening hunger. Aware of hoping. "I hate failing, Paolo."

"So do I, Laura."

"I didn't want to start this, going back. I told you to let it lie, but you insisted."

Paolo made a sound that might have been amusement. He wasn't sure. "That I did."

Again silence shaped the air between them. Paolo gathered a breath. "For what it's worth, I think about us, too, Laura. About why, about timing, about the things I did when I knew I shouldn't and was sorry for afterward. But I could never tell you that. Then."

Laura nodded. "I know. Me, too. I don't have any excuses for some of the things I did, either. They just sort of... happened."

"We just sort of happened, too."

"I know. That was the problem, wasn't it?"

They eyed each other, connected in the brief instant before uneasiness reared its head and made them uncomfortable again. Then, prompted by instinct, self-preservation, Laura's fingers stumbled back into her knitting, and Paolo's eyes made a determined effort to concentrate on the road.

"We should probably only go as far as Syracuse before we stop and grab a couple hours...."

A few hours later, wide-awake, Laura lay in the semidarkness of her room at the Holiday Inn, eyes cast toward the open doors linking her room with Paolo's, thinking that this sure as hell had to be the cliché of the month, a woman lying in her hotel bed fighting the hots for her ex, who was available a mere twenty feet away and thinking about her, too.

She turned over, listening to the sound the crisp sheets made rasping over her cotton pajamas. Probably thinking about her, that is, if he wasn't instead thinking about the three cars that had pulled into the hotel's courtyard right behind them, carrying two suited men apiece.

Paolo had identified them for her as they entered the lobby: the Mutt and Jeff team in the slept-in sport jackets belonged to Talon; the duo in the flexed-pecs-strained Brooks Brothers were Dunne's; the last two, the quiet, unassuming-looking ones in the military-style sweaters and slacks, Laura recognized from Paolo's apartment. He'd neglected to introduce them, but she assumed they were two of his finest; he rarely did anything by half measures.

While she'd tried not to stare, and at the same time tried to keep her heart out of her mouth, the men had dropped their bags at the registration desk and asked for rooms near Paolo and Laura—caravanning, you see, their eyes seemed to say. Got to keep in touch.

Then Talon's men had grinned at Paolo, one winking, the other sketching him a mock salute, and Dunne's men had acknowledged him with curt nods and a circumspect display of muscles against custom-tailored seams. Paolo's men, slipping silently between Laura, their F & S chief and the others, had made their loyalties clear with the soft single-word question "Boss?" to which Paolo had responded with an almost imperceptible negative shake of his head.

Stunned, Laura felt herself gaping at them all, feeling as if she were standing in the middle of some sort of ludicrous comedy production with macabre overtones. She'd looked for quick corroboration of what she saw to the registration clerks, who punched their keyboards and tore off their perforated paperwork, oblivious to the scene. Whoever had first said "better the devil you know" had obviously never been intimidated by these guys. How much more cozy and congenial could an unspoken threat get? she'd wondered, unnerved.

She'd turned to Paolo then, wanting she didn't dare think what, but he'd only given her the same slight shake of his head that he'd given his men, and bent to retrieve their luggage, a study in deliberate relaxation.

"Smile," he'd said quietly, motioning her ahead of him down the corridor to the elevators. "Don't let them see what you feel. They feed on fear. Don't give 'em that edge."

And she'd looked up at him, wondering if he realized how much like Gus he sounded, and then she'd seen it for the first time, wide-open in his eyes: the urgent plea for understanding, the self-control reining in the desire, the impulse to touch, to take, to give—to comfort and protect.... To be the person he wanted to be, the person who could give her everything she'd ever wanted or needed, everything she asked for, rather than be the person he was: a man who made a living playing footsie with the devil.

For her. And people like her.

The momentary fire in his eyes burned deep inside her, strengthening, weakening. Damn, she wanted him to touch her, wished he'd put his hand out, reach for her in some way— wished he'd acknowledge whatever it was she still felt for him that had kept her celibate and single for five years and made him the only man to visit her dreams.

She sat up in the bed, shaking. Why shouldn't they touch? What harm would it do? All she had to do was get out of bed, step to his door. There was undoubtedly an all-night pharmacy nearby, so why not let go? Not forever, just for a little while. Long enough to get them both through the night.

Because of the cost, she answered herself honestly. And the demands and the history lessons and the lies that seem like so much truth at the time you tell them, only you find out later they're not. Same reasons you won't reach for him first. Too old to lie to yourself anymore, too much to lose.

Way too much.

"I am what I do," he'd told her bleakly early in their marriage, not apologizing, merely stating. "I let one event shape my life for me, and what I have to do to fix it won't let me stop for you. I want to, but I can't. I owe too much."

Laura lifted her head and hugged the pillow up to support her chin, staring at the headboard. She knew the story of that event, or at least cryptic pieces of it—remembered it in the language in which it had first been presented to her, the terse, unemotional sentences of deep pain....

Beautiful younger sister receives red Lamborghini for her seventeenth birthday; she and a girlfriend take it out for a spin. Black car and black van box them in just outside the gates of the family's estate, force them off the road; sister is kidnapped, friend gets dumped outside father's Milanese bank with a broken arm and a list of demands for ransom and delivery. Big-brother, hotshot in the *carabinieri*, breaks all records for quick response, creates a few precedents for search and rescue techniques, but still takes five weeks to bring little sister home.

A month and a half later, alone in the Milan villa and in search of some final peace from the constant mental and emotional torment that never lets her sleep, little sister calls friend who was with her when she was kidnapped, then swallows a bottle of pills with a bottle of vodka....

The friend—Acasia Jones, Paolo's partner, in Paris at the time, suffering her own emotional distress over the kidnapping—had placed a frantic call to Paolo, who arrived in time to find Lisetta unconscious but still breathing. Though it had taken some doing, he'd managed to somewhat revive his sister and force her to vomit up half the pills before getting her to the hospital, where her stomach was pumped and every effort was made to rouse her again. Twelve hours later, she died anyway, without waking from her coma. Refused to live, the doctors said. Chose to die.

His family, for reasons Laura had never fathomed, blamed Paolo for Lisetta's death. Something to the effect that despite the fact that he had his own family and no longer lived at home, he should have been aware of his baby sister's state of mind, aware of the signals, should have gotten her help; he should have kept better watch over her, warned the family what to expect. Taken responsibility for keeping her alive, as well as for trying to find and prosecute the terrorists who'd kidnapped her.

She glanced toward the open doorway, where the lights from his room cast puddles of shadows into hers. Paolo always took more than his share of responsibility on himself; that was the problem. He was as hard on himself as he was on those he lived with, those he loved. He'd made himself culpable for Lisetta's choices, Maria's choices, his father's and his sons' choices.

Which left him with very few choices of his own.

Paolo put down the phone and glanced at his watch: 5:37 a.m., by its glowing digits, and the status, according to the night shift just checking in, was still quo—quiet and ominous, clouds against the horizon.

Not smiling at the analogy, he shot his wrists through the sleeves of a fresh pale gray shirt and secured the cuffs with onyx links; then, sliding a tie of charcoal silk under his collar, he headed for Laura's door. Her bed light was on, but she slept, hair spilled negligently like so much silk across her pillow, face puckered with worry even in repose. The room was filled with her scent.

His body tightened with need, want, loneliness, confusion—all things he couldn't afford. He thought about smoothing away the worry crease on her brow, but stayed where he was and knotted his tie instead, watching her, wondering exactly what it was he felt. Too much, too little...a hundred different things at once.

He shouldn't watch her, he knew, shouldn't remember what her skin felt like, how her mouth tasted, what it was like to be inside her. Shouldn't want to be inside her now. Shouldn't want any of the things he'd discovered while talking with her in the car that he still wanted with her. *Want* wasn't healthy in a situation like this. She'd only break his heart again—or he'd break hers. Better to maintain perspective, distance. Sentimental journeys down nostalgia lane while watching the beautiful ex-wife sleep were something only hard-boiled detective heroes in books took—usually just before the bad guys stepped in and beat them to a bloody, albeit sympathy-earning, pulp. A single moment wasn't worth all that ache. Physical or emotional.

He reached for her anyway, moving across the hotel carpet on soundless feet, drawn to soothe her sleep by something stronger than will. She heard him, or felt his shadow, or perhaps she simply found a kinder dream; she sighed suddenly and turned over, away from his hesitant fingers. He withdrew them, feeling lost, instantly reprieved.

He was almost back to the dividing door on his way to the phone to ask the desk clerk to give her a wake-up call when she sighed again and rubbed her face across the pillow, waking.

"Paolo?" she asked, sleepy or bewildered, he couldn't tell which.

"I'm here."

"Good," she mumbled, yawning into her pillow, almost settling in once more, but then she jerked herself up on her forearms, looking at him. She shook her head groggily, struggling for consciousness. He shut his eyes, closing himself off from that flushed beauty. She read his turmoil correctly, mistook the cause. "Has something happened? Is anything wrong?"

He shook his head. "No. No news. Everything's the same."

"You look—"

"It's fine, Laura. Let it lie."

She eyed him oddly, lips pursed against amusement or annoyance, but instead of throwing a "Like you did last night?" in his face, the way she might have once, she asked only, "What time is it?"

To which he responded, relieved, "Almost five-thirty." And then, when he saw her questioning eyebrow, he added, "Time to go."

Chapter 6

It was slushing in Buffalo.

Cars shushed through the streets in the gray light of still early morning, spattering waves of icy liquid over the curbs. Walkers in heavy coats and boots, tennies or once-immaculate work shoes hoisted umbrellas and hugged the insides of the sidewalks, away from the cars, slopping quickly between the puddles.

The encyclopedia said Buffalo's temperate climate made it one of the most healthful cities in the United States. Dubious, Paolo eyed the huge drops of half-frozen stuff splatting the Lincoln's windshield only to be caught in the wipers and shoved into freezing mounds along one side and the bottom of the frame. You couldn't prove healthful by him. He flipped the car's blower up another notch; just thinking about the onset of winter made him feel as though a cold were coming on.

Could move to L.A., he told himself dryly. No winter there.

He glanced at Laura, huddled in her coat in the passenger seat. No Laura, either.

"Do you think—" Laura picked at her seat-belt buckle, hesitating, glanced again at her sideview. She'd kept track of what was behind them all the way from Syracuse. "I can't see them. Are they following us?"

Paolo nodded. "We may have gotten out of the hotel before them, but you can bet they're out there somewhere."

"Oh." She swallowed. Afraid, but going forward.

"We don't have to do this, Laura," Paolo said quietly. "We can turn around right now and go back."

"Long drive for nothing."

"Doesn't matter."

She looked at him, captured his eyes, and for an instant the angry thing between them hung suspended, nonexistent, and they were just two people in a car, two people without a past, and the future was possible.

The instant passed.

Laura turned once more to the sideview. "Thanks," she said, "but I have to...follow through. I just don't want anybody hurt."

"We'll do our best," Paolo assured her. She nodded, but she didn't look like she'd heard.

With some concern, he eyed her between stoplights. She stared at the parks and buildings they passed without expression, her face remote, indicating their turns in a colorless voice. He wondered if actually being here to talk to Gus's mother was proving more difficult than she'd anticipated. He didn't want to, but he remembered how he'd felt carrying the news about Lisetta to his parents. They'd wanted to slay the messenger—and had, at least figuratively, when they disowned him. How much different could Laura feel?

He looked at her again: the wisps of hair haloing her head, the hands knotted together in her lap, the eyes that looked as if they'd been kissed by too many storms, and his knuckles whitened around the padded steering wheel. If he could, he'd reach down inside her and yank out her demons, wrestle them himself. But he didn't know how to, where to begin—even how to tell her he understood. Why would she believe him, anyway? He'd never understood her before.

He'd never tried.

It takes two, he reminded himself. But it didn't make him feel better.

In silence he turned where she indicated.

The house stood in the middle of the third block, a big, clap-board-sided barn of a place with peeling white paint and gleam-

ing red trim on a tree-lined city street that had seen better days.
A narrow, slanting drive widened at the back of the house, in
front of a three-car garage.

While Paolo parked the car, Laura studied the area, her
thoughts clotted with memory. Four years ago Christmas, she'd
come to spend two weeks with her mother and left after three
days, intending never to return. Funny the tricks circumstance
played on you.

Suck it up and move along, kiddo, she told herself, unclipping
her seat belt to step out of the car. A set of wooden steps attached to the side of the house led to a second-floor apartment.
Hand on the railing, Laura mounted them reluctantly, pausing
on the landing to draw a breath of dank air before she knocked.

There was a flash of silence, followed by a deep-throated
growl. The doorknob rattled, then something big and furious
assaulted the door from the inside, pounding to get out. Its bark
was menacing and businesslike, not a my-bark-is-worse-than-
my-bite kind of sound, but one that said if-I-get-out-of-here-you-
are-stew. Startled, Laura backpedaled quickly, banging into Paolo and nearly sending him down the stairs.

There was no time to notice the things that happened automatically: the visceral rush that snapped between them where
their bodies came into contact, the instinctive give of Paolo's
body to accommodate Laura's, Laura's intuitive knowledge that
he would not let her fall. The fact that they'd made physical
contact with each other at all. Instead, consciously, they struggled for footing, Laura grabbing the railing, Paolo shoving her
upright from behind. The dog displayed no signs of discontin-
uing its attack on the door; if anything, its offensive increased.
Erect once more, Paolo and Laura beat a breathless retreat to
the foot of the steps, then stared upward at each other in silent
consultation.

"Gus's mother doesn't have a dog," Laura concluded finally.

"Somebody does," Paolo said. "You said it's been a while,
maybe—"

"No, I don't think so." Laura shook her head. "She's afraid
of—"

Movement flickered suddenly at the corner of her eye, silenc-
ing her; a curtain brushed aside in a downstairs window toward
the front of the house. Inside, someone said something sharp,

and the dog upstairs abruptly quieted. A chain rattled, then someone cracked open the door in the wall beneath the steps. Sweet peach-scented steam escaped the house, and a huge, snuffling canine nose appeared in the crack. Behind it, an old, querulous voice called, ''Who's there?''

''Mr. Dinkens?'' Laura asked.

''Moved,'' the voice assured her, and someone tried to pull the dog's nose out of the slit to shut the door.

Laura stepped up quickly and pressed a hand to the frame. ''It's Laura Gia—Laura Haas, Mr. Dinkens. I used to live across the street. Remember me?''

''No.''

Definite and irascible. Stubborn old coot, Laura thought, and lifted her chin, equally obstinate. ''I'm looking for Mrs. Abernathy, Mr. Dinkens.'' The dog's nose pressed the door wider, reaching for her thigh. She edged sideways without giving ground. ''Does she still live upstairs?''

''Nope, gone. Took her away. Leave me alone now, or I'll call the police.''

''Who took her, Mr. Dinkens?'' Laura felt a sense of panic she couldn't have explained, a sense of loss—as though she'd laid her past away for future reference and found when she'd come back for it that it wasn't where she'd left it. ''Where?''

''Can't say. None o' my business.'' The antique voice hesitated, the person behind it making a decision: to shut the door and have these youngsters interrupt him again, or talk now and hope they'd go away sooner. Made accommodations. ''Mighta been her son—tall feller, fancy-shmancy suit, come with a ambulance. Took 'er out and I ain't seen her since.''

Laura glanced at Paolo. He shrugged, letting her lead. She turned back to the door. ''What happened? When?''

''Never heard. Long time—months. Get along now, girlie. Got my peach marmalade on the stove needs tendin', and I can't hold this dog no more. He don't like strangers.''

''Where, Mr. Dinkens?'' Something fizzed inside Laura: some memory, some stray bit of information that hadn't seemed to mean anything when she'd first heard it, so she hadn't paid attention to the gist of it. Something Gus had said. *Made out my will, Laura. Left the old lady to you. Take good care of her.* She'd thought he was joking, but retrospect changed perspective.

Finding Gus's mother was all at once desperately important. She pushed at the door, heedless of the dog. "Please. I have to know."

The old voice rose a notch, irritated by youth's impatience. "None o' my business, told you. Nobody says nothin' to me. Ambulance says Amherst something Rehabilitation. Fancy damn glorified name for a nursing home, you ask me, nobody did. Place to leave old folks to rot."

"But don't you—"

In the street, gravel crunched faintly. Paolo's head snapped sharply around; he stepped close behind Laura, blocking her from view from the curb. "I think we've taken up enough of the gentleman's time, Laura. Thank you, Mr. Dinkens, you've been a great help. We'll take it from here."

"Shouldn't wonder," the old man muttered, and shut the door.

"No, wait!" Laura rattled the knob, then swung on Paolo. "What did you do that for? He didn't even tell us—"

"He told us everything he knew."

"Not what happened. Not—"

"Laura." Her name was spoken quietly, a command given.

Laura looked at him. "You don't understand, Paolo. I need to know. Gus—"

"Later." He jutted his chin toward the street, where a dark gray Mercedes cruised dilatorily past the house.

She eyed it in silence, jaw working, face set. "Is that them?" she asked.

Paolo shook his head. "It's not one of the cars that followed us from the city, but it could be with them." He stepped across to his car and opened the door for her. "Time to go, Laura. We've risked enough here."

Laura nodded, staring at the house for a long minute, imagining ghosts. Then she climbed into the car and slammed a fist against the dashboard. "Damn you to hell, Gus," she said.

The Amherst ElderCare Medical & Rehabilitation Facility was listed in the yellow pages under nursing homes. They did indeed, the receptionist responded when Laura called to ask, list a Mrs. Lilah Abernathy among their residents, but could not extend further information over the phone. Mood as bedeviled as the color of the day, Laura returned to the car and gave Paolo directions to Amherst.

Adjacent to the Amherst Retirement Village, the continuing care-rehab unit was a low-slung series of modern smoked-glass and adobe-colored brick buildings surrounded by tall trees and gardens that would be pleasant in the summer. A high chain-link fence enclosed the grounds, keeping intruders out and any disoriented residents in; an empty guard shack stood at the entrance to the facility, the long-armed yellow-and-black-striped barrier, with its bright red stop sign, erect beside it. Noting everything, Paolo whizzed past without stopping.

A good distance beyond the complex's entrance, he cut a corner and pulled off the road behind a brick wall that marked the entrance to a wealthy subdivision. He let the engine idle a few minutes while he watched to see if they'd been followed despite the circuitous route he'd taken. But the surveillance so formidably blatant last night was frighteningly absent now.

Laura twisted beneath her shoulder harness, almost wishing their pursuers would appear. She didn't like being at the mercy of someone else's whims, manipulated by the gray world of her possibly dead partner and his unfinished business. The devil she'd been able to see last night was far less daunting than the invisible demon who was playing a wicked game of maybe-and-what-if with her mind today.

"Where are they?" she wondered aloud.

"Don't know," Paolo admitted. He picked up the car phone and punched a button, listened for a few minutes and hung up. Laura viewed him expectantly; he shook his head, frowning. "Nothing," he said. "No sign of either Talon's boys or Dunne's. Means they're really gone, or they're a hell of lot better at this than I gave them credit for." He didn't add, *Or my people aren't as good as I think they are.*

"If they're gone...if we lost them..." Laura hesitated. "If they can't find us, will they bother Mr. Dinkens? Will they..." Another pause, to swallow hard this time. "Will they hurt him?"

"No." Paolo heard the fear and reached out before he caught himself, withdrawing his hand before it quite closed around her fingers, afraid the contact would be inadequate. Afraid he'd forget himself and the situation if he allowed himself to touch her even once. Afraid of telegraphing what he felt. *Timing,* he thought savagely. *Damned screwed-up timing.* ''Talon's the law, and Dunne's not stupid,'' he said, trying to keep his voice neutral. ''Besides, the old guy's got that dog. No.'' He shook his head. ''They might try to intimidate him a bit, scare him—mind games—but they won't hurt him. No percentage in it.''

''Okay.'' Laura tried to let his logic, his nearness, reassure her. Tried not to stare at the hand that had nearly touched her, or wish he hadn't pulled it back. Tried not to think about the fizz of desire along her spine, or the ache in her heart, or the hole in her soul that he'd dug and was his alone to fill.

Almost succeeded.

In silence they turned around and went back to see Gus's mother.

''You don't understand. This is an emergen— It's about her son. I have to see her. Her son is—''

The charge nurse in front of the receptionist's station shook her head. ''No, I'm afraid it's you who don't understand, Ms. Gianini. I can't let you in to see Mrs. Abernathy without her doctor's consent, especially not if you have bad news. Her son stipulated the conditions when he brought her in, and we agreed to them. Only he is allowed to see his mother without talking to Dr. Drexell first.''

''Then let me talk to him.''

''Her.''

''*Her,* then,'' Laura agreed, irritated. What had made her assume the doctor was a man? she wondered in disgust. Only thirty-four years' worth of brainwashing, that was all. The same thirty-four years' worth of slanted education that had made her automatically want to describe the charge nurse as the doctor's goon. ''Will you *please* let me talk to her?''

''She's at lunch,'' the nurse said crisply, and marched away.

Laura banged her forehead on the high counter encircling the receptionist's station. ''How did I know she'd say that?'' she moaned, to no one in particular.

''From watching too many movies?'' Paolo guessed.

''Shut up,'' Laura said, and he grinned. This was the side of her he knew how to deal with, straightforward and crusty.

The receptionist—Patrice Winklerprince, according to the brass nameplate on the counter—cast sympathetic eyes up at them from her position near the phones. "I'm sorry," she said. "I probably should have warned you. Erica burns her bra every weekend. Ticks her off when people assume the doctor is a man. She figures that until everyone assumes first that a woman can do the job..." She shrugged. "I keep telling her she's got to quit taking offense over a pronoun—people gotta say something, and *him*'s what we're taught, but, well, you know..." She made a nervous clacking sound with her gum and rose to lean over the desk and scan the corridors in both directions. Her voice dropped. "What I'm trying to say is," she confided, "she only told you half the truth. I mean, the doctor *is* at lunch, but she's having it in her office, and I could check if you want—"

Laura grabbed the woman's hands in fervent thanks. "Please," she said.

In a vague sort of way, Clara Drexell had been expecting them—or Laura, at least.

Amid the plant-filled clutter of her office, she sat behind an old-fashioned oak-stained teacher's desk, a fifty-some-thing woman with long iron-gray hair tied back by a leather thong, direct hazel eyes, and a vivid smile that belied her years.

"Ms. Gianini." She rose and extended a strong-soft hand to Laura, then turned to Paolo. "Mr. Gianini." When Paolo did not offer his hand, she withdrew hers without apparent discomfort, turning the ignored greeting into a gracious gesture to her visitors to be seated. "So," she said, lining up a brown file folder with the edge of the desk. "What's happened to Gus?"

Laura and Paolo exchanged glances. Laura spoke. "What makes you—"

Dr. Drexell shrugged. "You're not the first person to bring us hard news, Ms. Gia—Laura. May I call you Laura? It'll make things easier. Anyway, a young man with as much on his mind as Gus Abernathy brings us his mother five months ago after a stroke, tells us he won't be able to make regular visits and leaves us sealed instructions about what to do if a Laura Gianini shows up asking to see her. This is a man who expects we'll need those instructions." She made a sympathetic that's-how-it-goes face and consulted the file in front of her. "So," she said again. "Is he alive?"

"No—I...that is..." The absence of emotion was the thing Laura noticed. She didn't know where to look, what to say, how to act. Her eyes slunk unconsciously toward Paolo, looking for...what? She was afraid to think about that. He stared back at her, coffee-colored eyes intense, filled with some message for her alone. She glanced away quickly; she'd gotten more than she'd bargained for, more than she'd known she wanted.

She wrapped her hands around her purse, holding on to the familiar for dear life. "I didn't know she'd had a stroke—Gus didn't say—" She stumbled over the words; uncovering the extent of Gus's deceptions hurt more than she could have imagined. The fact that he hadn't trusted her even this far after so much time... But what would she, could she, have done if she'd known about Lilah—besides feel better for not having been left out of Gus's confidences?

Men, she thought inconsequentially, *can't live with 'em, can't sell 'em for parts.* "I—we—only found out this morning that she was here, but not why. It—I mean, is there anything... Was it bad? How is she? Does she need—what does she need? Can I see her?"

There was no way to break some news gently. Long years of practice had made Clara Drexell blunt. "She had a massive stroke six months ago that destroyed everything. Her son told the hospital to put her on life support, even though her doctors advised against it. When he finally agreed to have life support shut off, she lived. He hired a private nurse and took her home to die. When she didn't, he brought her here. We've had her almost five months. Her condition hasn't changed." Her study of Laura was direct. "She's a vegetable, Laura. You can see her, of course, but—" She shrugged.

"I see." Shock left her with nothing to say. Her thought processes seemed muddled. This was supposed to have been a quick trip, difficult in content, simple in intent: to tell a mother about her son and lead all the other interests out there astray. Now the scope had widened beyond all comprehension, and she couldn't seem to focus, couldn't seem to remember what was important.

Keep moving, she thought. *Don't stand still. A moving target is harder to hit*. Oh, God, Gus's clichés again! Why couldn't she seem to think for herself?

"Laur—Ms. Gianini, are you all right?"

Dr. Drexell was up, coming around her desk. Laura dragged herself together and waved her away, reaching for Paolo without thought, without realizing he'd already risen and crouched beside her chair. He offered her a handkerchief, and she discovered that her cheeks were wet and she wasn't sure who she was crying for. Some kind of together woman she was. "I'm sorry." She mopped at her face with the hankie. "I don't mean—didn't expect—"

She looked at Paolo, at his fingers resting lightly on the arm of the chair beside her elbow. Never touching her, but always there. *Till death do us part...* She stifled a sudden hysterical giggle behind the hankie. Oh, God, caught between a lie and a paradox. *Get a grip*, she advised herself. *Hang on now.*

"I don't know what to do," she said to Paolo, throwing her self-imposed rules for being around him to the wind, because, gut-deep and despite everything, she trusted him. "Something's coming apart inside, and I can't think. Can they do anything—"

"Shh, Laura." He silenced her with a finger not quite placed to her lips, then turned to the doctor. "We came to tell Mrs. Abernathy that her son apparently drowned sometime early yesterday morning. You said he left instructions...."

"Joint partnership agreement and power of attorney." In disbelief, Laura slid the documents off the pile on the restaurant table in front of her. "Guardian of the trust to take care of his mother." She flipped another batch of the pages presented to her by the Buffalo attorney Gus's "instructions" had directed her to see. "In case of death, executor of his estate and holdings, principal beneficiary."

Boggled, she ran a hand through her hair, dislodging the comb that held it in place. It clattered unnoticed into the plate of chicken wings in front of her. "God, Paolie, what's he doing?"

"Putting you in the line of fire." Paolo eyed her over a belated lunch; she looked exhausted, emotionally spent, darting wounded glances at him every few seconds, as though asking when he'd let her down, too, and he wanted...way too much.

If—*when*—Futures & Securities found the bastard, Paolo would take great pleasure in personally living up to every Neanderthal cliché scorned in the feminist manifesto by taking the son of a bitch out.

Neanderthal love, he thought derisively. *Oogh, oogh, oogh...*

He swallowed a bite of stacked beef and wiped his mouth with a napkin instead of the back of his hand. Pretense of civilization. "Bastard needs a patsy, and you're it. If I didn't believe he was alive before, I do now."

"No." Swamped by awareness, she looked at him, ducked quickly away. More than Lilah Abernathy's condition had been revealed in Clara Drexell's office: Gus's motives, Paolo's motives, her own.... "Judging from all this legal mumbo jumbo, I think he's trying to protect me."

"Damn it, Laura, when are you going to stop excusing him?" He picked up the stack of documents, let it smack onto the table in front of her. "This stuff makes you a full-knowledge partner in all Gus's dealings. Talon gets hold of this and he's got ample cause to suspect you of—"

"Nothing," Laura said evenly. She riffled over a few pages, tapped a paragraph with a forefinger. "This says I have no knowledge of anything illegal..."

"If, indeed, anything illegal's going on." Paolo's tenor dripped with sarcasm.

"...and indicates," Laura continued, ignoring him, "that he's collected information—"

"That Dunne wants," Paolo snapped. "That he's probably willing to kill for, and that Talon can use against him—or you." Dark-circled eyes with impossibly thick lashes regarded him. He forced himself to meet them, no matter what the cost to either of them. Anything to protect her. "Look, Laura, you know as well as I do that legal bull can be manipulated to say anything the reader wants it to say. Hell, give him this, and all Talon needs is Gus's body to turn jargon into a murder indictment against you."

"He can't—"

"Wake up, Laura. He *can.*" Paolo snatched up the papers, shoved them into her face. "Look at the dates, damn it. Gus had these drawn up the day before he took his mother to Amherst.

He's been planning this for a long time. You go down, he goes free, Mom gets taken care of.''

"Why?" Laura's voice was soft, pained, direct. "How?"

Paolo's jaw worked. "Why? He's a coward, and you're available. How?" He looked at the table, at her. "I'm not sure yet. Right now it's a gut—''

"You sit behind a desk—you don't believe in *gut*." Laura threw long-ago admissions into his face like a handful of February snow, raw and stinging. "I need facts, Paolo. *Gut* doesn't prove anything. *Gut* won't make cases.''

"No, you're right, Laura, it won't. But gut's like paranoia. Use it right, and it'll protect you.''

Her voice as flat as her eyes, Laura asked, "Who's that talking, you or your partners?''

Paolo's lips whitened, knuckles tightened around the pages in his fist. Reconciliation interrupted by scenes from the marriage. "Just me, Laura, looking after you. Same as always.''

For an instant, dark eyes met dark eyes; silence seethed between them, waiting for the last word. Then Laura rose, picked up the check and headed for the cashier, giving action the final say. Paolo let her get halfway across the restaurant before he checked his pride with a violent "Damn!" and shoved back his chair to go after her.

She was out the door before he could catch her. Rain and slush had turned to wind and snow while they were inside; Paolo glared at the sky and turned up his collar. Laura was clicking down the empty street ahead of him, through the weather, oblivious to it.

Storefronts reflected her image, wind heightened the natural color of her skin, snow frosted the hair tossed back from her face. The worst weather brought out her beauty as easily as mood did, and Paolo felt the part of himself that was unable to resist her come awake inside him. "Laura."

She hesitated at her name, let momentum carry her a few more steps before she stopped beside an alley. Control was everywhere—in her rigid posture, in her face turned to look at him over her shoulder, in her voice. "You were right," she said. "This was a mistake. You and I can't deal with each other without things that shouldn't matter getting in the way.''

"This—" Paolo lifted the fist that still held the legal papers, then let it drop. "This isn't something that shouldn't matter, Laura. One way or another, this means your life right now. Gus—"

"Gus isn't part of this—" Laura waved a stiff hand back and forth between them "—this here. This is just us, Paolo, you and me, the way we've always been."

"If you mean you and I disagreeing about your partner's ethics—"

Laura took a step backward on the sidewalk and swung to face him fully. "I mean you and I doing our damnedest to hurt—"

There was the sudden squeal of tires in the street, and a long black blur jumped the curb, knocked over a parking meter and careened toward them.

Chapter 7

Stunned, Laura turned her head and watched the car bear down on them, unable to move.

Paolo reacted without thought. With an urgent sweep of his arm, he grabbed her and flung them both deep into the alley behind a Dumpster. The car's bumper brushed her thigh in passing before the vehicle fishtailed into the street and sped away, barely missing several parked cars.

Too shocked to think, Laura simply hung squashed between Paolo and the brick wall behind her, listening to her heart thump, feeling the pound of Paolo's, the harsh in-and-out of his breathing above her head, the shiver of his arms around her, the roughness of the wall at her back. His mouth was against her hair, his hands on her shoulders, her neck, her face. And she was shaking uncontrollably.

"Laura."

She opened her mouth to answer, but the only sound in her throat was a low keening. Reaction turned her legs to spaghetti, made her sag. Shuddering, she buried her face in his shirt, wound her fingers into the lapels of his coat and hung on tight.

"Laura." More insistent now, edged in panic. He lifted her face. "Are you all right?"

She wanted to nod, but it didn't seem possible; she managed to bob her head once. Something felt like it was thudding low in her right thigh, but it didn't seem worth mentioning even if she could have. Not now.

Frantically she tried to burrow deeper into his arms—or was that him trying to haul her closer? His mouth slid down the side of her face, and she turned to meet it.

Make sure she's alive. That was Paolo's excuse for touching her. His hands skimmed along her arms without direction, down her back and sides, roughly up her thighs to her waist, then around underneath her jacket and up her back again, over her shoulders. Catching in her hair. Pressing her into him and holding on...holding on...

Make sure nothing's broken, check for bleeding...

He felt her try to twist nearer, and reaction wracked him. His gut churned in recognition; he'd almost lost her, and she wasn't his to lose. Had to do something about that.

Her mouth skidded across his chest and lifted to him. He heard a roaring in his ears, felt sanity slip away. Laura soaked his senses, took possession of them, became sight and sound, touch and scent. The taste of her filled his mouth: the sweet, rough-slick slide of her tongue under his; the soft, plump-ripe underside of her upper lip; the smooth-sharp outline of her teeth; the faint iron-salt flavor of blood when a tooth nicked her lower lip.

He lifted his head for a breath of cold reality, and she strained to meet him, hands climbing his shoulders, arms twisting around his neck. A little desperate, but that was all right, he was desperate, too. He dropped his hands below her waist and rounded her bottom, rucked the plush, hoary knit of her slim dress up her thighs.

Her body softened, making accommodations to his; he felt rather than heard the low vibration rise in his throat when the cleft of her thighs met the thrust of his and settled. The sharp pleasure-pain in the hardening in his groin was like fire burning him alive. Laura's fingers brushed his face; she whimpered invitation, and he willingly threw himself full-tilt into the flames. Her mouth left his, her tongue rasped over his face, eager, furious, and the roar grew in his ears, his body. He'd been so long without her, so long....

He gathered her to him, and together they lurched down the wall, into the snow-dusted lumpiness of plastic garbage bags and sodden paper.

Laura awoke to the wet chill first. It permeated her dress, then her senses, then her sensibility. She opened her eyes and saw the darkening alley, the gray sky overhead, the garbage around them, and humiliation and futility flooded in. "No," she moaned. All the time she'd spent learning to squelch and live with her animal-primitive desire for Paolo, and here they were, the moment he touched her, behind a Dumpster in an alley. Didn't get much more depraved than this. "Oh, no." She shoved at Paolo, rolling out from underneath him and stumbling to her feet when he loosened his hold. "Oh God." She leaned against the Dumpster, feeling nauseous, one arm wrapped around herself, the other hand covering her mouth. "Oh, God, no."

In front of her, Paolo climbed to his feet. She watched the glaze leave his eyes and shocked reality set in. He took a step toward her. "Laura?"

"Don't." She waved him back and turned away, limping toward the street. Her soggy dress dragged along her hips and thighs, reminding her who she was with him. Not as classy as she liked to pretend. Not as civilized. Not in control.

"You're hurt."

He was at her side, slipping an arm around her waist to support her. She pushed him away. "I'm all right, it's only a bruise. Leave me alone."

He caught her again. "I can't, Laura."

"You have to, Paolo." She yanked herself out of his grasp and faced him, shaking with emotion. "Please. Don't touch me. I can't let you, not again, please. I don't know who I am with you. The first time we were in an elevator, a hallway, the floor right inside the door of my hotel room—we barely got the door closed. Now we're in an alley behind a damn Dumpster. We never seem to be able to touch each other without—"

"Exceptional circumstances..." Paolo offered hollowly, reeling under his own hormonal-emotional battle.

Laura's hands jerked into fists. "Don't offer me excuses, I make up enough of my own!" Her mouth trembled; she put a hand to her lips, stilling them by force, and shut her eyes. She hated this, but it had to be done. "I need your help, that's why

I called, but I should have remembered. Nothing's ever casual with you. Not how I feel, not how I am. I want you—God, I want you, I always do—but you make it too easy to lose myself in you. And after we're finished, then what? There's always that to think about—who will we be tomorrow?"

Her shoulders drooped, and her voice softened to a grieving tone. "I love you, Paolo, I love you, and I can't. I'm afraid of who I become with you, how possessive and obsessed. I can't go back to being that person, and God help me, I'm scared to death that I would, I will, if I let you touch me again." She lifted her face, and her mouth twisted; she turned her hands palms up in supplication. "I'm sorry, you've gone a lot of extra miles for me today, but—" She swallowed. "I feel dirty. Will you take me somewhere I can get cleaned up?" Another pause, another swallow, this one painful. "Please."

"Sure." Paolo jammed telltale fists into the pockets of his long coat, kept emotion out of his voice. The first time he ever touched her without waiting for an invitation, and he went and screwed it up. *Time and place,* he thought. *Can't get a handle on 'em.* "No sweat. Let's go."

He jerked his chin toward the street in a *c'mon* gesture and started down the alley in his patented Italian who-gives-a-damn swagger, without once checking to see if she followed. Aching inside and out, Laura huddled into her jacket and trekked after him.

God, it was cold. It was so damned cold....

You should have gotten a better look at the car.

The accusing voice in Paolo's head was as relentless as the car's tires humming along the Thruway.

You should have paid attention, gotten the license number, thought about the fact that the car might have been a blind for someone waiting in the alley to kill her. But no, you were too busy copping a feel behind a Dumpster like some oversexed kid.

Copping a feel? he asked himself with some derision. Where had he gotten that from, and what did it mean? And why was he comparing his reactions to Laura to those of a kid? A kid didn't have enough experience, enough years on him, to feel as primitive as he'd felt back there. Someone—Talon, Dunne, maybe even Gus—had upped the ante on this nightmare by aiming a couple of tons of steel and chrome at Laura, and he'd seen the car and stopped thinking straight, forgotten his professional self.

Fortunately, Futures & Securities' away team had been on the ball; while he'd been mauling Laura in the alley, they'd made and traced the car. Stolen, of course, with no apparent connection to Dunne, Talon or Gus, but Paolo had even less faith in coincidence than his federal nemesis, and none whatsoever in his own personal evaluation of the situation. Hell, he should know better—he *did* know better. But sometimes that didn't stop him from doing what he shouldn't and regretting it later—especially with Laura. No excuse, but where Laura was concerned his instincts—his libido—too frequently seemed to get ahead of his thoughts.

Except what had happened wasn't libido. The current between them ran far deeper than hormones, and they both knew it. Scared the hell out of them, too.

He glanced over the back seat to where Laura slept huddled beneath his coat, face pale and troubled in the flashes of light from passing cars. Four hours ago, as she'd requested, he'd found a motor lodge off the eastbound Thruway and checked them in. Without looking at him, she'd limped into the bathroom with her overnight bag and shut the door; the shower had run for an hour.

She'd emerged wearing more makeup than he remembered ever seeing on her, dressed in a shapelessly bulky, high-necked thigh-length copper-colored sweater and an equally shapeless black skirt that stopped at her heels. As though, Paolo thought bleakly, by covering up her body she could deny its existence, its response to him; as though by covering her face with makeup she could disguise her druthers, or her puffy eyes and blotched cheeks, or hide from him at all.

But he didn't really think it was him she meant to conceal herself from.

He took a quick look in the rearview mirror and changed lanes. He'd known letting her get to him was a bad idea, had denied to himself how bad. But knowing what was and accepting it were two different things.

First rule of business, he reminded himself bitterly: Know your enemy. Second rule: Don't start what you can't stop.

And if you'd met the enemy and it was you, and if what you couldn't stop had already begun?

Rule number three: Control the damage—ASAP.

The car phone buzzed; he picked it up. "Gianini... Have they? No, but I didn't anticipate they'd let it go this fast. Talon's got something in mind.... No, she'll want to go back to the beach.... Yeah, bring in the sweeper. If there are any bugs, I want to know, but leave 'em in place.... Ahhh..." He looked at his watch. "We should be in by two.... a.m., Jones, get with it.... Yeah...yeah... Will do. Listen, Casie—" He paused, swallowed, and followed rule number three. "Ask Jules to pick up Laura's things and meet us at the house. Tell her to plan to stay. No, I'll be in the office in the morning.... Mmm-hmm. G'night."

He set down the receiver and caught Laura's reflection in the rearview. She was awake; her eyes were vulnerable and sad. "Lawyer got your house released, you can go home."

"I heard." She sat up, wincing when her right leg made contact with the seat. "You're not coming." Not a question.

"No."

"The alley?" she guessed. "Damage control?"

She was, Paolo remembered, in business, too. He nodded. "Damage control."

Her lips tightened, formed over her teeth; she looked out the window. "Probably best."

For whom? he wondered, but nodded again. "Probably," he agreed.

"I'm sorry," she whispered.

Paolo said nothing. Typical, he knew.

It was a long road home.

Chapter 8

The beach was cold, dark and bitter, filled with the ever-present hush of surf on sand and rock. A barren sea of dune grass and dying scrub pine bent to the wind, holding their ground by making accommodations to it.

Laura's house sat above the beach, half a mile in off the paved road, where a weather-faded wood-burned sign still said Haas. Years of winter gales had swept large quantities of sand away from the foundation, left a sense of things standing rough-hewn and unfinished. By the light from the garage flood and the front porch, the house looked like what it was not: a stark, sand-scrubbed-gray cedar-shake-covered two-story three-bedroom home with high ceilings and loads of potential. It wasn't until you got around to the beach side that you realized the potential had already been fulfilled.

Full of some wary, dark anticipation, Paolo glanced at Laura, coming awake in the back seat, and stepped out of the Lincoln into the frozen mud of the rough circular drive. For the second time in three days, he eyed the place where, in retrospect, he'd spent too little of his life. *Too late now,* he mocked himself, and turned to appraise the area inch by inch, taking in the air of dishabille left by the police and marshals, the hurriedly slapped-

back-together-and-rein-forced splinter damage Talon's crew had
done to the front door—concentrating on Laura's safety rather
than his own regrets.

Now that he was leaving her, this stark, windswept land she
loved seemed a dangerous place too far away from anywhere
else. Too accessible to the ocean, the wind, Dunne, Talon, and
anyone else who wanted her on his agenda.

He faced into the weather, into the freezing rain, the kind of
cold that cleared the clutter from the mind and left only clarity.
Second thoughts, third thoughts, and fourth—where Laura was
concerned, he had them too often. In her arms and out of them;
before the divorce, during and after. He'd never totally found
his balance with her; without her it was worse. Decisions blurred
like the pattern on the crazy quilt that had covered their bed.

On the road it had seemed the simplest executive decision in
the world to bring in Julianna to watchdog Laura—certainly the
safest, sanest choice to make under the circumstances. Julianna
was cool, effective, and more capable than almost anyone else
he knew of following through on what had to be done when the
need arose. He'd entrusted Jules with his own life on more than
one occasion. Now he knew that his own life didn't mean as
much to him as Laura's did. He couldn't leave Laura with Jules.

Behind him he heard a car door click; with a groan, Laura
tried to ease herself into the night beside him. He bent to her in
an instant, reaching.

"Your leg? Is it bad?"

Without thinking, she gripped his hand and hauled herself
upright. "It's bruised. I'll manage."

Paolo slid his forearm under her elbow, supporting her.
"Don't be a hero, Laura."

Laura took a step, grunted, swore and leaned heavily on him.
"You should talk," she snapped.

"Maybe I should." Paolo placed Laura's hand on his shoulder, slipped his arm about her waist. "At least then we both
know that I know whereof I speak."

Laura's response was lost in her step, groan-under-the-breath,
curse, step, groan, et cetera toward the house. Somewhere in his
core, Paolo absorbed every wince, every caught breath that
shuddered through her. His fingers tightened on her waist. It was

a good thing he was leaving. "I worry about you," he said quietly.

She gasped a note of painful laughter and pressed her forehead to his shoulder. "Oh, God, Paolie! Me, too, about you. It's just never done any good."

"Not when you wanted me to quit being who I was because you were 'concerned' about me."

"*Concerned* is not a dirty word," Laura said stiffly. The old verses came back too easily. "And as for what I wanted, I don't think I ever knew. Except for you."

"Laura—"

She twisted toward him, stepping back at the same time. Her face was pale and unsure in the artificial light. Her eyes were afraid. "Don't go," she said.

"Laura—"

"I need—I want you to stay. I know what we decided, and, God help me, what happened, but I can't..." She shut her eyes, stiffened her tongue against the roof of her mouth to keep her chin from trembling. Fear was a weakening, galling, all-encompassing emotion, easy to deny, difficult to face. For the first time in her life, she looked at Paolo and dealt with fear, upfront and honestly. "I can't feel safe, can't—don't—trust anyone but you. Please. Stay."

Paolo felt more of the carefully maintained shards of ice inside him slip. Where he hadn't been able to do more than form the thought, she'd framed the words. She'd always had more courage than he to change her mind—and say so.

He leaned sideways, hoisted her up the five steps to the porch and set her down. "I'm not going anywhere, Laura."

"Good," she whispered. Then the door opened and Julianna Burrows, eyes full of censure, stepped aside to let them in.

The house was a shambles.

The carpeting had been torn up, the backs of the cloth-covered chairs and couch opened, the fireplace examined and sooty fingerprints left on the floor. Coffee grounds littered the kitchen, carelessly moved crystal lay smashed in the sink. Everything that had made the master bedroom an office had been seized;

only the metallic hollowness created by empty filing cabinets remained.

Down the back hall in the bedrooms, the mattresses had been slashed open, the pillows laid waste, the closets emptied. Nothing had gone untouched. Even the light fixtures had been opened and scrutinized.

Laura saw it all through eyes filled with shock, disillusion and anger. What she'd left in pristine condition had been handed back in tatters. She understood now that the federal search warrant, obtained and executed for Talon by the U.S. marshals service, allowed them to do exactly that: tear the premises apart and search it without regard for the property it contained—after all, it only belonged to an alleged perpetrator, right?

She sucked in the rank odor of suspicion made judgment without a trial, feeling betrayed, violated, not only by Gus, but by the system that had always had her trust.

Beside her, Paolo stood tight-jawed and read something different. The message was clear and succinct: *I'm in charge here, and I can do what I want. You'd better, too.* "It's Talon," he said quietly. "Talon did this."

"I'm sorry," Julianna said.

Eyes focused inward, Laura drew herself erect, apart, without seeming to hear. Paolo put out a hand, but didn't attempt to touch her, knowing she wouldn't accept the comfort even if he knew how to give it. He understood her need—not unlike his own—to fold into herself and find some composure before exposing herself to the impotent parade of *"I'm so sorry, is there anything I can do?"* that would begin shortly. Already he felt the words building inside him; already Julianna had expressed them.

Paolo bent to retrieve a piece of glass and a bright orange photodegradable garbage bag from the kitchen floor. "Let's get to work," he said.

Deep anger numbed at first, enervated, then revitalized. Fueled by it, Laura moved through the house like a dynamo, side by side with Julianna and Paolo, despite the throbbing protest of her leg.

The damage was more for show than anything, contained primarily to replaceable or reparable objects. The worst of it was the furniture and carpeting, which would have to be recovered and relaid respectively, and three garbage bags full of stuffing and glass. But, after ten years at the east end of the south shore, she was an old hand at the three Rs: rebuilding, repairing and replacing. If neither hurricane Bob nor E.T., the extratropical, had succeeded in turning her out of her home, it would take more than one ambitious federal agent named Talon to accomplish it.

With Paolo's and Julianna's help, she'd inventory the true extent of the destruction in the morning and get on to her lawyer about suing for compensation, take a stab at checking the balances of the system. Even if she failed, it'd be worth the aggravation to drag Talon into court and make him defend his excesses in the name of the law. An act of God was one thing, but this... She shook her head. She'd worked too hard for too many years to get the house the way she wanted it to let this kind of blatant nuisance harassment slide.

Not to mention the havoc it played with her reputation, self-esteem and emotions.

Eyes flat, she picked a once-exquisite Swiss anniversary clock off the floor beside the cherry sideboard. The bell cover was broken, the clockface folded, the hands bent outward at a ninety-degree angle from where they should be. It was a remnant of their honeymoon, the first thing—really the only thing—she and Paolo had ever bought together. Paris, midautumn, cradled in her hands.

She turned at a passage of shadow through the light behind her to find Paolo holding a fractured wooden box full of Paolo-and-Laura photos she'd stuck away in the back of the linen closet, waiting for some nebulous emotional statute of limitations to run out so that she could dispose of them. His eyes were exhaustion-bright, his hair was disheveled; there was an unprotected quality about him, a bruised defenselessness that Laura never remembered seeing.

She took one step toward him, he took one back and sifted a handful of memories, eyeing the battered relic she held.

"Brings it back, doesn't it?" His voice was rough with hints of Italian.

Clutching the clock tight, Laura nodded. "Whether we want it to or not."

Paolo's gaze flattened on a point behind her head, his mouth twisted. "Sometimes I do," he said.

He turned abruptly, headed who knew where, and Laura limped quickly, stiffly, around to stop him. "Paolo."

"No." He shut his eyes and shook his head, refusing to look at her. "I'm sorry, Laura. It's...damned romantic notions."

"It's—I know, I understand. I get them—"

He swung around to face her. "Don't," he said savagely. "Don't *understand*. Don't identify with me—that's where we began *and* ended, being too much alike. I couldn't...live through it again. So do me a favor and stay on your own side of the past, and we'll both be fine."

"Will we?" Laura taunted him quietly. "Will we? I'm standing here holding my side of the past in my hands, and I'm not fine. I look at you and I'm not okay. I think of you and I come apart inside. You reach for me and I remember what it was like the times we touched and the times we could have but didn't. I hold this clock and see that box of pictures and I remember Paris, and the rose petals you used to cover the bed, and making love on the stairs, and the minutes we had, and everything we might have been together afterward—and weren't. And now *our* clock is broken, and *our* box of pictures is torn, and it's like seeing some hope I didn't even know I still had dumped into the ocean, and I'm *not fine,* Paolo. Not fine at all."

"You think I am?"

"Aren't you?"

"No."

Anticipation, terrifying and intoxicating, stirred through Laura uninvited, pricked along her thumbs. Her bruised leg began to tremble uncontrollably; maybe she'd been standing on it too long.

Eyes on Paolo, she leaned into the sideboard and tried to still the trembling. "No?" she asked, daring him, like a grown-up child, to be honest.

"No," he stated, meeting her dare with his own. His gaze shifted to her leg. He moved toward her, put down the wooden box and took the broken clock out of her hands. "If you don't get off your feet, you'll fall down."

"I just want to—"

"Let it keep, Laura. It's as good as it's going to get tonight. You need some rest."

"I will right after I—" She took a step toward the kitchen, caught herself on the wall when her right leg crumpled under her. "Maybe you're right."

"Happens sometimes."

Surprised, Laura looked at him. Joking and cracking wise were not part of Paolo's usual mien. Laughter came out of nowhere, cleansing, healing. She shook with it, letting its relief scour the recesses where only shadows had lain for years. "I'm sure it does," she agreed when she found her breath. "Often."

"Well..." Paolo shrugged modestly.

Laura grinned, running her gaze over his silk suit. "You're overdressed for fishing."

"I was an altar boy, not a Boy Scout."

"Never learned to be prepared?"

"Only for death, not for life."

The statement was light, filled with the unemotional philosophy of a life lived. Caught by the unexpected truth, Laura's attention sharpened. She tilted her head to view Paolo from a new angle.

"What?" he asked.

"Nothing," she said. "Just something I thought I saw. Not to worry. It's gone now." She drew a breath and stretched, catching a yawn on the back on her fist. "I'm going to bed."

"Need help getting there?"

Humor and regret flitted across Laura's features. If Paolo were any other man, she might have to think twice before framing an answer to his question. But he was Paolo, and he meant exactly what he asked. "No, thanks. I'll lean on the wall."

Lean on me, Laura, he wanted to say—and didn't. He'd barely said half the things he'd really wanted to say in his life. Especially to her. "Laura..."

"Hmm?"

"Sleep well."

She looked at him, eyes once again looking bruised and vulnerable. The muscles in her throat bunched. "Maybe tomorrow," she whispered, and moved toward the shadows at the end of the house, pausing once to look back. "Paolo?"

"I'm here."

"I'm glad," she said softly. "Thanks for staying."

"No sweat," he responded, for the second time in twelve hours.

This time he meant it.

He couldn't sleep.

Stretched the length of her cream-on-cream couch, with its gutted cushions, his muscles were in knots; down the long back hallway at the end of her house, Laura was not near enough and she was too near.

He shifted beneath the heavy blue-green-purple-black afghan he'd found in the linen closet and listened to the tinkle of glass being sifted in the kitchen: Julianna cataloging damage. She'd wanted to leave when he'd decided to stay, but he'd talked her out of it. He trusted himself alone with Laura now even less than he had earlier, didn't feel he could rely on his own sole judgment if she were faced with immediate threat again. Safer for Laura to have a backup around in case his treacherous libido decided once more to divorce his brain, or his traitorous heart got the better of him, as it was threatening to do.

There were too many things about his ex-wife he liked, too many little things he'd deliberately forgotten, too many memories coming back. Of the light that used to darken and pool in her eyes if he simply ran a finger down her arm. Of the fire that ignited as easily as temper beneath her don't-touch-me surface. Of the unfettered I-am-comfortable-with-my-body arrogance that had, once upon a time, let her strip for him and tell him what she wanted, offer him what she had, accept whatever he could return, without embarrassment or restraint.

Of how it had felt to be skin-to-skin with her.

Of the many times she'd opened her heart and taken him in, despite the increasing provocation he'd given her not to.

Of how strangely peaceful it had been—despite their many storms—to simply love her.

With an explicit curse, he slid upright on the couch, swiveled and bent over his knees, face in his hands. His chest ached, and he felt like a man unraveling beneath the consequences of past mistakes and new admissions, fresh realizations.

It wasn't remembering the bad parts of their relationship that left his mouth filled with the taste of something bitter; he was haunted by the good. By the knowledge that he'd thrown away more than he'd bargained on when he'd thrown away Laura.

Blindly he reached for the coffee table to find the stack of faxes, phone messages and Federal Express packages Julianna had brought out from the office. Switching on the floor lamp beside him, he dragged an air-express Tyvek envelope out of the litter of reports, proposals and requests and slit it open.

Begin somewhere, he thought, and dumped the contents in his lap.

Black print danced before his tired eyes for a moment, then settled. Even then it took a minute to register that the documents were printed in Italian, not English. He stared at them without comprehension, numbed mind readjusting to thinking in his native tongue. Trying to assimilate, he glanced at the signatures at the bottom of the first page: Father Frederico Campanella, Maria DeSantes Gianini.

His mind froze, then switched on with a snap that jarred him all the way down to his heels.

Quickly he flipped through the top document, collecting understanding from the mass of words through single words and phrases: Roman Catholic, emotional distress, for the wrong reasons, dissolution of vows, *annulment.* The word stood out, corkscrewed its way to his center and weighted his lungs. After three children, seven years of divorce and twenty-one years from the date of their marriage, Maria had faced down the Church, confessed to their mistakes and gotten them annulled, as though they'd never been. He might have laughed at the anticlimax—if he'd been able to breathe.

Fingers pricking with premonition, he turned over the documents accompanying the dissolution decree. The first was a copy of the motive: a marriage license dated three weeks ago, six months after the annulment had come through. Maria had wedded a man whose name Paolo recognized as that of a family friend they'd both grown up with. He held on to the page for a silent instant, wishing them happiness, before skipping the handwritten lavender note attached to it in favor of the legal parchment underneath. And just like that, premonition was fulfilled.

Paolo stared at the pages in front of him, feeling as if he were

trying to breathe with the ocean closing over his head. His eldest
son, Edouardo, a man now of legal age, had petitioned the courts
to change his name from Gianini to his new stepfather's surname. Petition granted, no questions, no discussions, a fait ac-
compli.

Nerveless, he slid Edouardo's message aside to pick up the
final document: adoption papers for his youngest son, Giani.
"Please sign these," the note attached to it, written in his fifteen-
year-old's scrawl, requested. "It will make things easier for everybody, and it's what I want."

Somewhere inside him, Paolo felt the corkscrew twist deeper,
find his heart and draw blood.

He'd spent five weeks in Milan this past spring—from Palm
Sunday to the first of May—and no one had said anything to
him about any of this. He'd always known he was missing huge
chunks of his sons' lives, but he'd never imagined missing the
cues to something like this. He looked again, but there was nothing in the packet about his second son, Mauro; hope rose, but
he squelched it, sure it was merely an oversight to be corrected
with the morning mail.

The roar of silence grew in his ears.

God, Maria and his mother were right. He was a lousy father,
a lousy brother, a lousy son. When it counted, he was absent,
too busy dealing with death to pay attention to life, tilting at
impossible windmills and skewering ghosts.

He ground the heels of his hands into his eyes. Damn, how
had it happened? He'd never wanted to become his father, had
fought it with everything he had. Tadeas Gianini lived for his
work, scheduled appearances with his family, gave them everything money could buy—except his time. Now here Paolo sat,
twenty years out of boyish ideals, and just like Tadeas, sched-
uling his life around the timetable pride and honor had drawn
around him.

In his twenty-year quest for absolution for Lisetta, to find her
true killers and establish some kind of peace for his family, all
he'd done was lose his sons. Hell of a price for something he'd
only lately begun to realize had never been worth the cost.

But that was Tadeas's legacy. Pride and honor were ferocious
companions, bred in the bone, impossible to ignore. For twenty
years now he'd paid homage at their altar, just like Tadeas,

unable to escape his genes. And now Edouardo was following in his footsteps, and the other boys were close behind. Some examples they'd had to follow.

God, Paolo thought, somewhere along the way he was going to have to figure out how to let go of his dead sister and embrace what was left of his one-note life. Before he lost anything—any*one* else.

Unseeing, he stared at the spot in the corner of the room where the drapes gapped and let in a subdued dawn. From far away, through the mess of his conscience, he thought he heard the sough of slippered feet on thick carpet. Heard them pause.

"Paolo?"

Laura's voice, Laura's scent, infiltrated the gloom. He didn't turn. "Yeah?" Too brusque, he realized, and too late to call it back.

He closed his eyes in silent apology and felt her hesitate, then move closer.

"What's happened? Is something wrong?"

"No. Nothing. Everything's fine. How's your leg?"

"Sore." Paolo felt her measuring his answer while she considered her own, knew his came up short. "I got up for some ice."

"Talon leave any?"

"Don't know yet. Have to see." Paolo listened to her open the freezer door, heard the clatter of ice against hard, frozen plastic, the sound of it rattling into a plastic bag. "Just enough. Guess nobody needed to frisk the ice."

He tried to chuckle at the joke and failed miserably. "I guess."

Too late, he heard the thickness in his own voice, knew at once she wouldn't miss it. But she surprised him. She studied him thoughtfully for an instant, then turned to go without a word.

Chest tight, he watched her limp toward the hall, suddenly remembering the times they'd played this scene in their marriage: one of them wanting or needing something from the other without saying so, leaving manipulative little clues for the other to pick up on, the other pressing the former for response and getting nothing, so pressing harder and more irritably until all that was left to either of them were short, clipped sentences and slamming doors and the unsatisfying anger that they'd somehow been looking for in the first place to mask the needs they didn't want—or didn't know how—to handle. Only this time, Laura was strong enough not to play, and he was glad.

A deep, spacious calm filled him. "Laura," he called softly. "Stay. Please."

She stopped and turned; her voice was strained. "I want to, Paolo, but I promised myself I wouldn't let us do this. I can't unless you talk to me."

"I want to," he said, "I need to, but it's tough to do what I've never done."

"Try."

He glanced at the papers, looked at Laura. "She remarried last month."

"Who?" Eyes on him, she crossed to perch on the coffee table, balanced the bag of ice on her injured leg. Confusion became comprehension in a flash. "Maria?"

He nodded. "Papers came today. She worked on the church annulment for a year. It came through six months ago, and I didn't know."

Laura went still, her emotions tangled. "How does it feel?"

He shrugged. "I don't know. Might have made a difference once, now it's anticlimax."

"What about the boys?"

Paolo hunched over his knees, eyes flat. "They're old enough to make choices, and they have."

"Paolo—"

"'Douardo changed his name, and Giani's asked me to sign adoption papers. There's nothing here from Mauro, but..."

It was inadequate, but she said it anyway, because she meant it. "I'm sorry."

"Yeah, me too."

"Is there anything—"

"You're here."

"Fat lot of good that does you."

Paolo took in her thermal-knit pajamas and sheepskin slippers and flashed her the remains of a smile. "You're underdressed for fishing."

Her smile held her heart and his pain in it. "Yeah, well..."

Dark eyes to dark eyes, they shared a moment's silence. Then Laura asked quietly, "What are you going to do?"

"I don't know. It's done." He shrugged; capitulation was painful. "Half of me says let go, they're gone, don't make things worse for them. They're so far away, and I can't be there all the time, and they've known this guy longer and better than me—maybe the best thing for them is to love them enough to let them go."

He rested his elbows on his thighs, let his hands hang between his knees; his thoughts were far away, his expression was distant and ferocious. "The other half," he said flatly, fiercely, "the other half reminds me that I am not bleeping Solomon, and that, while I may not have loved their mother, I do love them and I don't want to let them go without a fight. Maybe I can't do anything about Edouardo except take the slap standing and let him know his decision doesn't change our relationship as far as I'm concerned, but Giani and Mauro... Maria may control how often I see them, but her husband can't adopt them without my signature, and—"

He stopped suddenly, breathing hard to let the wind out of his emotions, and grimaced at Laura, eyes blank. "Like I said—" he made a two-handed gesture of defeat "—I don't know. There's no tidy way to handle it. Long-distance relationships..."

His voice trailed away. Laura set what was left of her bag of ice on the floor and moved onto the couch beside him. "Go," she said softly.

Paolo looked at her. "What?"

"Go," she repeated. "Don't stay here for me."

"Go?" He sank back into the couch, chuckling mirthlessly, and ran a hand through his hair. "You may not realize it, but that's easier said than done."

"Why?" Laura skimmed her knuckles over the back of his neck. "I'm business, this is family—your children. They take precedence. Go."

Paolo closed his eyes, focused on the warmth where her knuckles lingered. "You're not business," he said thickly. "Anyone said you are is either a fool or a liar."

"You told me. I told you."

"Then we're both liars." He turned his head, met her eyes. "We're both fools."

"Paolo," she whispered, just his name, nothing more. Paolo felt her fingers scrape the back of his neck, up into his hair, down into his collar, halfway up again, and pause.

Inside him, everything froze, every muscle and nerve concentrated on her fingers, on the touch he'd imagined too often and wanted too badly. The hair on his nape fuzzed, sensation skittered up his spine like dry leaves along pavement on Halloween night, tangible, uncertain, reckless.

Next to him, he sensed Laura go still, felt her fingers stiffen against his neck and fist slowly into her palm. Opening his eyes, he looked at her, all at once recognizing something in her expression he'd seen often when they were married but never understood: she thought he'd just rejected her.

Insight was swift and stunning. Communication between man and woman was in more than what they said to each other. It was in nuance and expression, tone and response.

In the blink of an eye, a montage of unexplained moments rivered through Paolo's mind. Moments when he'd been sure they were growing close and she'd turned away. Fragments of expression, of a hesitancy that had grown in the years they were married.

He'd grown up without much in the way of physical contact, without even really knowing that he'd missed it—until the first time Laura touched him. Every time he'd frozen because he wanted to savor the feel of her so badly that he was afraid moving would break the contact, he'd sent her a message he didn't intend to send. By stiffening, as he inevitably did when she touched him, he told her "hands off", not "stay," as he meant.

He felt Laura start to draw her hand away, and the cold, alone place inside him panicked. His nerves screamed, *Don't go, touch me,* but for some reason he'd lost both the words and his ability to say them. God, for the first time in his life he knew what was wrong in time to fix it—and he couldn't get the words out. He, Paolo Gianini, so skilled in the arts of negotiation and verbal persuasion that government experts consulted him on ways and means to handle delicate political intercourse, couldn't find a way to tell this woman he'd loved that the signal she'd read wasn't the one he'd meant to send, that what he wanted was the opposite of what his body was telling her. She had to know. He'd screwed up telling his sons, but Laura had to know that she meant more to him than the stray moments he'd once offered her implied.

Awkwardly he arched his neck up to find her fingers, turned his head and pressed his cheek to the back of her hand. *Help me, Laura*, he thought. *I'm not sure how to do this, but please don't go.*

He opened his eyes and met hers, and she must have seen it on his face. The muscles in her throat bunched when she swallowed. She smoothed back his hair, held his cheek in her palm. He didn't reach for her, but it wasn't for lack of desire, it was because, as always, he wanted her too much and was afraid of scaring her with the extent of his need.

Instead he tilted his head down, found her wrist with his lips. Her pulse fluttered and moved frantically beneath his mouth, then resumed its normal steady pace. She released a long-held breath.

"I know," he heard her whisper. "Me too. But go slow." She repeated it tightly for emphasis. "Slow."

He nodded, brushing dry lips across her palm. "Get it right this time," he agreed.

Then he raised his head and looked at her again. And in that immediate place and time they both understood what was possible; both retreated in fear. The question *How can I trust you?* seemed to fill the atmosphere, to haunt it with longing.

"Laura." His mouth framed her name without sound.

She blinked, and moisture glinted in the corners of her eyes. She put an unsteady finger to his lips and shook her head once. "Don't," she said, and eased herself off the couch, picking up what was left of her sack of ice as she went.

"Laura." Her name had substance this time, the sound of it as thick as the weight in his throat.

She faced him, trying to catch her breath through the ache of distrust in her lungs. "I'm sorry," she whispered. "I—"

In some distant reach of the house, a phone rang. Laura turned toward the sound, greedy for distraction, but Julianna had already reached it. Backlit by the harsh glow from the fluorescent light over the stove, she stood in the kitchen doorway, studying

first one, then the other, of them. Her gaze settled finally on
Paolo, ice blue and accusing. As plainly as words, it reminded
him: *The involved professional is the dangerous professional.*

How well he knew.

"Goddard checked in," she advised him coolly. "She thinks
she and Cronkite have Abernathy treed in Cutchogue. It's your
case. You call it."

Paolo glanced at Laura and rose, dragging his jacket off the
back of the couch and snapping his cuff links into place, torn
between the uncontrollable desire to get his hands around Gus's
throat and his inability to leave Laura's safety in someone else's
hands. The choice, as always, between relinquishing control in
one area and retaining control in another. A matter of priorities.

Again he looked at Laura—harder, deeper, this time—taking
in the flawless skin and slender jaw, the occasionally quiescent
mouth that had the ability to reduce him to shreds in a heartbeat;
the eyes that refused to offer compromise, challenging him instead to decide for himself, to choose. He knew without a doubt
that the easier choice by far would be to put on his shoes and
go after Gus. Easier, not necessarily better.

The annulment and adoption papers on the coffee table
seemed to demand his attention; he was all at once keenly aware
of where *easy* had gotten him thus far.

With a twinge of trepidation, he pulled at the knot he'd just
cinched in his tie and turned to Julianna. "Tell Cronkite and
Goddard to stay put," he said. "You're on your way."

Chapter 9

Silent as a ghost sidling through the night, Laura hugged her heavy wool greatcoat to her and slipped past Paolo—sleeping for the third night in a row on her tattered couch, instead of in one of the guest beds—and out the window wall onto the terrace.

The morning that greeted her was windless, clear and cold, bright with stars. Against the horizon, as though rising out of the Atlantic itself, she could see the edges of the sun, a faint pinkish-orange glow that made promises she wondered if it could keep.

Automatically she scanned the beach, the ocean, as she did every morning, looking for late-season fishing dories or the whales she always hoped to spot at this time of the year. Looking, she supposed with a sense of revulsion, for Gus, who had not been at Cutchogue—or any of the other villages along the Forks that Julianna had spent three days combing through. But the sea was flat and empty, a gray wilderness without a mark that stretched to meet the dawn.

Inside, she felt what she always felt looking at it: a sense of immenseness and awe, a thrill of apprehension and expectation, a case of lungs and imagination that could never expand far enough to breathe in the ocean's possibilities. Like Paolo, the ocean was beyond her ability to control and, therefore, both dangerous and appealing. Both called to her wherever she was, refused to leave her alone. Neither belonged to her, but both were part of her, and she, somehow, belonged to—or perhaps with—both.

November storms and winter wastes notwithstanding. Speaking of which...

Guiltily she glanced over her shoulder at the house. From its glass prison, her reflection peered nervously back.

Like a child promising a parent to be good, she'd promised Paolo that she'd stay in the house, away from the windows, until they figured out what it was that Dunne wanted badly enough to kill her for—if not for her own sake, then for the sake of Paolo's sanity. Simply by standing out here she courted storms, but she'd needed a breather.

For the past two days, all they'd done was keep the drapes pulled and sit together in half light and caution, going through the files Futures & Securities had culled from the disks Paolo had purloined, studying the federal seizure inventory her lawyer had messengered out to her, reviewing the papers from Gus's attorneys, tracing and retracing the computer trail that had led Laura to her own suspicions about Gus.

She shivered a little inside her coat, and her right leg knocked against the bars of the iron balustrade. The deep ache of greening-purpling bruises made her wince, reminding her once again of the car, the alley, and a host of things she'd rather forget.

Gus had a lot more than his disappearance to atone for.

Talon had come out day before yesterday, smug and gloating, to announce that early that morning, in a hotel between Buffalo and Amherst, a maid had discovered the body of a man slain execution-style, on his knees, wrists cuffed, one bullet at the base of the skull. His fingerprints twinned those in an FBI file on a reputed wiseguy with apparent ties to one William Dunne. They also matched a partial thumbprint lifted from the front seat of a stolen car found abandoned on a Buffalo side street. The car matched the description of the one Futures & Securities reported had attempted to run down Laura. Talon had then introduced them separately to file photos of the dead man and William Dunne, wondering if Laura could identify the man as someone who'd had any connection to Gus.

The face of the dead man had meant nothing to either Laura or Paolo, but the pictures of Dunne had disturbed her. There was something familiar about the man, something more personal than the possibility that she'd simply seen his picture in the society pages. Still, she hadn't been sure that Dunne's familiarity wasn't simply wishful thinking, a desire to point a finger and get out of the mess, so she'd said nothing.

When Talon had left, she'd gone back to reading files with Paolo, more certain the longer she looked at everything that something was missing, something important that she had to remember, wanted to remember—besides all the things she'd spent the past five years trying to forget about Paolo, that is.

In the two days since he'd received the papers from Maria, she'd watched her ex-husband changing before her eyes, losing a measure of himself. It hurt.

For as long as she'd known him, Paolo had been arrogant, impatient, obsessed, driven—battling demons over which he'd never accepted he had little control. The Paolo who sat with her now was a quiet, vulnerable man, haunted by the choices he'd made, an aging dragon-slayer who'd begun to question his reasons for continuing with the hunt at all—to question the quality of the life he'd created.

Though he'd mentioned nothing more about the boys, Laura knew that he'd waited up late or gotten up early to call Maria, Edouardo, her parents, his family, her lawyer—anyone who might offer insight into what he might do to change events already in motion. She knew, too, that he'd gotten through to no one but Maria's lawyer, and that whatever the man told him had cut to the bone; when she'd gone to him after and touched his arm, instead of shying away, as she'd expected, Paolo had turned into her arms and let him hold him—something he'd never done, not even once, when they were married.

They'd stood a long time beside the same phone table in her foyer where the dead pigeon had lain less than a week before, holding on, sharing nothing more than warmth and grief and darkness.

She'd attempted once again to tell him to just go to Milan and take care of what he could, but he'd simply shaken his head in the hollow of her shoulder and mashed her tighter to him, mumbling something about having to learn when it was time to let go of one piece of your life to make room for another, about the cost of impetuous decisions, and about hindsight, wishing that when he'd met Laura he'd known what he knew now. And, without wanting to, Laura felt the not-quite-dead embers of an impossible emotion begin to glow inside her.

For better or worse, she wanted to hope again. And Talon and Dunne and Gus, with his magic money-laundering slash embezzlement slash trust-fund-to-take-care-of-Mom schemes, be hanged.

Fingers clenched around the terrace's iron railing until they turned white and purple, Laura looked at her piece of the beach, carved away by November's storms, then at the dead ocean, somehow ominous in repose—like chaos lying in wait.

The truth was, she'd intended to keep her promise to Paolo to stay in the house, but she couldn't. Paolo himself made it impossible. His nearness irritated her nerves and her hormones; the protective grip she'd kept on her emotions for so many years was loosening.

She'd changed the house completely, purged her environment as best she could, but she couldn't turn around without finding something of him where it didn't belong. She couldn't breathe without finding the taste of him in her lungs, and she'd begun to anticipate their accidental brushes with the greed of a clandestine admirer who hasn't apprised the object of her affections of her desires.

Gus had often accused her of seeing more with her heart than her eyes. Her heart, she had as often retorted, was more honest than her eyes, saw what her eyes too often missed. Her heart had seen and believed in the good parts of Gus, even as her eyes and mind had seen something else. Lucky for him, he'd agreed, grinning, then sobered and reminded her where her heart had left her standing with Paolo. Her heart was the part of her that ached when she looked at Paolo and remembered....

She shut her eyes until they stung; it didn't help. Physical hunger was becoming its own precarious universe, with Paolo at its center. Something as straightforward as the backs of his fingers grazing the backs of hers over an investment report had become filled with erotic moment, made her think of roses and rain and...

Paris.

She stuck her hands in her pockets and leaned into the railing for support. Funny, until she'd picked up the clock the other morning, she'd forgotten that trip. What kind of woman forgot her honeymoon?

The kind of woman who chose to.

Had she, she wondered sadly, chosen to forget?

Maybe. Memory was selective at best, and that had been a good trip, a good time. Maybe she hadn't wanted to remember. Easier to excuse the break, make it clean, if she forgot.

They'd been close in Paris, physically, emotionally. Difficult not to succumb to the city of lovers. They'd held hands, wrapped arms around one another, shared kisses in the falling snow. They'd made love, hot and uncontrolled, on the steps beneath a bridge, and again on impulse between floors in the antique elevator at the hotel. Then in bed through the night, lost in one another, passionately learning the way to each other's souls.

And they'd talked—night talk, secret and revealing, about dreams and fears, about who they were, and what—and held on to each other with careful hearts and trembling hands and made love again at dawn.

She'd wakened to the scent of roses on her pillow and found the bed littered with petals, the room filled with flowers, and Paolo naked beside her, with one deep red rose in full bloom centered like a surrogate fig leaf on his sex.

She'd looked and blushed and reached for the flower. He'd hardened, and the rose had lifted willfully into her hand; she'd blushed brighter until he'd drawn her down and whispered against her lips, *"Je t'aime,"* and other, more poetic, more erotic things the formal and inhibited Paolo could never say.

Things he wanted to do to her, with her, what he felt—all the things that were in his heart.

And she'd forgotten.

She shut her eyes. What else had she forgotten, what other insanely special moments had she discarded because they hadn't lasted long and had been too far between to make up for Paolo's unexplained absences, his frequently inhibited formality, his inability to say or even remember the things she needed to hear when she needed to hear them? Why was the negative so much easier to recall?

Paris wasn't Paolo's style; neither was the alley. Both were

too gritty, too uninhibited, too lacking in the unrevealing formality that was part and parcel of his life. But the man who'd
surprised her with Paris had been with her in the alley the other
afternoon. Passionate, impulsive, uncontrol-led...intimate. And
she had responded then as she had seven years ago, with the
same willingness to be seduced by his hunger, his need for her.

A current passed through Laura, an emotion more obscure
than anger, more reckless than love. The woman who'd seduced
her husband on those dark, secluded steps in Paris had wanted
to be taken in that alley three days ago, wanted to remember
what it felt like to be that uninhibited, that heedlessly free.

She gripped the terrace's cold iron railing with hands more
chilled than the weather had made them, and sucked in air filled
with reality instead of Paolo. Better to risk a few stabilizing
moments of abstract danger in the open than to stay inside
watching him sleep, remembering how easy it was to love him.

Better to flaunt her presence to Dunne or Talon or whoever
than to dwell on knowing without a doubt that, when she'd
retired the past two nights, she'd gone to sleep in the wrong bed
and in the wrong room, and that wherever she slept he should
be with her.

Always.

The thunder rose inside her without warning. Called beyond
reason, or perhaps *to* one, she stumbled backward and slid the
double door open on its soundless tracks. Paolo stood near the
sideboard, sliding the knot of a fresh tie to his throat, even
though, as far as Laura knew, he wasn't planning to go farther
than the living room today. A cup of steaming coffee and a
holster-with-handgun sat on the buffet near his elbow. He
glanced sharply at her, startled, then concerned, then rapidly
furious.

"What the hell were you doing out there?" he demanded.

She eyed him, distracted. "Breathing," she murmured without breaking stride, drifting by him and down the hall to the
office that had once been their bedroom.

"Laura," he insisted, following. "What are you—? What's
going—?"

One hand to her mouth, she waved him back with the other.
"Can't," she whispered. "Not now. Please. Have to...let me...
figure it out."

"Figure what out? Laura."

Again she waved him off. Shaking, she stepped into the middle of the room and stopped, waiting for she wasn't sure what. *Revelation.*

The room was different from the way it had been before Talon and his posse came. There was a vacancy in the light slap of her slippered feet on the oak floor, a sense of hollowness in the atmosphere, as though whoever lived here were in the process of moving on. The desk and chairs still sat in the middle of the floor, the filing cabinets were in their niche, but the drawers were open and empty, the files seized, and the computer monitor, the hard drive and the other office machines were also gone, confiscated by the marshals.

Oblivious of Paolo, confused and concerned behind her, Laura shivered and ran her fingers through her reflection in the heavy glass that protected the inlaid desktop as though she could wipe out what had happened and erase her image with the dust on the glass.

It wasn't only the room that was different today; she was changed, too. She felt as if she'd lived years in the past few days, experienced a lifetime. That was what it was like with Paolo, always: intense, exhausting, confusing, frightening and rewarding. A process of never quite knowing where she stood, but being intoxicated by the possibilities.

Drawn by the room's reflection, Laura moved toward the windows, wondering what she'd find if she could somehow crawl through the looking glass. Hope ghosts flaunted their come-hither, *maybe* shadows at her from the corners of the room, and she remembered the woman who had once lived in this room suspended above the winter beach, who'd paraded naked and modeled silly hats to her husband's laughter, and who'd known how to play, and she wanted...

She felt Paolo's familiar presence come within inches, his warmth close but without invasion. For the second time in five days, his reflection wavered indistinctly against hers, connected in illusion. She flattened a palm against its window image, trying to touch the essence of who she-he-they'd been, to remember what she'd hoped, and why she'd hoped with Paolo.

Less than a week ago he'd told her that there had never been anyone else for him. Three days ago, in the middle of trying to tell him something else, she'd told him she still loved him. He'd reached for her without quite connecting how many times? She'd turned to him without meaning to how many more?

Verbally they shoved each other back, emotionally they reached. The messages might conflict, but the signals were clear.

She wanted him.

He wanted her.

Together they were a bundle of misplaced need.

She covered her face with her hands. Her head hurt, and she felt fifteen; everything was out of whack. He thought he was a stark, unemotional man, but she knew differently: Paolo had more emotions than she could count and he could handle. Why else would she still be so drawn to him?

Well, li'l missy thing, her mother's voice whispered from the shadows. *Still haven't got the sense God gave a flea, have you?*

Can't help it, Ma, never did. You always said there's no way for a woman to feel mature with a man on her mind, and you were right. I haven't been mature since I met him. Not once.

Damn it.

She met Paolo's eyes in reflection. His hands hovered near her shoulders for an instant, then dropped to his sides.

"Damn you, woman," he muttered fiercely, "you're scaring me. Talk to me."

"And say what?" she asked, abruptly spinning to him. "What do you want me to say?"

"Anything," he answered. "Tell me what's going on in your head. Tell me what's bothering you. You can say anything to me."

"Since when?" she demanded, putting distance between them, all at once needing space to use her hands to help her talk. "Tell me when I could ever say anything to you. You never wanted to hear anything."

"That was then," he said softly, intensely. "You were different, I was different, the situation was...*different.* This is now, and *now* I'm telling you, damn it, say it. Whatever it is."

"Oh God, Paolie." Laura swung her arms wide, her laughter choked with pain. "I wish that were true. I wish I could...tell you."

"Why can't you?"

"Because *I'm* not the same person I used to be. I'm a lot

more careful about who gets to see all the little pieces of me, but you, you're still on the other side of the room, so what's different, Paolie? How has anything changed?''

His jaw worked in silence; he studied the windows, as though looking for answers in the ocean. She could have told him the sea never offered explanations, kept mysteries locked tight in a fathomless safe. But then he pocketed his hands and faced her again, eyes steady, mouth firm, and she felt the breath *whoosh* out of her. He had answers and he intended to reveal them.

''I want to be over there with you, and I can tell you that,'' he said quietly. ''I couldn't have done that before.'' He took his hands out of his pockets and turned them palms up, offering them to her. ''I want to touch you and hold you and make things better, and I can tell you that, too. That's how things have changed.''

''But you're still—''

''Do you want me over there? I'm willing, but I'm no good at—'' He paused, looked away, then back at her, revising as he went. ''I don't trust myself. I don't know what you want. I—'' He swallowed. It was harder than he'd imagined it would be to say what he meant. To her. ''I need the words, Laura. Say them. I'm here. I'll come.''

Of all the things in her life she'd ever wanted, the only one that came to mind at present had his name on it. It was the one thing she'd wanted for him five years ago, and she wanted it for him still. She wanted him to let go with her, to forget himself and all the reasons he *shouldn't* and come apart in her arms.

Sound stuck in her throat, part laughter, part hiccup, part sob. She covered her mouth with a hand and faced the windows. ''Damn it, Paolo, do you know how long I waited for you to be able to tell me that? But your timing stinks, because I don't have the f—.'' She bit her tongue, refusing to give in to the obscenity. ''I don't have the words anymore.''

He took two steps toward her. ''Maybe I could help—''

''No.'' She raised a hand to stop him. It bobbed in the air between them for a moment, before she gathered her fingers into a fist and let it drop at her side. ''No,'' she repeated, and strode from the room.

''*Laura.*''

He was after her in an instant, moving fast, trying to get around her, but she skittered away.

There was only so much room she could allow him in her life at the moment; she didn't want to be seduced by her memories, nor by the fact that they were both in need of a little human kindness, a little human contact. And he was much too close to crossing that particular emotional threshold for comfort.

"Don't Paolie, I can't take this."

"Not till you talk to me. I've waited a long time to hear me say things to you, too, and I—"

"No." Laura swung through an open doorway—any door would do, so long as she could close it, with him on one side and her on the other.

She had no idea where he wanted to get to out of all this, if he'd considered end results at all, but she knew herself. She knew what she wanted at this moment, and where she wanted to wake up six and ten and fifteen years down the road. And she knew what would happen if she stayed out there talking to him.

It would be so easy to give in to the temptation to give him her body again, to partake of his. To soothe a craving she had no business indulging; to accept a moment that she knew from past performance wouldn't last.

"Where I am," she said unhappily, wishing she could make him understand, "may not be the greatest place in the world, but it's a damn sight better than some of the places I've been, and I'm not going back."

"You can't go on, either." His voice pursued her relentlessly through the wood. "Not without facing me first."

"I can try."

"That's not what you said the other night. You told me to look at us. You pushed me to meet you halfway, Laura. I am. Now it's your turn."

"Yeah, well, that was you." Gnawing her thumb, Laura paced the rectangle of fake fur on the floor of her bathroom. "I don't want a turn."

"Too late." Paolo twisted the doorknob and heard the lock click into place. "Damn it, Laura. I didn't make you do this through a door."

"You wanted me to do it. I don't."

"God, woman, I hate this part of you."

"I'm not particularly fond of it myself."

Chuckling, Paolo rolled back against the wall. "At least that's honest. So what now?"

Laura hiked up her coat around her. "You could go away and do security things so I can think."

"I can do security things just fine from here, thanks."

"I'm not coming out until you leave."

"Settle in for a long wait, then."

"No problem," she shot back, moving over to sit on the only thing there was to sit on in a bathroom. "I'll just make myself comfortable right here and—"

Splash.

Knees tucked beside her ears, mouth gaping to her chest, Laura sat in the bowl, suffering a curious montage of reactions, ranging from disbelief to outright fury.

Cold water penetrated the heavy wool of her coat, lapped merrily against her backside. Two days and three nights he'd been in this house, and already she was up to her ears in the toilet bowl because men had to be men and leave the damn seat up.

Righteous outrage simmered and came to a boil during the three tries it took to lever herself upright, and the two tries it took to undo the lock and yank open the door.

"Good," Paolo said affably before he got a look at her face. "You changed your mind. Now maybe we can get—"

Laura grabbed the lapels of his suit jacket and shoved him against the hall wall. "You unbelievable, arrogant, insensitive, inconsiderate, ignorant *male!*" she ground out. "Two days, two bloody days, and you can't remember to put the damn seat down in the bathroom."

"What?"

"What do boys' parents do?" She tightened her hold on his jacket and yanked him forward as far as she could—almost an inch and a half—and shoved him back into the wall. "Take them into the bathroom when they're two and say here's your throne, you're the only one who's ever going to use it, so go ahead, leave it open, and aim high?"

"What the hell are you talking about?"

"You, me and the bathroom," Laura said evenly. "I'm wet. I fell in. You left the seat—"

A sudden vision blindsided her from out of nowhere. Three days after their last fight, he'd moved the last of his things back to the city. She'd been lonely, distraught—aching, glaringly aware for the first time that this was how life at the beach would be from here on out. The house was hers and hers alone again. Empty, no aggravations, no fighting for space, no need to make accommodations to anyone else's idiosyncrasies—everything tailored to her specifications, everything the way she liked it, time for the hurrahs.

Instead of cheering, though, she'd stalked into the bathroom, slammed down the lid on the toilet, decided she didn't like the way it looked, so perversely jerked it open again—then burst into tears. For two years she'd fought with him over the position of that lid, and the minute he left, there she was leaving it up herself, because she missed him and his quirks more than she'd dreamed possible, and this petty little thing made her feel less alone, allowed her to live, for a fleeting instant, with the sense that she had someone coming home to her.

Fury evaporated without warning, left laughter in its place.

Laura choked on it, reveled in it and sagged against Paolo, using his crumpled lapels to hold herself upright. "You left the seat up," she howled, hysterical. "I'm all wet."

"So you said," Paolo agreed uneasily, uncomfortable and dumbfounded, trying to figure how to handle this. As far as he knew, no one had yet written a manual on the proper etiquette to deal with a faux pas of the commode variety. He had no idea if a simple note of apology would cover it, or if he should send flowers. In lieu of either, he made an awkward attempt to steady Laura by her shoulders. For some reason, she seemed to laugh harder. "I'm sorry."

"Don't be," she sobbed into his shirt. "I'm not."

A curious warmth stole through Paolo—a kind of fuzzy static-electricity sensation he wasn't sure he'd ever experienced before.

He looked down at her sleep-styled dark hair plastered across his chest, at her tear-streaked, laughing face, and felt the seed of an emotion that had taken root inside him when he'd first met her push through the soil and blossom.

"Are you all right?" Before he realized what he was doing, he'd lifted a hand and used a fingertip to push aside the strands of hair caught in her mouth. "I don't think I've ever seen this side of you," he murmured.

"I know, it's too bad, isn't it?" Laura gurgled, raising her face to him and sobering a little. "Think of the trouble it would have saved if you'd met this side of me sooner. But I was always so busy trying to be somebody serious who fit the image of the sophisticated business world I thought you—and everybody else I was dealing with—lived in that I sort of…laid aside the things of a child."

"That is too bad. I think I'd like to have known that side of you."

"You'd have run away screaming. Would have saved us a wedding, a divorce, and me a lot of therapy trying to figure out why I failed so miserably at something I wanted so much."

A look of pain flitted across Paolo's face. He set Laura away from him. "You didn't fail." His eyes were dark and emphatic, his voice laced with a passion that said he'd thought about this a long time and believed every word. "We…" His hands balled at his sides. Even when he was willing, mistakes were hard for him to admit. "*We* made mistakes. We forgot…to make accommodations to reality. We… It was so easy at the beginning, we forgot that somewhere along the way it would get to be work. It did."

"You don't own it till it costs you?" Laura asked softly. "Until you…accept the cost and go on?"

"Yeah, maybe."

Something unnamed rippled down the long hallway and hung suspended between them. Something like an invitation, a place to begin.

All at once Laura knew she wanted him back, wanted him where she could reach him as often as he'd let her. Wanted him where she could let him go, if letting him go was the only way left to love him. It was a hell of a lot easier to stop being married than it was to stop caring.

To stop loving.

She touched his face with her fingertips, let them rest lightly on his chest. "Do you own it yet, Paolie?"

He looked at the wall behind her head, down at her and offered up a lopsided shrug. "I think I'm still negotiating the price."

"I'm sorry."

"Way it goes—isn't that what you say?" She nodded, and his eyes pinned her suddenly, shrewdly. "What about you? You still ready to back away from the hard things, Laura?"

"Between you, me, Gus, Talon, Dunne, and the man in the moon?" He nodded. She shrugged, watching her feet. "I'm working on it."

"Good," he muttered hoarsely, and Laura was suddenly intensely aware of the sodden drag of her coat against her legs, of the chill along her backside, of the knots her stomach was tying itself into—of the warmth that was Paolo beneath her hand. Funny, for all his reserve, he had the warmest hands of anyone she knew. Even at his coldest, he radiated enough heat to melt the eastern seaboard in February.

She leaned her forehead against his chest, wanting a little of his heat for herself, needing to take the chill off. To get close—but not too close. Just...nearer...

Paolo felt his muscles stiffen, then relax, where she touched. She had an uncanny knack for getting to him, giving him what he wasn't even aware he needed, at the very moments when, left to himself, he would have chosen to move away. She had the ability to reach inside him and rearrange his soul with a flick of her finger.

He swallowed. Her hair was soft, tickly, beneath his chin; if he bent his head and breathed, he could smell the ocean air that lingered in the syrup-colored strands, taste the essence of the woman.

Peace seeped through the chinks in the wall he'd built around himself, settled, deep and tranquil, in the pit of his tormented gut the way Laura shifted and settled the length of his chest—unthreatened, unthreatening.

Sighing, he lifted a fist, watched his fingers unfurl and brush gently through the silken mass resting near his shoulder, found his other arm coming up on its own to round her shoulders and gather her in.

"Tell me, Laura," he said softly, "what do you want?"

She turned her face up to him. "You," she whispered. "I want you."

Chapter 10

The tension coiled inside him, stunning and ferocious. Her mouth hovered bare inches below his, soft and pliable, full and promising; heat seared every place their bodies made contact. He couldn't breathe.

"Laura—"

"You asked," she said fiercely into his hesitation, "I'm answering. I want your hands on me, Paolo. I have for days. Put your hands on me."

"Here?" He felt lost, unsure, unaccustomed to having his own desires echoed so plainly in so many words. So easily. He had to be sure. "Don't start what you can't stop." A warning.

"Don't want to stop." Her hands moved restlessly inside the folds of his jacket, down his sides. "Never stop."

She'd learned something inexorably important in the moment he'd brought his arms around her, something she'd been too blind and too dim-witted to realize when they'd been married: Paolo could neither touch, nor be touched by, someone he didn't love.

He had, now and always, given her every part of himself he knew how to give, shared none of himself with anyone else. Let no one else touch him, allowed no one else to comfort him to any degree at all. Not Maria, not anyone. Except her. Ever.

The knowledge was heady, shaming, shattering, electric—and it opened doors her heart had no choice but to go through.

She dipped her fingers inside the shoulders of his jacket, ran them over his shoulders and along his jaw, framed his face with them.

"Laura." Just her name, a shivery brush of air across her lips. His eyes darkened, his breathing was short, harsh against the press of her breasts, and her own breath quickened. "Laura." His fingers flexed in her hair. "Tell me."

"I want you," she whispered. She straightened slightly and, with a roll of her shoulders, let her coat fall away. "I want you with me, I want you inside me, I want—"

"Here?" he asked it again, desperate, feeling his hands tremble when they skimmed her throat and caught in the wide collar of the soft knit sweater she wore, baring her shoulders. She lifted the satin skin into his touch, laced her fingers into the buttoned edges of his shirt, and he felt his senses scrambling for control, his reserves fading. Nothing mattered except this minute, nothing existed outside it.

It would feel good to take her here, flat against this wall, to ease the ache of years and let the burning inside him become a conflagration. To forget himself with her, only with her.

No one else could do what she did to him; no one else made him feel this...this frantic desire to crawl inside her and never leave, to drown in her—to consume, and be consumed by, her.

Celibacy was a state he'd observed by choice for five years without considering the alternatives because, for him, there were no alternatives, neither in time nor in inclination. This feeling of need, desire, *desperation* to mate, to become a part of someone else, belonged only to Laura. Inside her lay a piece of him he hadn't even known was missing, the key to his senses, the balm for his heart, the serenity for his soul. God, he needed her.

He'd been so long without this, without her....

"Damn, Laura." His breath savaged his lungs, his body was tight, ready to explode. He dragged her against him, hands riding her hips, rounding her bottom, and ground himself against her. "You don't know what you're doing. Please know what you're

doing. Don't do this unless you mean it, because I can't—can't
hold on..."

"Then don't hold on. Let go." He felt her tug, heard the tear,
listened to the clatter of pearl buttons along the wall. Felt the
rush of air across his chest. "Let me love you, Paolie. Here—"
Blood boiled, heart pounded. "On the floor—" Her mouth was
open and hot, her teeth sharp, tugging at his nipple. He arched
convulsively into that welcome heat, caught his hands in her
hair, urging more. "In the bathtub—" Her fingers were sure,
releasing his suspenders, impatient at his zipper. "I don't care,
Paolie, any damn where at all. Just..." She rubbed her hands up
his chest and into his hair, tipped her face to him. Her eyes
glistened with emotion, her lips were parted, hungry with anticipation. There never had been anyone for her but him. "Just put
your hands on me."

Too fast, he knew it, and he didn't care. It would have taken
a saint or a choirboy to resist her, and he was neither. He caught
her face in his hands and brought his mouth down on hers.

Everything promised in that dark kiss of days ago was here,
open to his marauding tongue and greedy lips. Heat and silk,
fire and fury, reckless speed—she offered and he claimed them
all. When she came up on tiptoe to wind her arms around his
neck, fitting her length tight to his, he groaned deep inside and
grasped her waist, turning them until she was the one with her
back to the wall. No time to think about tomorrow. With Laura
there was only today.

He bent his head to find her throat; her skin tasted of salt tang
and cold air and primitive needs. He traced the length of her
neck, her collarbone, with his mouth, tasted the hollow between
her breasts with his tongue. Her sweater was soft and hairy,
tickly against his lips. He hooked his thumbs into the big, stretch
neckline and slipped it lower on her shoulders, exposing her to
his caress, then slid the heels of his hands along her sides to
find the roundness of her breasts, the hard pucker of her nipples.

She made a hungry sound deep in her throat and braced herself on the wall, arching upward and fitting her hips urgently to
the rigid ache of his. He made an inarticulate sound of understanding, caught her hips and lifted her against him.

Her skirt was a soft plum corduroy with a deep front slit that parted readily when he bunched the fabric high and brought his thigh between hers.

"We should slow down." He heard himself rasp it from a distance, even as he tucked his hands under her skirt to rid her of her underwear and she released the hard, aching length of him from his. "Make it last."

"Later," Laura responded raggedly. She hooked a knee around his thigh, wrapped her arms around his neck and surged toward him. "Right now, just come home, Paolie, please. I need... Come inside, let me hold you. I want to...hold you."

"Laura—" He shuddered violently, losing his train of thought for an instant, when she pocketed a hand between them, stroking. "Laura, don't," he gasped, catching her hand. "I don't... want it...to be...like last time. I need you...more than that. I need—I want—*us*...right..."

She went still at that, withdrawing to tilt her head back so that she could see him. "Slow?" she whispered. "Like wait?"

"No." He shook his head, laced his fingers in her hair. "I mean slow like undressing you, touching and kissing every inch of you, feeling your hands on me. God, Laura, I want your hands on me..."

A wealth of feeling honeyed through Laura. Power, hunger, love...mischief.

She tilted her head, and her lips curved as she considered. "Like this?" She dragged her nails up his chest; his muscles rippled and clenched, and he groaned.

"Where's our bed?"

"In the wrong room, but we can move it."

"Now?"

"Do you want this right or not?"

Frustrated, Paolo laughed and buried his mouth in her hair. "You are the most aggravating—"

"You brought it up."

His chuckle was filthy, seductive, intimate. He hauled her against him, belly to belly, rubbing. "Uh-uh, not guilty. You did."

"Well..." she agreed modestly, and Paolo grinned and turned her around, spooning her into his hips and urging her down the hallway.

"Lead me astray, woman," he suggested into her ear—then

suddenly stiffened and whipped around at a faint click in the foyer.

"What—" Laura began, but he shushed her with a quick finger to her lips.

"I heard something." He tugged his pants together and reached automatically to the back of his waistband, swearing when he realized he'd left his gun sitting on the sideboard. Some bodyguard he made—which, if he remembered correctly, was exactly why he'd called Julianna. "Stay put," he told Laura, "I'll take a look."

Carefully he eased himself along the wall toward the kitchen doorway.

Floorboards creaked in the kitchen, and something thumped onto the breakfast table.

"Hey, Gianini, look what I got," a cool British alto called at the same time Paolo slid along the last bit of wall and rounded the doorway to smack face-on into his partner.

Tall, an inch or so over six feet and model-slim, Julianna squared off against him instinctively, as though she were a teen back home in the east end of London, before either her modeling or her piloting years had begun. Her carrot-colored hair was long, braided down her back and tucked into the collar of her navy turtleneck to keep it out of the way; she had on black jeans, black running shoes and a worn leather aviator jacket that should have made her look tough but somehow didn't.

"What the—"

"Damn, Burrows…"

"…give a person heart failure…"

"…knock once in a while."

"Not my job, boss. I'm supposed to be here." She stepped back and looked Paolo up and down. "You look like hell. What hap—" Her gaze strayed past Paolo to land on his gun on the sideboard, to find Laura disappearing down the dusky bedroom hall to change out of her wet clothes. "So." She lounged lazily against the doorjamb, regarding Paolo through eyes that were the pale blue of polar ice, and almost as warm. "Am I too late, or just in time?"

Paolo felt his jaw tighten, the muscle tick in his cheek. Guilty by being caught. Julianna always had been both too bloody quick at detail and too uncompromising to let it slide. "None of your business."

"No?" Julianna planted her feet and splayed the aviator jacket wide over her hands on her hips. "You louse up when I'm working with you and it's my life. Corporate Affairs 101, Paolie—keep your hands to yourself, don't mess with the clients. It makes you dangerous. You taught the class."

"Class dismissed," Paolo said evenly. "And since when have you paid attention to anything even remotely corporate?"

"Since you turned forty, talked us into a board of directors and started examining your life like it was your conscience— and since Casie got married, became insufferably happy, fixed her priorities and got pregnant. Somebody's got to be responsible while you both angst your way through midlife."

"And that someone is—"

"Excuse me," Laura interrupted, reappearing to place a hand on Paolo's arm. She got halfway through "Didn't Julianna say she had something to show you?" before he reflexively jerked his arm out of her fingers as though she were someone he didn't know instead of the woman with whom he'd been about to make love.

Too late, Paolo saw the shutters drawn on Laura's face and realized what he'd done; repeated mistakes were the easiest to make, the habits of a lifetime the hardest to break, misinterpretation and misinformation at the crux of most of life's snags. Before he could think how to correct the situation, however, Laura had slipped around him and Julianna and was at the kitchen table, examining the shoebox-sized chunk of metal the latter had brought in.

It was beige, weighed about sixteen pounds, had the words Colorado Data Systems printed on a label embedded in its front and looked exactly like the external hard drive Gus used to keep his files on.

Paolo suddenly forgotten, Laura shut her eyes and felt the bottom drop out of her stomach to be replaced by some curl of alertness, some cold, bottomless pit of tension.

The kitchen seemed to darken and close around her, became the Abernathy and Associates office of a week ago. Whispered by the voice behind the ski mask in the darkness of her office, the demand had barely registered over the terrifying bang of her heart. Even now, hearing the words in her head, she couldn't move; her limbs seemed weighted with shock, and her heart and lungs appeared to have expanded and seized high behind her ribs.

"Find your partner and tell him there's no place to hide," the voice within the ski mask growled. "Tell him we want the money and the files back. Tell him he's got two days. Tell him next time…" A bodiless hand traced the line of Laura's throat, over the high collar of her knit dress and between her breasts to the soft belt at her waistline. "Next time we're not polite."

Then hand and voice were gone.

Heart slamming, Laura steadied herself against the table and breathed. Of course, she thought, how simple, how obnoxiously obvious—and how like Gus, damn him.

Now she knew what was missing from the list of items the feds had seized, what the hooded intruder wanted from her, what she'd felt was missing from the desk when she'd arrived home to find Gus's suicide note taped to the computer down the hall— the evidence that Gus himself had alluded to hiding in the papers from the Buffalo attorney.

His files.

Just that fast, Laura felt dizzy. "Where—?" She took a deep breath, trying to control the sudden trembling in her voice. "Where did you get this?" she asked Julianna.

Julianna glanced at Paolo, who took a convulsive step toward his ex-wife, then back at Laura. "The trunk of his car. He turned it in to the leasing company you use in Sag Harbor for its regular tune up the morning after he supposedly died. Company hadn't heard about the trouble you're having. Abernathy told their service department he'd be gone for a while and wouldn't need his car back, could they park it for him. They figured the drive had to be important, but when they tried to call, nobody answered so they decided if nobody'd missed it enough to call and ask them about it by now, they'd wait and return it to you next week when their mechanic picked up your car for servicing."

"I see." Containing herself with an effort, Laura gripped the edge of the table. Gus was alive; she'd known it all along. The bastard. God, when she found him, childhood history be damned, he was dead meat. Sliced, diced, and roasted slowly over a hot fire. Alive. All she had to figure out now was where to find him before Dunne did. And she would. Guaranteed.

She drew a breath of decision and lifted her chin. "So what now?" she asked Paolo. "Make a copy of everything on the disk and see where it takes us?"

Steeped in senses still filled with her, in obligations brought back to him by Julianna's presence, Paolo nodded at Laura from the doorway. "If Dunne wants it badly enough to threaten you to get it, it must form at least part of the connection Talon needs to force an indictment against him."

Laura paled slightly. "And me in lieu of Gus?"

Paolo hesitated a fraction of a second, then nodded again, once. "Probably."

He watched her fingers contract around the edge of her sweater, glimpsed the war she waged within herself to hold her ground and not flee in the face of fear, and his heart clenched. She'd told him once she was a terrible coward when it came to facing the unknown, but he knew better. A coward didn't face the unknown.

Warmth rushed through him. He wanted to go to her, but he held back, knowing suddenly, without knowing how he knew, that she'd prefer to fight this particular battle with herself without his interference—the same way he'd had to fight too many of his own battles over Lisetta, Maria and the boys without sharing them with her.

Awash in druthers, he turned to Julianna. "How did you find the car?"

Julianna shrugged negligently. "Luck. When we went out the second time, we canvassed anyplace we hadn't hit before—used car dealerships, Rent-A-Wreck agencies.... Reports don't say anything about lease cars—or any cars at all. Didn't anyone ask?"

Laura shook her head. "The car never occurred to me."

"Why not?" This from Paolo.

"What?" Laura eyed him as though she hadn't understood the question.

"Why didn't you think about it? Why not look for it? Why assume Gus was even here? Get ready for it, because Talon's going to ask you, Laura. It'll be your word against the evidence."

"My word against—?" She stared at Paolo in disbelief. "What evidence? That's...lunatic. Why *would* I think about his car is more to the point. I mean, for God's sake, he left his clothes on the beach and a suicide note in our old bedroom while some guy violated the sanctity of my office and made threats upon my person. Three days ago someone tried to run me down in Buffalo—we reported it, and I've still got the bruises to prove it. So I mean, really, just pardon the hell out of me for being distracted and not thinking about Gus Abernathy's damned car."

"Laura..."

"Damn it, Paolie," she snapped, all at once angry with herself for allowing shock to skew her ability to turn two and two into a reasonable sum about Gus a whole lot sooner, and with Paolo for...for reasons that didn't make enough sense and were too numerous to go into right now. "What do you want from me?"

"Everything," he said quietly, and Laura looked at him. His face was intense, passionate, and she knew suddenly, without a doubt, that they were no longer talking about Talon, Dunne or Gus, but something else entirely.

Heat swelled and washed through her limbs, unnerving and ferocious. She caught her breath and let it go slowly; what he could do to her with a look should be boxed and regulated along with the rest of the world's lethal weapons. Patented, that look could bring the world to its knees—or maybe it was only her. To her knees, to his bed, to anywhere he wanted her to go, anything he wanted her to do...

Dangerous to let a man have that much power over you, her mother's voice whispered. *Look what it did to me. Look where it's gotten you.*

Shut up, Ma, I know. I'll be careful. Just shut up.

Willing away the echoes of another day, Laura closed her eyes and sighed. Wanting and loving Paolo had always been an emotionally tricky proposition. The ache from both cut jagged and deep, but it was childish to let her temper get away from her because, simply and gallingly put, she was too frustrated to be nice to the man she'd spent five years trying to quit loving, and who wouldn't let her touch him in front of his partner.

She had to face it—the size and bent of Talon's brain weren't Paolo's fault. Neither was Gus's desertion, nor Paolo's own current state of... She couldn't decide precisely what Paolo's current state was, but her own was...confusing, to say the least. Frightened one minute, calm the next, then angry— Lord, why did she always let the *him*s in her life get to her? She wasn't a novice at this with either of them; her heart shouldn't be so tender. Gus was only being Gus, nothing changed there. But Paolo...

She looked at him and sighed again. Maybe she was letting old wounds drain where they didn't belong, water under the bridge and all that. Maybe that little arm jerk he'd given her had been about his own frustrations and not about her-them at all. Maybe...

Hypersensitive, that was what she was. No excuse, just the facts.

Benefit of the doubt, she thought, turning it into a mantra. *Benefit of the doubt. We all deserve a little benefit of doubt.*

"I'm sorry," she said to Paolo. "That was...inex-cusable."

"Me too," he returned softly, and Laura, looking, found something in his face that she'd wanted to see for a long time but was afraid to recognize now: wary hope and tentative promise.

She ducked her head, idly tracing the pattern on the hard drive's label, trying to still her heart and put her thoughts together.

"The car?" Julianna prodded.

Laura hesitated, thinking. "I didn't think about Gus's car," she said finally, "because I assumed it was in the garage and I didn't use the garage when I came in. I was...frightened and not thinking straight. I parked in the drive outside the front door and came in to try to find him, or see if I could figure out where he'd gone so we could straighten everything out. Instead, I found his note, then his clothes, and—"

She swallowed and shrugged. "Anyway, afterward no one asked, and I guess I assumed his car was confiscated with everything else. Just now, I realized that I've been trying for days to figure out what was wrong with that inventory Talon gave my lawyer. Gus's car wasn't on it, and neither was this drive."

"What's on the disk, Laura?" Paolo asked. "Do you know?"

"His files," Laura said, looking straight at him. "Anything that wasn't joint business. Anything he wanted to keep...private. I think..." She hesitated, hearing the voice clearly in her head, as chilling as it had been in person. "I'm pretty sure…it's what the guy in my office said. They wanted them back, the files and…and…the money."

Paolo and Julianna looked at one another.

"I'll get the laptop," Julianna volunteered, and clattered down the foyer stairs after it.

From the wide living room entryway Laura watched Julianna arrange the Futures & Securities laptop computer with hard drive, miniprinter, fax machine and telephone modem on top of the smoked-glass coffee table. They were linked by technology to Futures & Securities' offices, a hundred and forty miles away, able to receive and transmit information in an instant. Paolo had said they called this office-in-a-box the No Excuses Box—as in no excuse for not staying in touch—and issued a briefcase-sized version to any F & S operative going into the field.

It was not, he'd admitted, a completely foolproof system particularly—he'd glared at Julianna behind her back—when issued to certain people, but for the most part the technology worked well, equipping them to work faster in areas like communication and identification than they'd ever worked before.

The physical setup of the system was much the same as the one Laura and Gus had used to stay in touch with one another, the office, the world financial community and some of their clients. Both at their individual homes and in the office, they'd kept their programs and data bases on unwieldy desktop personal computers, but their files and records were kept separate from the programs. Laura carted a notebook-sized laptop and floppy diskettes around with her, but Gus kept his private files on the external drive, claiming it was easier. Now Laura remembered why. All it took to make it work was a cable and a port in the computer to connect it to. Remove drive and cable, and no one who didn't know the office setup would ever know anything extra had been there. Especially not if you kept the desk dusted but slightly disarrayed and covered the bare spot with the telephone.

The last time Laura had been home before Gus's disappearance, the drive had been on the back of the desk, in its usual spot when Gus was working at the house. But the morning he'd apparently died, it had been gone. Without realizing it, Laura had missed the hard drive when she'd come in to phone Paolo that morning, because she'd automatically reached for the corner of the desk where the phone normally sat, but the phone had been at the back of the desk, covering up the "hole" where the hard drive no longer was.

She'd also unconsciously missed it again yesterday and the day before, when she'd gritted her teeth and gone into the office-née-bedroom to use the phone to call each of her clients.

For whatever good it would do at this late date, she'd wanted to try to reassure them about their investments and stem the tide of media-generated conjecture and inaccuracy about the IRS lockout and what was going on behind the doors of Abernathy and Associates. She might not be able to conduct business for them at present, but she knew that even a meager amount of contact from the person who handled their money would go down better than none at all when insecurity rose to a premium. She understood that where many of her clients were concerned, their children might *be* the future, but their investments insured it.

Sadly she narrowed her eyes and concentrated on watching Paolo connect Gus's drive to the port in the laptop. Between human paranoia and the IRS, she was well aware she'd have to start from scratch to rebuild lost trust and a damaged, if not destroyed, reputation. But, even when she wanted to, she couldn't blame Gus for everything, couldn't shirk her own responsibility in this. She had an obligation to admit culpability where it lay: in an eye unforgivably blind to the events that had unfolded in front of her nose.

"All set." Paolo straightened from his crouch beside the coffee table, twisting to unkink his back. His first turn brought Laura into view, and he was instantly aware of some subtlety in her posture, of a sadness quickly disguised in her expression. He took a step toward her, agonizingly conscious of his own inability to reach out to her in Julianna's presence—aware that, even if he could, Laura might not want him to. As ever, his ability to make love to her had served to emphasize, rather than decrease, the distance between them. "You all right?"

"Fine." Laura nodded.

"You want a minute before we do this? Even if we can guess what's coming, it might be difficult—"

"Don't baby me, Paolo, do it. Turn the damn machine on and let's get this done."

Torn between what she said and the ache that lay behind her eyes, Paolo regarded her unyielding figure for a moment. Then his mouth folded into an expression of quiescence and regret and he returned his attention to the computer. "Okay, you got it. Let's do it. Gus put any kind of protection on his files?"

Laura shook her head. "I don't know. Probably." She tucked her hands into the pockets of her skirt and rocked on her heels, looking anywhere but at Paolo. "I put macros on my files. You—" She met his eyes directly, dropped her gaze. "You taught me how at the conference where we met—string a bunch of consonants together that no one knows but me. Like a money-card personal identification number. Don't use vowels, because it's too easy to want to make a word that someone might guess." She grimaced and flipped a hand. "It's simple and effective, except that I have to keep the codes written down so I don't forget them."

"I remember," Paolo said, and Laura raised her chin and faced him squarely again. Awkwardness charged the atmosphere with that living thing between them, made it uncomfortable. Down beside the coffee table, Julianna squirmed but held her ground. Running interference between him and Laura, Paolo realized.

He stooped, abruptly aware that he didn't want the interference, that regardless of what else was going on, there were things he and Laura had to straighten out—by themselves, immediately, before things went any further. Except—he flipped the switch on the side of the laptop, turning on the system— whatever happened here concerned not only Laura's personal welfare, but her life, as well.

Two days of brooding quiet, with no word from Talon, no threats from Dunne, and, up till now, nothing on Gus, did not mean she was out of danger. It meant storm clouds gathering out at sea, hurricanes on the horizon.

With the bulk of Gus's files in her possession, she would be a target now more than ever, pursued by both Talon and Dunne until one or the other got what he wanted from her or she was dead. Even if she gave Dunne what he wanted, the likelihood that he would let her walk away without exacting a price was almost nil. Paolo couldn't let that happen. The view of mortality he'd gotten when he'd seen that car bearing down on her, the gentle, generous way in which she'd handled him when he'd told her about his sons, the scant moments they'd spent wrapped together in the hall—each new minute he had with her demanded care, reminded him of both what he'd discarded and what he'd lost.

He watched the system's checklist cross the screen, listened to the beeping and grinding as the machine came to life.

Time and experience had taught him many lessons: bitterness, distrust, resentment, anger…easy lessons, with easy fires to fuel. But neither time nor experience had taught him the hard things, the important things: to admit his shortcomings, to forgive.

To understand that what had gone wrong between him and Laura had more to do with impatience and reaching for quick fixes to solve problems that required time, attention and commitment than with her insecurities or his putting too many other obligations before her. It was Laura who'd finally begun to teach him that, in the past six days.

He looked at her, conscious of every nuance in her expression, of every emotion he'd ever experienced with her, of the turbulent shimmy of blood through his veins when he remembered how freely she'd offered herself to his heat, and everything inside him clenched. He desperately wanted to touch her, take her, wrap himself tight within her, except— He swallowed, looked at the floor. He'd done that once before, and look what they'd become.

No, he thought, what he *needed* now, more than anything, was the time to go forward with her, time to review, time to… He shut his eyes and let himself think about it: time to lie in bed and think of nothing more important than giving, receiving and sharing pleasure. Time for him and Laura to get comfortable with one another, to learn to trust.

Time to learn the rest of what she had to teach.

Which meant he had to find a way to bring the business of the drive, the money, and possibly even Gus, back to Dunne himself, then ladle the results into Talon's hands. Shouldn't be too difficult, right?

Beside him, Julianna muttered under her breath and banged on the keyboard, forcing Paolo's attention back to present business.

"I don't know what kind of protection he's got on here," she grumbled, "but it's good. We're going to have to send this stuff through the office decode program, and that's going to take time."

"How long?"

"Five, six hours. Maybe more."

He felt the warmth of Laura's thigh against the side of his back where she'd perched on the edge of the couch near him. Five or six hours, a lifetime and no time.

No choice in this business, he thought, except to hurry up and wait.

Taking a deep breath, he glanced over his shoulder at Laura, then settled himself deliberately on the carpet and pressed himself back into the cradle of her knees. After a moment's hesitation, he felt her legs part slightly to accommodate him, felt her fingers drift lightly through his hair and withdraw. *Welcome.*

Stifling relief, he nodded at Julianna. "Go," he said.

Chapter 11

Another day without results, tensions growing high.

Black clouds piled against the horizon, promising a storm they had yet to deliver. Paolo glanced through the kitchen blinds at the sky, then down at the pages in front of him. Decoded and hard-copied, Gus's files were no more enlightening than they had been locked inside the beige lump of metal and technology that William Dunne had threatened Laura to find and hand over to him. Certainly nothing that obviously tied Gus to Dunne in any fashion that would interest Talon and the IRS.

He flicked a rude finger at the copy. It was no wonder that bankers, accountants and investment counselors were so popular as fictional perpetrators of white-collar crime: shuffling and hiding numbers among all these other numbers, where only another expert might—not necessarily would—find them, had to be not only a tempting game, but one that was challenging and fascinating, as well. An easy ego trip. And hell, it was only paper, right?

Yeah, Paolo mused wryly. Paper worth millions.

He sighed and ran a hand across his face, adjusting the pages again. His eyes prickled and itched, and no matter how long he stretched his arms, the words on the green-and-white-striped paper eluded him; lately, every time he read a newspaper or an office report, his arms seemed to get shorter.

He shook his head, and the lines of print suddenly came into focus; it was like jiggling a camera lens. Somewhere in here there had to be a pattern Laura had missed—something his unbiased eye might spot. But he only saw what Laura had seen: There were discrepancies in a couple of the accounts, but nothing to point at, a penny or two here, a nickel there. Nothing excessive or unexplainable, nothing that hadn't balanced exactly when statements went to clients. Nothing Laura had overlooked or ignored—nothing even Talon's most suspicious mind would be able to make something of. A lot of nine-thousand-dollar-transactions would have suggested that Gus was laundering money for some of his accounts, since all transactions over ten thousand dollars had to be reported to the IRS. But there was nothing like that, no simple pointers. No, if Gus was laundering money for anyone, he was doing it with more circumspection than Paolo could discern. Probably embezzling it from them, but not laundering it.

Paolo sat back and considered that. With the kind of money Gus handled, embezzlement was certainly a possibility—hell, all he'd have to do was round down any extra percentage points from his clients' profits instead of rounding up. For someone in need, someone who understood computers and handled accounts, it was an easy way to accumulate funds, and generally unnoticeable. But, like the proverbial penny, three-quarters of a percent here and a half a point there added up—especially when multiplied by the kind of profits someone like William Dunne had to hide.

Paolo shook his head; without evidence, he wouldn't have given Gus credit for the nerve it would take to steal money from Dunne. The smarm and weakness to slide into business with him, sure, but not the strength or the guts to try to hoodwink him. Not without one hell of a provocation.

Paolo paused, suddenly thoughtful. Desperation to provide for a terminally ailing parent might prove exactly that.

The numbers blurred and became fuzz on the paper again.

Yawning, Paolo rubbed his face, making a rueful mental note not to cancel his appointment with the ophthalmologist next week. Simple pride had made him hold off the inevitable as long as he could, but middle age was a ruthless adversary. His battle with it grew more academic every year.

Time for a reality check, his body seemed to say, but he guessed all it really meant was that it was time for him to give a little ground. Age and experience both demanded compromises from a person—only some of them physical.

It disturbed Paolo to realize abruptly that he was thinking about Gus and his mother, Lilah, wondering how hard he'd feel pushed to make untenable compromises in the same situation. He'd made hundreds of...question-able...concessions on various occasions in the guise of duty, but to be faced with the same kind of sudden, unthinkable loss, then to be presented with the catch-22 option of hold on or let go...

He spread a thumb and forefinger over the bridge of his nose, smearing the unanticipated sting from his eyes. If Lisetta had lived, if the doctors had been able to bring her back but she'd remained in a coma... If there had been any choice to make at all, would his father have succumbed to the constant financial pressure of having to care for an invalid daughter twenty-four hours a day, seven days a week, for an undetermined number of years? Would he have given in to the temptation to filter funds from the money that passed through his hands at the bank? What would Paolo himself be willing to do to care for Edouardo, Mauro or Giani if the need arose? How far would he go for Laura?

A long way, he realized, sadly and without surprise. As far as necessary, and maybe farther. When your back was against the wall, you did what you had to do.

He blinked. However much he didn't care to think about it, Laura had made suggestions along those lines in the restaurant in Buffalo: that it was hard, if not impossible, to let go of someone you loved sometimes; that Gus had set his wheels in motion after his mother's stroke; that spending day in and day out looking at the numbers that represented the capital needed to keep Lilah situated had presented too much temptation. That Gus was doing what he felt he had to do to care for someone he loved.

Making excuses for Gus, Paolo had thought angrily at the time. But now he wondered bleakly how often Laura had made excuses for him, Paolo, too. Out of love.

Swearing, he sat back, again trying to force himself to concentrate on the numbers in front of him. Details, he reminded himself—crime pays when the good guys get careless over the details.

Yeah, but why is it always me gets stuck with 'em? he wondered. God, how he hated details.

The names on the pages before him changed. Paolo skimmed them rapidly, looking for any he recognized. A William E. Dunne appeared as one of Gus's accounts, as did a Bill Dunbar, a Dunstan Williams and a Liam Donne, but the money involved was minor—a few conscientious middle-class investors apparently gambling on the future. Of the roughly ten million people in the metropolitan New York area, Paolo decided, it would hardly be unusual to find more than one person named William Dunne, or variations thereof. Coincidental, yes, but not unlikely.

Yeah, right, instinct said. Tell me another.

Paolo cocked his head at the movement of shadow across the kitchen window, thinking hard, because he didn't believe in the voice of intuition. He'd been an administrator—a suit, not a player—for too long. He'd been trained to believe in what he could see, hear, touch, smell, taste—five senses, not six. But there was no other explanation for the larger-than-life awareness that trickled along the back of his neck and played insistently down his spine. Intuition, coupled with coincidence, said it all. He just didn't have all the pieces yet.

He swung around in his chair. "Laura, did you see this—" He stopped. Laura's scent drifted around him, through him, unnervingly close.

He could feel the weight of her eyes on him, could feel it in his pulse, in the rush of heat through his belly, when she paused in the tenth circuit she'd made in as many minutes from hallway through kitchen into foyer around living room and back and looked at him.

He swallowed, struck by her, taking her in. Her appearance was quintessential Laura. It was a picture he'd seen many times before: fine dark hair drifting around her face, clothing soft and carefully fitted, computer printouts dripping from her fingers, features serenely belying her restiveness, eyes dark and deep and...

Defenseless.

His insides twisted. There was an unaccustomed rawness in

her expression, a sense of emotions exposed, of a spirit ready for fight or flight, wondering how much she had to regret.

He wondered that himself, felt his hands shaking in response to the tension coiling through him, although they looked perfectly still. The feel of her skin lingered on the pads of his fingertips, the impression of silk remained on the backs of his hands, and on his palms where they'd tangled in her hair.

Things between him and Laura had changed since those moments in the hall yesterday, but he wasn't sure the change had been for the better. The acknowledgment of possibility drew them together and set them apart—the old once-burned-twice-shy effect. With Julianna in constant attendance, they couldn't seem to find a balance between them. Laura was irritable, and he, himself, seemed all thumbs.

Hurry up and wait seemed to be all they did, was a hazard of his business, left too much room and too much time for imagining, for awareness. Too much time unfulfilled.

After twenty years, he should be used to living with unfilled time, he knew. Waiting, biding time, choosing the optimum moment to act, were among the primary functions of his business, required a kind of smoldering tenacity that seemed almost eternal, the ability to retreat into oneself and block out everything else while remaining constantly alert. He couldn't allow himself to forget why he was here: to protect her, to be the voice of reason when her initial panic slid into fear and then anger, became the need to act, to revenge, then the simple necessity to get this business over and done with. To get things back to normal. To make sure she remembered that even during the days when nothing happened, she was still at risk until this was over. To ensure that she not become desensitized to the threats against her.

And that he not become one of them.

He shut his eyes and dipped his head, wishing he hadn't said her name, opened this door. Looking at her, he couldn't concentrate, couldn't remember what he'd intended to say. Every nerve in his body felt as if it were on point, overloaded, waiting for the infinitesimal final straw that would make it snap.

Anticipation sharpened by experience made the hunger deeper, more painful, more breathtaking. Made the reasons to refrain both more understandable and more in-tolerable. Made the ache less physical, more cutting, emotionally impossible to ignore.

Since yesterday, they had been more aware than ever of things they didn't want to be aware of: heat, hope, hesitation, history; of how it it would feel to lose themselves in one another, to ignore the problems of past and present and simply go to bed. Making love for the first time with someone you cared about held its own special, incredible wonder, the pleasure to seek and explore, experiment and discover. But to make love with someone who was familiar with every intimate inch of your body...

Paolo's fingers convulsed, crumpling a corner of the printout he'd wanted Laura to look at. A particularly uncivilized fantasy of himself and Laura, coupled on the steps beneath the viaduct in Paris, filtered through his mind, caught him off guard, then switched without transition to a memory of one of the countless times she'd reached out to him later in their marriage, offering him the simple body-to-body comfort he so badly needed and couldn't accept, the times she'd undoubtedly known he would reject her and had reached anyway.

Regret seared a jagged, painful path through him, compelled him to open his eyes and see her. As though she'd been privy to his thoughts, Laura caught her breath and steadied herself on the edge of the counter just inside the kitchen doorway. Her eyes on him were first startled, then sad, then longing, then openly hot and imperative; they held an element of an act committed—sent heat and urgency arcing through Paolo, drew him from his chair.

Three strides across the kitchen, Laura held her ground, lips parted slightly, calling him without words. He came toward her hungry, without question or hesitation, giving her that power to move him with a glance, to make him crave her.

In the living room, Julianna groaned and stretched full-length on the floor amid the sharp rustle of papers. "Soddin' stuff makes no sense," she muttered, to no one in particular, and Paolo and Laura stilled in their tracks, eyes on one another, regretfully aware of the world around them.

"Listen, Gianini," Julianna called. "Does this make sense to you? If you can believe what you read, Abernathy has never done a wrong number in his life."

With an effort, Paolo yanked himself back to the here and

now. "With you in a minute, Jules." He turned to Laura. "I'm sorry."

She shook her head. Her voice was soft, tired, ragged around the edges. "Don't be. It's probably better this way. We have to stop doing this to each other."

Paolo nodded. "Yes," he agreed. Then he did one of the things he wanted to do anyway and reached out to rub the pad of his thumb roughly across her lips in a kiss he couldn't trust his mouth to supply and stop at. "Rain check?" he suggested. "Maybe when this is over?"

Shuddering, Laura took a breath and reached up to span the distance between them, brushing her fingertips across Paolo's mouth. "Maybe next life," she whispered, "if my defenses are better." Then she gathered herself together with the continuous pages in her hands and backed toward the living room. "Now, what was it you were asking me about...?"

Midnight. Somewhere in the house, a phone was ringing.

Logy and disoriented, Laura struggled out of a restless sleep, kicking at the covers tangled round her legs.

Outside, wind thundered along the coast, bellowed through the crawl space beneath the front porch steps, howled down the eaves. Below the house, the Atlantic tattered the beach, carving slim rivers deep into the shore. Hail battered the roof and bounced off the windows, sand and sleet scudded across the terrace, scouring. Accommodating and resilient, the house creaked and muttered under the winter's onslaught, while underneath the sound and fury the phone continued its imperative trilling.

Panic hovering just below the surface of exhaustion, Laura jerked her feet out of the blankets and slung them over the side of the bed before she remembered the cordless phone tucked into the recess in her headboard and reached for it. Midnight phone calls were never good.

"Hello?"

"Have...found..."

The line was wide-open and crackling with static, the voice on the other end too garbled to understand at first. Jumbled in the darkness, Laura's thoughts flew instinctively to list family, friends, horrible possibility, memory. Daddy had gone out to help at a fire after a midnight phone call and never came home; Grandpa had called in the middle of the night to say Grandma had died; the news that her brother John had accidentally shot a bully in a bar brawl in West Virginia had come by phone at 2:00 a.m.; her marriage to Paolo had, in part, ended over not one, but many, phone calls in the wee hours of the night.

"Hello?" She jiggled the compact receiver, feeling nausea curdle in her stomach. Maybe it was a wrong number, a crank call by some kid looking for cheap thrills on a stormy night. And maybe it wasn't. "Hello?"

"Laura." Paolo stood in the doorway holding out the foyer phone, with its long cord. "Use this. Signal's stronger, and Jules can get a trace."

Trembling, Laura nodded and took the receiver from him, felt him hunker in beside her where he could hear, too. "Hello?"

"Have you got it yet?"

The voice was male, clearer now, but still muffled, as if whoever it was were holding a handkerchief over the speaker to disguise himself. Familiar. *Find your partner and tell him...* No, she thought wildly, it wasn't it.

"Have I got what? Who is this?"

"Time's running out, Laura, better get cracking. Every second costs. I need that money and those files. They may have missed you in Buffalo, but they won't next time."

"You have to tell me what I'm looking for. I don't—"

"Thursday, Laura. I'll be in touch," the voice advised, and the line went dead.

"Wait—" Laura tried, then pressed her lips together hard and let the hand squeezing the phone drop into her lap.

Paolo was already up and out of the room, calling sharply to Julianna, "Did you get it?"

"Every digit."

"Where?"

"Close. Somewhere in Amagansett."

"Get someone—"

"Done," Laura heard Julianna say crisply. Their voices dropped to a murmur. It didn't matter, she wasn't listening anyway.

Tell your partner there's no place to hide, she heard the

masked man in her office rasp. *Tell him we want the money and the files. If we have to ask again, we won't ask nice.*

Time's running out, Laura, better get cracking, the voice from the phone said. *They may have missed you in Buffalo... Have you got it yet?*

No, she thought, rubbing her temple with shaking fingers, as if doing so might unnumb her brain. They're not the same person. The first man had been someone she didn't know, she was sure, but the second was...someone she'd spoken with before. Someone she'd...met.

Someone she knew.

The telephone receiver dropped from nerveless fingers.

Come on, Laura! Gus's monthly shout echoed around her mind. *Time to get the accounts out. Let's get cracking.*

Then, again, the voice from the phone: *Time's running out, Laura, better get cracking...cracking...crack—*

Air seemed to catch in her windpipe, choking her. On the floor the telephone receiver began to beep, and a recorded voice urged her to hang it up or seek assistance, but she didn't hear it. All she heard was the voice in her head, the inflections, the enthusiasm, the damning years of familiarity in the final straw of knowledge that told her it belonged to— Gus.

Stunned, hands knotted between her knees, Laura sat on the edge of the bed and absorbed shock and betrayal the way she hadn't a week ago. In a second, the years of education, of refinement and control, of first pretending to be, then becoming, the person she was now, were stripped away, leaving in their place the wide-eyed tomboy from Upper Jay who'd moved to Buffalo with her mother and two brothers twenty-three years ago, after her father's death. There she'd met Gus, a smart-aleck con artist of a West Virginia mountain boy, three years her senior, whose parents were divorced and who'd spent summers until he was fifteen fishing off the Carolinas with his father.

By her third day in Buffalo, Gus had tried to scam her little brother, Bobby, out of some prized possession their mother had bought him and that they couldn't afford, and Bobby was buying into the scam. Laura had told Gus to back off. He'd laughed in her face and said, ''Make me,'' and then he'd gone back to his teasing.

Incensed, she'd shoved him, and he'd sat down hard in the

mud of her front yard. Too furious to remember his superior
years and size, he'd come off the ground swinging, and she'd
knocked him down again, just the way her older brother, John,
had taught her: stamp on the instep, knee to the groin; hit low,
then high, ears are especially vulnerable to pain; whip, rather
than punch, with the outside of your fist so you don't break your
hand. It had worked like a charm. Gus had limped off the bat-
tlefield an adolescent with a somewhat wised-up perception of
his own limitations, and a new respect for women who said what
they meant and meant what they said.

The following afternoon, Gus had arrived at their door to
make apologies and return a quarter he'd conned Bobby out of
two days earlier. Laura had recognized him then as someone
capable of manipulating a scorecard to his own advantage, a
sloe-eyed, good-looking schemer who would always find a
means to charm his way through life. She'd managed to remain
aloof to his efforts to sway her opinion of him for two entire
days.

At which point she'd gotten herself into more trouble than
she could handle at school and he'd stood up for her, and, well,
after that there wasn't much choice. He, exalted ninth-grader
that he was, had shared his lunch with her, a lowly sixth-grader.
She, eleven years old and beginning to find herself susceptible
to chivalrous acts, had forgiven him his trespasses, accepted the
fact that he would undoubtedly commit further transgressions
throughout their relationship, because it was in his nature to do
so, and taken him on as her third brother and friend.

God, what a stupid thing to do.

Why, she wondered, savagely shoving herself erect, was it so
easy to love what was bad for you, like donuts and easy living
and men who needed saving from themselves and who would,
in the end, drag you under with them? Why not love salads and
a disciplined existence and men self-sufficient enough to solve
their own neuroses, but also sensitive enough to know when it
was time to let you in on them? Men who knew when it was
time to hold you, when it was time to let go, and when it was
time to simply love you through your mistakes? And who'd
given them the right—however justifiable their motivation—to
think they could just...work things out however they liked and
get away with it because they were so sure, not only that they

were right about everything all the time, but that when they screwed up you'd trail along after them with the Dustbuster, cleaning up the fallout?

She shut her eyes and massaged her bruised leg, and anger—bold, brittle, brilliant—washed through her. Damn Gus, *damn* him and his glib tongue and ready apologies. Damn his gee-hawed ethics and his impatience and his compulsion to take care of his mother no matter who it cost. Damn him and his schemes and his fear and his weakness and his humanness—and her ability to excuse and forgive him no matter what he did. Damn him straight to hell without reprieve.

She knew what he'd done.

But more than that, clear as leaded crystal, she knew *where* he was.

In the instant of realization she was out of the room and down the hall, colliding with Paolo on his way back to her.

"Laur—"

"Where are the files?"

"Wha—"

"The printouts we were looking at the other day, Paolie, where are they?"

"Kitchen table."

"No." Laura pushed by him impatiently. "Not those, not the ones from the hard drive, the ones from the disks you picked up off the desk the day Talon took the house."

"Living room, but—"

"But nothing." Laura swooped down and scooped printouts off the coffee table, switched on a light, fanned pages. "I know where he is, Paolo." She looked up at him. "I know where he's been. I know where he will be at six o'clock this morning, but I've got to make sure."

Furiously she let pages spill onto the floor. "It's so damned simple it's scary, but I'm not good at simple, I'm good at complications—creating them, seeing them, living them. Put something basic in front of me and I'll find the most difficult and devious explanation for it—dramatic, my grandmother used to call me. I mean, look at you and me. I love you, you love me, what could be simpler? But no, I gotta complicate it, dig a lot of holes—and you didn't help. Gus always goes straight to the point—*if I do this, what will happen?* Ask me that question and

I list ten or fifteen possibilities and the dozen or so probable
consequences for each one. Gus lists two, the worst thing that
could happen and the best thing that could happen. Then he says,
I can live with that, and he does it. Twenty-three years he's
Peter damn Pan and I'm his spring-cleaning conscience, Wendy.
Son-of-a-bitch bastard— Sorry, Lilah.''

Paolo stared at her, seeing, for the second time in two days,
a side of her he'd never understood existed.

There was nothing cool and cautious, centered and serene,
about this Laura; this one was all fury and action, passion and
intervention—was, he realized with a start, the Laura who, from
beneath a compassionate, calm-waters exterior, had reached out
and gathered him in the night he'd met her. The same Laura
he'd taken to Paris. Only this Laura was funny.

He felt laughter fizz inside him, worked to stifle it, because,
good as it felt, it didn't seem quite appropriate to the moment.
"What are you talking about?"

"Gus," Laura snapped. "Try to pay attention."

"I would if you made sense."

"Don't bait me right now," Laura advised him icily. "I'll
take your head off."

"Bravo." Julianna propped a shoulder against the kitchen
doorjamb, applauding. She looked at Paolo. "You have better
taste in wives than I gave you credit for, Gianini. Too bad you
have so much trouble holding on to them."

"I don't see Charlie hanging on to your coattails," Paolo
retorted mildly, referring to Julianna's own long-departed and
unlamented ex. Spoiled relationships were a hazard of the trade;
he'd suffered various versions of this conversation with his partners before.

"I don't keep his picture in my desk drawer where I can take
it out and pine over it when I think no one's watching, either."

"You don't have a desk."

"Knapsack, then."

"You keep my picture in a knapsack?" Laura asked, glancing
distractedly at Paolo. It was late, she was mad as hell, and she
was getting punchy. Had to be it.

"No, I—" Rubbing his eyes, Paolo caught the direction of
the conversation with an effort, changed its course. Someday he

would figure out how he always managed to wind up *here* from *there* with Laura. Then they'd see. "Gus?" he prompted.

"Hm? Oh." Slightly befuddled, Laura separated two perforated pages from the rest, thrust them at Paolo. "Look, I think he's here." She pointed out a string of small private accounts, all with addresses in the fishing villages of the South Fork. "These are some of Gus's first accounts. He's bailed them out once or twice during some bad times—they'd do anything for him."

"Hide him from Dunne or the police?"

She nodded. "Small towns and fishermen, us against them. He's one of their own."

Reading over Laura's shoulder, Julianna suddenly snatched the printout from her, snapping a finger at an address. "This is near where we got the trace. Same town, same street, few numbers down." She eyed Paolo speculatively. "He couldn't have been here all along. Talon or the FBI or someone would have questioned his clients—especially the ones around here."

Paolo shrugged. "First couple of days, maybe, but they'd need a warrant to search premises for him, and they couldn't get a warrant without cause, and with him apparently dead they had no cause."

"I went through his client list and called everybody on it," Laura agreed. "Nothing. Gus has that, I don't know, that *something* that makes people who normally wouldn't lie to protect themselves lie to themselves to protect him. He's...genuine, somehow, he appeals to people. They want to take care of him." She made a moue of regret. "At least I did."

"Past mistakes," Paolo said softly, almost to himself, and Laura looked at him. "Love is blind, deaf and hopeful." He rubbed the back of his neck and glanced at her, shrugging. "Isn't that what you used to tell me?"

"My grandmother used to say it."

"It's true."

"Paolo—"

Julianna interrupted her. "You said you know where he'll be. Not where he is."

Laura pulled herself back from the brink of private admissions and turned to Paolo's partner. "It's the end of the season around here, a lot of the fishermen have moved on." She pointed to another of Gus's accounts. "The ones who haven't will meet here, at Syl's Cafe in Amagansett, for coffee before they go out. I think Gus'll be with them."

"Think?" Paolo asked neutrally.

"His father was a bayman," Laura responded without offense. "Gus grew up with it. It's a natural place for him to hide where no one would think to look."

"Except you."

"I almost didn't."

Paolo nodded thoughtfully. Julianna pursed her lips. "I'll put a crew together," she said. "We'll pick him up." She jutted her chin toward the phone, eyed Paolo. "You want Talon in?"

"No." He shook his head, eyes flicking automatically toward Laura. "I want to chat with Abernathy first."

Something about the intensity of his manner drew Julianna's gaze. "Gently?" she suggested.

Paolo's mouth curved in response; the humor didn't reach his eyes. "We'll see."

Julianna made a sound of censure, but all she said was "I'll let you know when we've got him, then." Then she picked up the phone.

Chapter 12

It was 2:14:13 a.m. by the bright red digits on the kitchen clock radio. On the other side of the slatted blinds, the sky was as pitch-black and starless as Laura had ever seen it.

She let the shade slap back against the window. *It was a dark and stormy night,* she thought giddily; then, breath catching in a moan, she buried her face in her hands. *God,* she wondered, suddenly exhausted. *What have I done?*

Delivered up her oldest friend unto his enemies, that was what. Never mind the position he'd put her in. Never mind what he'd done to her, nor that she'd cheerfully filet him alive if he were here right now—nor even that she realized that the best way to extricate both herself and Gus from his mess was to turn him over to Paolo. It didn't help. Some destructive little worm in her mind, like the fist twisting in her chest, insisted she'd betrayed him.

She heard footsteps on the basement stairs, listened to them pause on the landing below the foyer at the door that opened into the garage.

Muted voices—Paolo, Julianna, and the F & S operative who'd arrived within a few minutes of Julianna's phone call—exchanged words Laura didn't attempt to overhear. The garage door opened and closed, car doors slammed, and an engine roared to life and departed. Then the house was quiet except for the click of seconds on the clock and Paolo's light expulsion of breath as he mounted the foyer stairs.

"They're gone," he said unnecessarily.

Laura didn't turn. "I feel like I've betrayed him," she said softly.

Paolo understood; the cop in him, that infinitesimal piece of his code-of-honor-trained brain that still valued loyalty above all else, understood her guilt at betraying her partner. "He turned on you. You have to protect yourself."

"Don't." Laura swung on him savagely. "Don't tell me not to feel what I feel."

"Okay." He didn't apologize. "But you did the right thing. You're not the only person Gus was hurting."

"I know." She dropped her head back on a sound of pain. "I know. But it doesn't matter, it doesn't change the way I feel. I hate Gus right now, and that doesn't change anything, either—not who we were, not what's been, nothing. I still love him like my brothers, I'll still be there if he goes to trial, I'll still make sure his mother is taken care of, but I can't ever trust him anymore, and that hurts worse than anything." She looked over her shoulder at Paolo. "I hate it. Nothing's ever hurt like this, not even you. I always knew, if I had to, I could trust you. For anything. If the kitchen faucet was dripping and I called, you'd be there."

"I knew the same thing about you."

Pulled away from herself, Laura's attention keened, a question mark.

Paolo smiled sadly, answering. "That day at court, you waited outside for me. You wanted to talk, but I kept going. If I'd stopped…"

Laura looked at her hands. "Maybe," she admitted quietly.

"Maybe what?" he asked.

"It was a long time ago, you didn't stop."

"Maybe what?" he repeated, stepping nearer, almost pleading.

She shut her eyes and twisted the hem of her shirt as she would have liked to twist the memory in her hands. "I think I'd have asked you to try again, to stay." She swallowed convulsively, opened her eyes, and the years drifted backward to that damning moment on the courthouse steps. "Right then, I'd have done anything, begged, to make you stay. Please stay."

She looked at Paolo, and the moment receded. "It's been a long road since then, but I'm glad you didn't. I've learned a lot because you didn't, things I had to learn to grow up, maybe, a little. Maybe."

Eyes on her, Paolo admitted quietly, "I didn't grow up, I hurt. I learned to hate you, because that hurt less."

She nodded, without flinching. "Yes."

"I missed you. When we were married and I had to be gone, it felt like some piece of me was being torn away every time I left. I felt guilty about leaving Maria and the boys and convinced myself, somehow, that it would be poetic justice if you left me. I became obsessed with the thought that it would happen—was happening. I couldn't live, couldn't work—couldn't concentrate on anything else, so I stopped sleeping with you to make it easier on myself when you finally did leave." He shrugged, grimacing. "Call it a self-fulfilling prophecy, but it made sense to me at the time."

Laura didn't pull punches. "It was stupid."

Paolo's mouth formed a hard, bitter, self-castigating line. "That, too."

A rushing silence filled the room between them, separating, enclosing, measuring. Tension fizzed along the invisible wires that seemed to have connected them from time immemorial, coupling desire and denial, longing and lust, love and despair.

Eyeing Paolo, Laura again fiddled with the hem of her pajama top. Watching Laura, Paolo stood stock-still, unblinking, barely breathing, hands loose at his sides.

Within each of them, instinct warred with reason: to reach out or to withdraw, to touch or to withhold. Each word they'd spoken to each other, every emotion they'd shared in the last many days bound them; uncertain memories pushed them apart. Around them lay unmapped territory filled with dark ravines, hidden snares, and no footsteps to follow in.

Eyes wary on each other, they breathed, soft, shallow breaths in perfect rhythm. It could happen if they let it.

It and *if.* Small words, big consequences.

Step careful, but make your own path or die with the rest of the lemmings, Laura's grandpa used to say.

She blinked, seeing the drift and play of shadow across Paolo's face. Darkness shielded the color of his emotions, but she knew they were there, raw and electric as hope, dangerously inviting as anything she'd ever known. Sensation swept up her spine, raising goose bumps.

I love him, she thought, not for the first time, but for the first time the feeling didn't frighten her. I want to move our bed, put it back where it belongs.

Such a strange response to the skitter of emotions through her, so basic, so simple, so direct. Straight to the heart of things—and except for the night she'd first met Paolo, Laura didn't think she'd ever gone straight to the heart of anything in her life.

Carefully she reached out, outlined a button on his shirt, measured the carved metal texture of his tie tack with the tip of her fingers. It was the middle of the night, but he was working, so his only concession to the hour was an open collar button and a marginally loosened tie.

Her lips curved slightly, and she lifted her face to him. "Help me move the bed?"

Paolo shut his eyes and expelled a long-kept breath, then opened them and framed her cheek in the curve created by his thumb and forefinger. "Okay."

Quiet dark, disturbing dark; voiceless, but full of sound: the tick of the furnace, the soft exhalation of breath, the desk skidding and scraping when Laura shoved it out of the way; the sough of the mattress they'd once shared when Paolo slid it across the polished oak floor and let it sag into place in the center of the room.

Their room.

Paolo watched her move, graceful and precise in her shapeless flannel pajamas, and his heart fisted behind the pulse in his throat. Some fleeting smidgen of happiness stood within easy reach, and he was afraid to trust it. He was damn well certain he didn't deserve it. His priestly teachers had often warned him that ecstasy never came without a price—one he wasn't now certain he could afford to pay.

"This where you want it?" he asked hoarsely, straightening the skewed mattress with the toe of his shoe.

Laura finished easing the desk into the far corner of the room and turned. He couldn't see her face. "More to the left I think," she said.

Hands sweating, Paolo nodded and bent to make the adjustment. Sheets and blankets tangled round his fingers, hindering.

"Need help?" Laura asked.

He shook his head. He'd make a fool of himself if she came near him now.

Wrapping her arms about herself, Laura faced the bank of windows overlooking the beach. Thin drops of rain or sleet dotted the panes of glass; clouds diminished reflections. Night lay all around them, seductively obscuring reality even as it promised truth. It wasn't, she realized uncomfortably, as easy as she'd thought it might be to simply make the decision and do the deed, to acknowledge feelings she'd nurtured and avoided for what seemed a lifetime.

Preparing for, and thinking about, love required far more courage than she and Paolo merely attacking one another in the hallway would have—made the act far more precious, the consequences far more obvious. Left the future far cloudier than it had ever been. From this moment, where would they go, what would they feel, how would they behave?

Love, as Laura had unwillingly been left the time to learn, was so much a matter of becoming more than you were, of compromise and disillusion and coming to terms with matters you never had to think about when you were single. Like raised toilet seats and someone else's viewpoint and learning to leave enough room on signature lines to accommodate all the letters in Gianini when you were used to leaving only enough room to spell Haas. Because in the end, it was always the little things that did a relationship in, never the big ones.

Worrying the inside of her bottom lip, Laura glanced across the room to where Paolo stood, a taut-strung shape in the inadequate darkness. The heaviness of anticipated pleasure pooled and spread down through her breasts and belly, into her lower limbs. Despite her best intentions, she knew, it would take but a touch of his lips, a fingertip against her cheek, to make her heart abduct her mind and head south permanently.

A frisson of expectation sent pleasure shivering down her spine. Not that letting her heart and mind head south with Paolo would be so bad.

She peered again through the dark windows at the cold isolation of her beach, and south seemed a good place to go, a magical, mystical place more amenable to impossible dreams than a stark winter beach could ever be.

Godspeed, she whispered to her soul, and turned once more to face Paolo.

On hesitant feet he crossed the room toward her and paused at the edge of the window's darker than dark shadow encasing her. She was an arm's length away; he could reach across that distance and claim her, with her permission, but he faltered. His heart pounded behind his ribs, heedless of his efforts to calm it. So much depended on what happened here, so much could be lost, so much gained, in the twinkling of a moment. His whole life hung in the balance.

He couldn't discern her expression, but he watched Laura lift her chin, felt the sweep of desire he'd always experienced when she shook her hair back away from her face to see him better. He could imagine her features: the cool, dusky, come-hither invitation in her eyes that belied the fire beneath had tormented his dreams forever. Too late he'd learned what an irreplaceable piece of his life she was.

He felt the sweat tingling in his palms, the strain of nerves too long denied her.

The first time he'd touched Laura, he'd needed his wounds healed. She'd supplied the balm and they'd gone on from there, their relationship stunted and lopsided because she'd mistaken his momentary emotional crisis for the whole man, while he'd managed to mistake the healing, nurturing aspects of her heart for the whole woman. Without intending it, they'd managed to set themselves up as victim and savior—and become entrenched in roles that befitted neither of them.

They were each, Paolo knew now, more than pigeonholes in a desk, each human, each divine, weak and strong, turmoil and serenity, solid ground and quicksand. When they bridged the gap between them this time, it would not be a random occurrence, a happenstance of time, place and needs. This time it was by choice, with eyes wide-open to the foibles that could separate—or bind—them if they chose.

And so Paolo stopped before crossing into the shadows to savor the moment, the chaos of his emotions, the uncertainty in his head—the heady, electrifying scent and taste of Laura in his lungs.

She loosened her arms from about herself and dropped her chin, suddenly shy, twisting back toward the window.

He invaded the black length between them in two quick steps and slid his fingertips down her shoulders, cupped her arms in his palms.

For an instant her cheek dropped to her shoulder, and time suspended, waiting. Then she turned to him, into his arms and they became not two individuals, but one being.

There were no questions, no pauses, no tacit acquiescence, merely the actions of two people who had long understood—and loved—each other far better than either of them knew.

Softly, gently, they touched, without impatience—over clothing, hands along arms, forehead to forehead, nose to nose; caressing, exploring, wondering...seeking and finding renewal.

Laura touched his face, let his hair slide like silk through her fingers. Paolo smiled. His fingertips sought Laura's jaw, his lips found her mouth. Her hands made a loving foray along his chest and around his sides, flattening on his back. He laced one hand through her hair, cupping the back of her head; his other hand settled on her hip. Laura's lips curved and parted, inviting, and he was lost.

They were not tender people by nature. They were treacherous, icy surfaces with volcanic underpinnings. In their own ways, they both devoured life, supped violently of its offerings—took no prisoners.

Tenderness surprised them.

Desire was no longer merely an ache in their loins, but a need to find and belong to each other; to be together, separate but unified. They touched each other with infinite care, moved together, fluid and graceful, anticipating and meeting each other's movements in ancient choreography—allowing the fire to build and consume without destroying.

Buckles, buttons, zippers and knots all gave way to gentle

persuasion. Plaid flannel pajamas and silk shirt, tie and trousers, coupled together on the floor, fabrics blending like the lovers who'd worn them, creating a new material.

Beneath Paolo's fingers, Laura's skin was washed silk, impossibly soft, a sensation to drown in. Under Laura's hands, Paolo's skin was rougher, a pattern of subtle textures and tactile treasures to be sought and found and cherished.

Lips, teeth, tongues and hands created mindless sensation, left heat boiling in their veins, made their motions feverish, seeking the means to cool the fire.

"Laura." Paolo's voice was ragged, greedy, urgent. He slid a taut palm over her hip to round her buttocks and drew her thigh up, pressing to fit her. "I...can't...wait. I'm sor—"

"No." Laura locked her arms around his neck and hooked her leg around his waist, tightening the embrace as she tipped herself frantically to meet him. "Don't wait anymore, Paolie, please. I need...I...need...."

That was all it took; that simply did she undo what remained of the civilized being inside him and call the primitive from the darkness into the light.

Catching her about the waist, he lifted her to him, bent his head and took her mouth in a bruising kiss. His tongue swept her lips in reckless abandon, thrust between them as though to devour her.

She would not be devoured.

She took his tongue in her teeth, nipping, sucking, tormenting, with the same passion and purpose with which she twisted her hips and took his length into the white-hot melting center of her. He gasped and went rigid, tearing his mouth from hers and throwing his head back, dragging air into his lungs as though it might also hold reason—fighting the need to empty himself into her already, fighting to make it last.

Without success.

His control was gone, he needed her too badly—and Laura, with her face pressed tight to his shoulder, her body stretching and straining against him and her breath shuddering in her lungs, told him the same.

She needed him and wanted him.

All of him.

Now.

Paolo's fingers clenched around Laura's thighs. He'd meant to share the bed with her, to reclaim the symbol of a union that had gotten the better of both of them, but urgency ravaged intention. The desk was closer.

With a growl of desperation, he settled Laura on the cool glass surface and plunged into her, tearing a sob of satisfaction from her lips even as she took from him every last ounce of reserve that had once estranged them.

Again and again he drove into her, deep and hard; Italian, the language of his birth and his discarded heritage, poured from his throat, raining down about them with his tears.

"Mia bella... Mia sposa... Amóre mia...." Then her name, over and over: "Laura..."

Heart full, fingers threaded in his hair, arms straining around him, Laura held Paolo tight and went with him. When he came apart in her arms, she held on to him.

Undone. Rebuilt. Completed.

There was no nuzzling softness, no sighing laughter, no tickling, no teasing, only a fierce, dark passion, the compelling desire to make up for lost time, to reclaim and renew.

Time and again they came together, lost in the slick sensations of sweat and greed and voiceless demands—and ghosts. Leaning among the shadows, jeering at them, wondering what had kept them apart so long, the ghosts brandished questions neither Paolo nor Laura chose to answer. There were no answers, anyway, only this place, this time, five years of absolute denial and a husband and wife who had legally disentangled themselves from each other, but whose hearts remained forever bound.

Without words they spoke of the separation—and banished it. At least temporarily. Neither of them was ever as sure of anything by daylight as in the darkness. When there was no light to see by, certainty was always more incontestable, forever more constant.

Emotion overpowered them. They couldn't get enough of each other.

They touched as though holding were the answer to a question never asked, consumed by sensation like madness. Pleasure was a by-product of what they found in one another; they did not seek it. They sought to belong, to become part, to absorb each other—to become one. In this one thing they were certain of where they stood together; within physical consummation, loneliness faded.

Man-woman, husband-wife, Paolo-Laura...eye to eye, body to body, lover to lover...whole.

At last, wrapped together in the hour before dawn, exhausted but unsated, Paolo and Laura slept.

A hand clapped across Laura's mouth, pressed her nose.

Startled, Laura came awake struggling to face a gray daybreak and Paolo's naked body angled across hers, his face close to her own. He shook his head once and placed his lips at her ear.

"Someone's in the house," he breathed. "I'm going to check it out." Then he raised his head and looked down at her again to be sure she'd understood.

Swallowing panic, Laura nodded. Paolo took his hand away from her mouth, brushed her lips with his thumb. For a bare instant he rested his cheek against hers, absorbing her warmth, gathering strength. Then he eased himself across her and onto the floor to collect his pants and find his gun. Heart banging loud against her ribs, Laura followed.

"No," Paolo ordered immediately. "Stay here."

Laura shook her head, located her pajamas and slipped into them. "Whither thou goest," she whispered back, but her fingers, stumbling to fasten the buttons of her shirt, belied the bravado of the retort.

Paolo caught her hands. "Laura," he began firmly; then, seeing the apprehensive but stubborn set of her jaw, he sighed and worked the buttons for her. "Keep behind me."

Gun held high in his right hand, he took Laura's hand and drew her close, and together they crossed the shadowy room and eased into the hall. Placing their feet carefully, hugging the wall, they edged toward the front of the house.

Stillness lay around them like a dangerous fog; Laura's ears keened to it, trying to hear through the dense blanket and discover what lay ahead. Something foreign seemed to exist within the stealthy quiet; premonition pricked through the nerves in her thumbs. The furnace whooshed on when they passed under the ceiling vent, and she started and cut her lip on a tooth in her attempt to remain silent. Paolo gave her hand a reassuring squeeze, but didn't look back.

Daylight had not yet penetrated the kitchen blinds or found its way through the cracks between the drapes in the living room. When they reached the foyer, Paolo let go of Laura's hand and paused before whiplashing his head around the jamb for a quick reconnaissance, then back for a longer look. Seeing nothing, he motioned Laura to follow when he slipped across to the opposite wall and followed the same ritual at the kitchen doorway before recrossing the foyer and continuing the short distance to the living room.

A faint scratching sound reached their ears. Paolo held out a hand to halt Laura and swiveled himself until his back was flat against the wall, then he ducked his head to survey the living room. Shifting his gun to his left hand, he reached around the corner to find the wall switch. He flicked the lights on at the same time he went into a crouch and swung himself gun first into the room.

Chapter 13

Taken by surprise, Angus Abernathy—Gus to everyone but his mother—started and dropped the dulcimer he'd just removed from its spot on the wall. Eyes popping, hands wide from his body, his posture wary, he stared at Paolo—or Paolo's gun—and didn't breathe.

"Well, well, well," Paolo said softly. Without lowering his gun, he straightened from his crouch and motioned Gus away from the dulcimer.

"Gus?" Suddenly indefinably cold, Laura stepped out from behind Paolo and wrapped her arms around herself, kneading her shoulders. The world seemed suspended, unreal, around her. Movement seemed to flow through her at some delayed speed—as though she consciously had to think of an act before her body would perform it.

She eyed her sandy-haired, green-eyed, guileless-appearing partner with shock. She hadn't expected to ever have to face Gus again this side of a witness stand, but there he was, looking gaunt and hollow, wild-eyed and desperate, full of despair—apparently paying dearly for his cowardice and duplicity. Face-to-face, it wouldn't be as easy to filet him alive as she'd imagined. "What are you doing here? What do you want with my dulcimer?"

Hands outspread in supplication, Gus took a step toward her. "Laura, I'm sorry. I never dreamed—"

"Don't," Paolo warned. "Face down on the floor, hands behind your head. Spread 'em."

Uneasy about Paolo's motives, Gus hesitated. "I'm not carrying."

"Do it," Paolo snapped.

"Paolo." Laura stepped away from the wall and placed a hand on her ex-husband's arm. Automatically interceding on Gus's behalf, as always. "Can't you just—?"

"No." Paolo shook his head. "I can't, and neither can you."

"But he won't—"

"What, Laura? Hurt you? He does that by breathing. I don't care who he was to you—who he is now is what counts. Because of him, you were nearly killed. Because of him, Talon would happily send you to prison, so don't give me 'he won't.' Look at him with your eyes for a change, damn it, instead of your heart."

"I am," Laura said, quietly, intensely. "Because of him, you're here."

For an instant, Paolo's gaze slipped her way and softened, darkened. Then warmth was gone, exchanged for an absence of emotion so terrible that Laura was afraid to name it, and he returned his attention to Gus. "On the floor," he repeated almost gently. "Do it."

Aware that Paolo meant business, Gus nervously did as he was told. Eyes on his nemesis, he carefully placed one knee, then the other, on the carpet, prostrated himself and laced his fingers behind his head. Transferring his gun to his left hand, Paolo moved in behind him, toed Gus's feet apart and made a great and decidedly rough show of patting him down.

"You're clean," he announced, with what sounded like regret. For a thoughtful moment, he eyed the straight, clean-cut, light reddish hair that covered the slight hollow at the base of Gus's skull. A small-caliber bullet, placed just *there*, would lodge in the brain and produce very little blood; a couple of weights, a quick trip out to sea, and a heavy ocean would take care of the rest....

Sighing, Paolo discarded the pleasant fantasy. No, satisfying as it might be to get rid of him once and for all, death was too humane a punishment for Gus; a far more exacting revenge would come from keeping him alive to face the consequences of this drama he'd wrought—and making him participate in the outcome.

Smiling grimly, Paolo retrieved Laura's dulcimer from the floor and stepped away from Gus.

"Can I get up now?" Gus asked.

"Keep your hands where I can see them," Paolo agreed. He waved at the newly reupholstered overstuffed chair angled near the fireplace. "Have a seat." He waited for Gus to comply, then demanded answers to the questions Laura had only asked with a simple, laconic "Talk."

Gus swallowed hard and looked at Paolo, at Laura, at his hands, seemingly shepherding his thoughts. Paolo started toward him impatiently, ready to shake an explanation out of him. Laura pressed close again and stayed him with a light touch on his arm.

"Gus." Her tone was soft, delicate, but with an unmistakable core of steel. "You have to tell me. What are we into? What have you done?"

Paolo watched Gus straighten and pale under her scrutiny, and viewed Laura with renewed comprehension and respect. Gus's name might be on the door of Abernathy and Associates' offices, but when push came to free-for-all, Laura was the spine.

Just as she'd been the spine in their marriage, the bowed but unbroken survivor of their divorce.

Something tightened in his chest, an odd swirl of feeling choking him: fierce pride in her, love for her, and the unexpectedly terrifying, catastrophic recognition of a knowledge he'd actually possessed for a long time. He loved Laura, but love had degrees and, sometimes, marked perimeters where it should be unconditional. His were obsessed in the extreme. He'd go to the ends of the earth for Laura. He'd sell his soul to the devil and spend eternity in hell's embrace—for her. Her presence in his life was vital to his well-being. He'd deny her freedom and access to his personal crises to protect her. From him. Because, more than anything in this world, anyone in this life, in order to do more than merely "get by," he needed Laura. Beside him, in his pocket, a captive of his soul.

But Laura, though she might not realize it, didn't need him—not the way he required her, anyway. And the kind of overpowering, possessive need he felt for her necessarily went part and parcel with everlasting love.

Didn't it?

Rocked to his toes, Paolo leaned a hip against the arm of the couch beside him and tried to adjust his balance in an unbalanced world. Damn, whoever said you couldn't have your cake and eat it, too, was right.

"Gus," Laura prodded again. Though still gloved in velvet, the steel undertone was sharper, less merciful. Struck anew by the sound, Paolo listened hard—and nearly missed seeing the hand Laura fisted and pressed tight to her side to keep it from trembling when she asked Gus, "Why are you here?"

Gus snorted as though the answer to that should be obvious. "I saw the vultures gathering." Censure was faint but present—even though some part of Gus must know he had no right to feel it. "You told them where to find me. I wondered if you would."

"You can't set me up and not expect me to fight for my life."

"I didn't think it would be your life," Gus shot back. Then he slumped over his knees in despair and dropped his hands, pleading with her. "Look, Laura, I'm sorry. It's no excuse, but I really didn't think it would go like this—I didn't think it would get so out of hand." He looked at his feet, sounded exhausted. "I thought...I guess I thought..."

His voice wavered; he passed a hand across his eyes and blew his cheeks out on a sigh. "Maybe I pretended I thought that everything would work out all right if it looked like I was dead. It seemed like the only way out at the time, the safest thing for everybody." He shrugged. "You'd find the hard drive and the offshore bank accounts and give everything to...to Paolo, and he'd contact Dunne and arrange to give everything back and explain it was all a mistake." Another sigh. "But then they caught up with me that last day and made some threats—showed me pictures of you alone out here, my mom in her room, your mom...your brother John in the prison yard, and Bobby with his kids, and they said it was a shame how easy accidents happen

and I...panicked and left the drive in the car and didn't have a
chance to get the account codes out of the dulcimer before..."

"Why, Gus?"

He glanced up at her, let his gaze slink away, denying culpability. "Look, Laura, if I could take it all back, I would, believe me. But I...didn't know who Dunne was at first, and then
I was in too deep. I wanted out, but they wouldn't let me—"

Something harsh, something that might have been laughter,
shuddered through Laura, interrupting Gus. "I don't think I believe that, Gus." She ran a hand through her hair, dropped her
head back and made a sound of disbelief. "How can I?" She
perched on the edge of the coffee table and leaned forward on
a knee to study him intently, looked away and rubbed a hand
across her mouth. "I mean, God, Gus! You always knew who
the players were—you warned me about them, made me stay
away from them. How can I believe you didn't know?"

"I don't know, Laura." For the first time, Gus met her gaze
directly. "Maybe it was as simple as I didn't want to know. Or
maybe I just figured it was better not to."

"Why?"

Gus sat back and shrugged. "Lilah's stroke," he said bitterly,
referring to his mother by her first name, as he'd often done
when he was younger and angry with her. "You were in West
Virginia visiting John when it happened. You had your own
problems, I couldn't talk to you, and the temptation was..." He
hesitated. "Always there. It got to the point where I'd come into
the office every day and try to remember where I'd drawn the
line. Needing the money to take care of Lilah just made giving
in to what I'd always kind of wanted to do anyway...acceptable.
Justifiable."

He made an offhand gesture, avoided looking at Laura. "Most
people don't see the world with the same eyes you do, Laura.
Most people aren't as sure of who they are, but you always
knew, 'this is right, this wrong,' no in-betweens." He grimaced.
"Makes your standards hard to live up to."

"I never expected you to live up to my standards."

"Ah, Laura." Gus's chuckle was harsh. "Maybe not. But you
sure expect everybody to have your standards. And when they
don't..." He glanced toward Paolo, and Laura suddenly under-

stood exactly what he was saying and blanched. He eyed her apologetically, hunched into his shoulders, went on.

"Anyway, when it came right down to it, it was simple, really. About six months ago I got an inside tip on an upcoming stock split from an old girlfriend. I didn't have the cash, so I wasn't going to act on it, but then Lilah got sick. I borrowed money from a couple of our biggest accounts, figuring I could put it back with interest within forty-eight hours. The tip backfired, and everything was gone. It might still have been all right, but we were coming up for an audit soon and I needed a way to replace the funds fast." He licked his lips with a dry tongue. "So I...took in Dunne's laundry. If I hadn't gotten greedy..."

His voice trailed away, and he dropped his hands between his knees and looked at the floor. "Anyway, it wasn't very long before that IRS agent, Talon, started coming around trying to, um, *flip* me, I think they call it. Said they'd protect me if I cooperated—even hinted there might be some sort of 'arrangement' he and I could make, just between us. And if there wasn't, well, he'd be sure to make it look like I'd, er, assisted him anyway, so no matter what, I was dead. I finally decided to beat everyone to the punch, take myself out. That's all."

He looked at Laura again, his misery plain. "I never... considered...what might happen to you. I'm sorry. I don't have any excuses. I ran."

"Oh, Gus," Laura whispered, sickened.

There was nothing else to say.

Silence thickened and dripped audibly about them. Outside the windows, morning expanded and found its way between the drapes. Paolo studied the shaft of weak sunlight and found the stray shaft of illumination appropriate to the moment. When he felt the weight of Laura's eyes on him, he shifted his in her direction and regarded her steadily for a moment. To her silent question, he tipped his head in unspoken reply—*you're doing great; go ahead* and waited for her to lead.

She pursed her lips and raised her chin, gathering courage, and returned her attention to Gus. "So what now?" she asked him.

He raised his head. "You call it," he offered bleakly. "I don't want to hurt you anymore, Laura. Scares hell out of me, but I'll play it however you say."

* * *

Three hours later, in a snow-drizzly, misty morning that felt far colder even than it looked, Laura stood on her terrace, looking out to sea.

Any pleasure she'd once taken in the view and the weather that went with it was gone. Even the vague sense of defiance she'd experienced when she'd approached the terrace doors had been denied her. Paolo had said nothing to stop her when she'd slid open the glass wall, although she'd looked at him, expecting—perhaps hoping for?—some admonition about still-lurking dangers. But none had been forthcoming.

It was as though something subtle had changed between them during her exchange with Gus, and she had no idea what it was.

Food for thought, she'd decided numbly, along with everything else that had happened since just before dawn.

Gus was gone, on his way into the city with Julianna and two of the Futures & Securities operatives who'd been with her. Paolo, Laura and the one remaining F & S agent were to follow shortly, in an attempt, Laura supposed, to confuse and dismay the enemy.

Once safely within the confines of the F & S offices, Gus had agreed, he would dictate and sign a deposition detailing what had occurred as exactly as possible since he'd begun laundering money for—and embezzling money from—Dunne. The statement would include Gus's allegations regarding Talon's suggestion that he'd consider accepting "payment in exchange for services" and would contain the location and nature of all corroborating evidence—beginning with the slip of paper with the offshore banks and account numbers on it that was taped inside one of the larger of the four heart-shaped cutouts on the face of Laura's dulcimer. When that was done, Paolo had said, they would see about putting together a sting to tie both Talon and Dunne up in the same neat package, ready for disposal.

There was no telling how long that might take.

But, as Paolo had said, Futures & Securities had handled liaison-type negotiations with the bad guys many times in the past. And, since F & S had a solid reputation for square dealing, resolution should be nothing more than a matter of time.

He'd also expressed the opinion that William Dunne was a businessman above all else, and whatever his "rank" in his "business," he still had higher-ups to answer to. Something in the way he'd said it, Laura reflected with a sense of fear, had made that opinion sound a great deal like a threat. She didn't want Paolo risking himself or anyone else over the likes of Gus, Talon and William Dunne. And the old saw "someone's gotta do it" be damned!

All in all, it had not been a pleasant morning. Especially when she'd realized that just when it should be at its least, the distance between her and Paolo seemed wider than ever. Her fault, his fault, or Gus's, it didn't matter. All she really knew was that she hadn't asked for comfort after Gus's revelations, and Paolo hadn't offered it. They'd retreated into the old habits their separate lifetimes of self-sufficiency had taught them, burning the very bridge last night's ferocious joinings should have built.

Why she who recognized it couldn't close that widening gap, Laura didn't know. Fear, pride, awkwardness and, of course, some natural predilection were all undoubtedly to blame in part, but she didn't want to have this sort of reticence with Paolo anymore, had never wanted it.

To waken in Paolo's arms after a mindless night of cherishing was something Laura had wanted for a long time. To gain that intimacy, then lose it for a reason she couldn't name in what seemed the space of a breath, made her heart ache—and her resolve stiffen. No matter what Paolo thought to deny himself, or how unhappy he thought he deserved to be, she would not go passively this time.

She was no longer a naive, insecure little twenty-seven-year-old. Heck, no, she thought wryly. She was a grown-up with the IRS and the underworld after her. She was someone to be reckoned with. This time, she wouldn't make it easy for Paolo to withdraw over something that, she suspected, he felt he should have total control of and didn't. She would not stand there and take his manly silences and numb remarks that alluded to a thing but didn't say it; she would dig in her heels and know *why*. Hell, if she had to climb some barbed wire fences to get through to him, well, she'd snagged her clothing and been scratched up to get what she wanted before. What she needed.

No matter how long it took.

Because the hard fact was that, as Gus had said, adult life *was* a constant battle to balance the compromises between the black-and-white principles and idealism she'd grown up with, and the concessions she had to make to day-to-day living. A going in and trying to remember where she'd drawn the line every single day.

When she viewed things that way, it wasn't so difficult to understand what had happened to Gus, to comprehend Paolo's difficulty in accepting emotions, needs, occurrences, over which he had no control.

She looked at the tips of her carefully manicured fingers, at the ruthlessly white winter sky, and remembered the mistakes she'd made in loving Paolo, the expectations she'd had of love and marriage, expectations that no one, not even Paolo, could ever have lived up to. The sad truth was, she was a bit of a control freak herself, sometimes, and she had to live with the fact that her onetime desire to control who she thought her husband should be was at least fifty percent of what had screwed up her marriage. And since nothing ever really changed in a minute, no matter how badly one wanted it to, until she was sure she had her own head screwed on straight about everything that was happening around them right now, some distance between her and Paolo might not be such a bad idea.

"Making things right always costs you in the end, kiddo," Gus had wryly warned her, offering up a lopsided grin on his way out the door with Julianna. *"Don't forget to watch out for that."*

Sighing her regret over how easily she'd managed to talk herself out of something simply by thinking it over the way Paolo did, Laura turned her back on the ocean, shook winter out of her coat and hair and went into the house to get dressed and face a long day fielding questions in Paolo's office.

When Paolo was seven, he'd decided to become a priest.

At twelve, when he'd been an acolyte for five years, he'd decided to become a playboy, because playboys got more girls than priests.

At fifteen, painfully awkward, shy and suffering a bad case of adolescent rebellion over having to snap-to every time his father said "jump," he'd run away from the seminary-style boarding school he'd attended since he was five to become a monk.

It had taken the carabinieri a week to find him and return him to his distraught parents, who thought he'd been kidnapped. Paolo had spent a great deal of that week cold, wet, hungry and thoughtful, too stubborn to return home on his own, too steeped in the realities of deprivation to want to follow through on his monk plan.

His time with cold, wet thoughts had taught him something, though; it had spelled out in stark letters exactly what he didn't want in his life: he didn't want to be directionless, he didn't want anyone telling him who he was and how to live, and he didn't want to be a banker like his father.

He'd also decided that the best way not to have to take orders would be to give them. He wanted authority, and he wanted to thwart his father. Joining the carabinieri had seemed a viable means to both ends.

Until Lisetta had been kidnapped, brought home, taken her tranquilizers and died. Then authority had no longer been enough; he had needed power and a means of revenge.

At its inception, Futures & Securities' sole purpose had been to negotiate the release of kidnap victims and to act in the capacity of liaison between kidnappers and the victims' families in a country where kidnapping was fast becoming a prosperous trade. Negotiating and engineering a quick release for the victims while remaining the coolheaded third party had been all that mattered to Paolo—to begin with.

Being, as it were, a civilian contractor in a world full of uniforms had been a plus: Paolo hadn't had to care about bringing his criminals to justice, only about getting victims home in the shortest time possible. The business had been of benefit to everyone—including, unfortunately, the kidnapping trade—but in the beginning, Paolo had made that compromise willingly, aware of his limitations and obsessed only with saving lives and expediting the release of victims.

Then he'd located Acasia Jones.

Just released from the United States Army and returned from the revolution that had resulted in the formation of the new South American dictatorship of Zaragoza, Acasia had been a woman with an ax to grind and a past to live with. Daughter of a jewel thief who traveled a lot, she'd been Lisetta's best friend at the Swiss boarding school they'd both attended, and had been

with Lisetta when she was abducted. The terrorists responsible
for the crime had used Acasia as their go-between; when Lisetta
committed suicide, Acasia had felt responsible, guilty because
she hadn't found some way to control the chaos churning around
her.

Trained by her father in the fine art of thievery, and imbued
by the army with a means to put her illegal skills to good use,
Acasia had enabled Paolo to expand Futures & Securities' activities to include hostage location and retrieval. She had also
offered him a means to cooperate with and advise local, state,
federal and international authorities in hostage situations: F & S
collected the victims, the cops got the perps.

By the end of their third year in business, Acasia had met and
contributed pilot Julianna Burrows to the partnership, and within
a short time Futures & Securities had gone international, opening
offices in London and then New York.

Over time, the partners had expanded the firm's capabilities
to provide what their expanding clientele required, be it security
systems, executive antiabduction survival training or personnel.
According to an article in an issue of last year's *Forbes,* after
fifteen years in business, Futures & Securities, Inc., was one of
the premier private security companies in the world, with
branches in Tokyo, Rio de Janeiro, Los Angeles and Bonn, in
addition to the branch in London and the corporate headquarters
in New York.

Something to be proud of, Paolo reflected late that morning
when he and Laura alighted from the car in front of the copper-
glassed building where Futures & Securities occupied the top
three floors. By building Futures & Securities, he'd accom-
plished everything he'd set out to accomplish almost twenty
years ago, and then some. Not everyone could say that. So why
didn't he feel better about it, why didn't it mean more? Especially since, because of his insistence on Futures & Securities'
existence, he had the means at hand to truly…take care of Laura.

A brisk wind whipped along the street and tossed dust into
his eyes, stinging them. He pinched the bridge of his nose with
his thumb and forefinger, spread them across his eyes to wipe
away the sensation. Hell, who was he trying to convince, anyway? Last night, the past few days, had reminded him what he'd
thrown aside to get here. He'd destroyed everything that creating

F & S was supposed to preserve, anything that might have made him more than the business, more than a man on a quest for redemption for a twenty-year-old crime he hadn't even committed: two marriages, three children, his family and Laura.

Laura, who made him more than he was. Better.

He looked at her as they crossed the concrete plaza to enter the building. Head high, shoulders squared, she was dressed in bold red and black, from one of the simple, slim, soft hairy-knit dresses she favored to her wide black belt and big, round earrings, down to the tips of her matching red three-inch heels. Her hair was pulled back, French-braided and tucked under off her neck, displaying the fine lines of her face to best advantage. Her makeup was light and sure, defining and enhancing her lips, eyes, brows without overstating them.

She made, Paolo thought with a flash of pride and pain, one beautiful power statement if ever he'd seen one. And it was part of his job to be an authority on power statements. Laura wielded color like a weapon, to intimidate any opponents at the same time she sought to bolster and defend her own confidence.

An image of Laura dressed to the elegant nines, genteelly but succinctly cutting an attorney with a fractured set of principles down to size, came to mind, and something inside Paolo inadvertently smiled.

He held open the lobby door for her, whisked her past the Futures & Securities-run security station and into the alcove that housed the elevators. How could he possibly have missed seeing this side of her when they were married, missed discovering all the women she was? Consigned her to such a tiny, background, supporting role in his life, when she was obviously so much more?

If he had it to do over, he would never make the same mistake again.

If...

His eyes met the same turmoil, the intensity, in hers when their shoulders touched as they stepped into the elevator and they looked at each other. Who and what they'd been together in this morning's predawn darkness washed over him in a suddenly staggering flood. His mind rang with the sounds of their lovemaking, her eager moaning and pleasured gasps, his own uninhibited groans and mindless demands; the harsh, pleading, primordial language one exchanged only with one's mate.

He saw her as she'd been then, glistening and sweat-slicked, her head tossed back, her body bowed into him, her movements hungry and ferocious: milking him, feeding him...straining to take him deep and deeper, to swallow him up and release him whole. To free him from the prison of himself.

He stood packed against her, breathing her scent, feeling the tingle of her warmth and proximity course through him in the crowded, rising elevator, and saw himself mirrored in her eyes. Wondered, with a stifled curse, what she saw in his, what truth or lies his eyes told.

Windows to the soul, one of his teachers had once called a person's eyes. Poetic, but untrue of most people, Paolo had learned since. Too many people lied with their eyes; he rarely trusted what he saw through the soul's windows, and he had a great deal of trouble placing any faith in words, too. Consistency in actions was what counted in the people he trusted and respected, unfailing follow-through from words to actions and back again.

Last night, in the aftermath of climax, she'd wept and said, "I love you," as easily and unthinkingly as she'd said it the first time they'd made love. And she'd meant it, he knew.

Last night, when he had, out of habit, turned away from Laura in his sleep, she'd turned with him, spooned along his back and wrapped her arms around him, holding him close. He'd groaned and half awakened, only to sink back against her and then sleep the deep and dream-filled slumber of a haunted man.

When he'd started awake to the sound of Gus entering the house, she'd still been wrapped protectively around him, holding him, warding off his demons. Loving him.

Suiting actions to words.

It was quite something to be loved by somebody. Sometimes it was even almost just about enough to be loved.

Almost just about enough.

Emotion started somewhere deep inside him, and Paolo came back to the now of the slowing elevator two floors before their stop. Laura's dark brown eyes regarded him inquisitively, sadly, offering him half a smile filled with her own doubts. He felt his mouth quirk in some wry, bitter, wish-filled response that remembered where they'd begun, where they'd ended. Where they could wind up again, human foibles being what they were. And the possibility of trying again only to end again scared him to death.

She slipped her fingers inside his and squeezed. His lungs filled and expanded with something tremulous and unwilling, and he gripped Laura's hand hard in return.

"You all right with this?" he asked, not sure whether he was referring to the coming interrogation and planning session or to the limbo their doubts about themselves and each other kept them in.

"No," she returned quietly, equally unsure which question she answered, "But we'll get through it anyway."

"Laura," he breathed—not a question, not an answer, simply her name—and brushed two fingertips across her lips. Then he turned to face the elevator doors that were opening at his floor and loosened his hold on Laura, letting go.

And concentrated on what he could do to free her from Talon, Dunne and Gus, instead of on what he would shortly have to do to free her from himself.

Chapter 14

Pandemonium accosted them the moment they stepped out of the elevator and into the Futures & Securities lobby.

Normally cool, calm and womblike, in Paolo's favorite pale dove gray, with accommodations to color made by accents of soft rose, sea-foam green, slate blue and amethyst in the gentle Japanese prints that decorated the walls, F & S's atrium was the scene of general chaos. Water dripped from the ceiling and ran along wall seams, separating the textured decorator paper from the plasterboard, soaked the carpeting and overflowed the stone pots containing ferns, palms and bonsai arrangements in the combination greenhouse-waiting area of the foyer. F & S staffers dashed back and forth alongside building maintenance personnel with buckets, mops and towels at the direction of an enormously pregnant blonde in a pair of tall rubber boots, well-worn bib overalls and a violet-plaid flannel shirt that seemed to match the color of her eyes.

Acasia Jones Smith, Laura guessed with an unexpected flash of amusement, sidestepping a particularly large puddle accumulating underneath a sputtering light fixture. According to all reports—namely Julianna's and Paolo's—Mrs. Smith, pregnant and riled, was the stuff of which dictators were made.

Which, Laura decided, swallowing a grin as she watched Paolo's senior partner deploy her troops with all the finesse of a General Patton, was undoubtedly a kindly understated assessment of the woman. Trying to contain her amusement, she glanced at Paolo, flycatching beside her, with his jaw practically gaping to his chest.

"What the hell—?" he thundered, then fell silent, turning to survey what had once been his pride and joy in disbelief. Around him everyone stopped in their tracks, seeming to draw and hold a collective breath. It never paid, he reflected blackly, ignoring Laura's uncharacteristic enjoyment of the situation at his expense, to take life too seriously, because it was always just when you thought you'd finally brought some order to the confusion that the toilets backed up on you.

"Paolie!" Acasia exclaimed, a good deal too affably for comfort.

Paolo eyed her darkly. She removed her hands from the baby-enhanced vicinity of her hips and turned her palms up, shrugging, giving her head a resigned shake. "A mess, isn't it? Apparently the sprinkler system shorted out or something, and the water ran all night. We've got it shut off now, thank God, but we had to turn off all the water up here to do it. Don't flush the toilets. Electricity's been cut to most of the offices, too, don't know for how long, which means the computer lab and most of the faxes are down. We've rerouted everything through London, but you know how well that works...."

She hitched up her Farmer Johns and squished across the carpet in her oversized Wellingtons to place a consoling hand on Paolo's shoulder. Her voice dropped to a confiding level. "Couple other things have, ah...come up, too."

She bunched her nose up toward her eyes, grimaced broadly. "We have a, kind of a...delicate situation here. Jules has that Gus person stashed somewhere in a dry closet upstairs, and a special agent...let's see if I can remember his name." She rubbed her jaw, thinking. "Claw? No, Talon, that's it, always reminds me of a claw...anyway, he called and said something about wanting to arrest you for obstruction of justice if you didn't get this Gus what's-his-name's body—he didn't use that word, but you get the picture—down to his office soon. I told him we'd temporarily misplaced you, but as soon as we located

you again.... Then there was this Mafia wiseguy or somebody
looking for you, says his boss, you'd-know-who-he-was, wants
to arrange a meet. We told him to get in line and, then, oh yeah,
ah—''

She cleared her throat, dropped her voice lower still. "Ah, it
seems that, ah, hmm, Maria's decided to, er—'' She paused and,
eyeing Laura apologetically, drew Paolo a few steps away. "Apparently Maria's decided to forgive you your trespasses. Or
something like that, I guess. She's, um, sent you some...stuff. I
put it in your office. It's a little wet. For what it's worth, I'm
sorry, but before you...see it, you and I should maybe, er, talk.''

"Talk? With you?'' Acasia never wanted to talk to him about
anything—at least not without a lot of argument—and certainly
never about anything, er, as she would say, personal. Staring at
his partner in consternation—much as if the wrath of God had
suddenly descended upon him, Paolo missed seeing the elevator
doors open once again and Talon step into the lobby.

"I think that's my line,'' the federal agent said sardonically,
joining them, and Paolo and Laura both started and turned.
Laura muttered something explicit under her breath.

Grinning as if at some private joke, Talon spread his coat and
placed his hands on his hips, displaying the badge tucked into
his belt at the same time that he showed Paolo the shoulder
holster with its Colt .45 bulge beneath his arm. Silently assuring
him that this little meeting would be all threat and no bluff,
government-backed employee to corporate civilian: cooperate or
else. "Fill me in.''

Paolo smiled slightly and placed himself deliberately between
Laura and Talon. Sick as he was of them, he was good at power
games. The trick was to wield the power, not play with it. It
was a fine differentiation that Dunne would understand, but
Talon, smart cop though he was, never could. That and an inability to know where to draw the line on his games would keep
Talon in middle management forever. If Paolo didn't find some
way to cost him his job first. "On what?''

"Don't play coy with me, Gianini. We know you picked up
Abernathy this morning. Turn him over.''

"Got a warrant?''

Talon flapped open the front of his sport coat, showing Paolo the paper stuck in his inside pocket. Paolo made a "gimme" motion with his hand. "Let's see it."

Talon shrugged and handed him the folded piece of legalese. Paolo accepted it and shook it open, turning as he did so to place a hand on Laura's elbow. With a barely perceptible shake of his head to the questions in her eyes, he urged her in the direction of his office, jerked his head at Talon to accompany them.

"How wet is my office?" he asked Acasia over his shoulder.

"Drier than anything out here," she replied, "but—"

"Good. That's where we'll be. I don't want to be disturbed." Acasia tried again. "Paolo..."

He waved an impatient hand at her. "I know, you put some stuff in there. I'll get to it later, Case."

Acasia threw up her hands in a "why me Lord?" gesture, then tried again. "Paolo, I really wouldn't. If you go in there, I don't think it'll wait—"

"*Later,* Case," Paolo returned firmly, oblivious to Acasia's attempt at circumspect warning. Acasia Jones had never been circumspect about anything in the twenty-some-odd years he'd known her, after all.

Laura, however, heard something in what Paolo's partner didn't say and looked back at her in time to see Acasia puff her cheeks out in an "I tried" sigh, shrug helplessly and mouth, "I'm sorry," at her. With a sense of apprehension that had nothing to do with Talon or his warrants, Laura faced forward and followed Paolo into the office corridor.

One eye on where he was going, Paolo proceeded toward his office, studying the warrant with interest, then glanced over at Talon.

"Satisfied?" Talon asked.

Paolo lifted a shoulder. "It's in order," he admitted. His face grew thoughtful. "Trouble is," he said, "I'm not sure exactly where Abernathy is at the moment. Unfortunately, this—" he indicated the warrant "—allows you to take him into custody wherever you find him, but it doesn't specify searching my offices for him." He made a regretful face, handed the legal papers back to Talon. "Sorry."

Fury seemed to color Talon's eyes for an instant; then he pulled control back around himself and eyed Paolo coolly.

"Harboring a wanted felon, Gianini? I thought your business—" He cast a meaningful glance at Laura, who drew herself up and matched his expression, ice for chill. He ignored her, returning his attention to Paolo. "—or your ex-wife's reputation meant more to you than that."

"You unbelievable bastard," Laura said softly.

Talon nodded. "Count on it."

For the space of a heartbeat, Paolo felt rage against Talon's treatment of Laura surface and threaten to consume him. Then, like a phoenix rising from the flames, he remembered the allegation Gus had made about the federal agent's suggested method for dispensing with Gus's case. He looked at Talon. "Like you counted on Gus to feather your retirement to let him off the hook?" he asked.

Beside Paolo, Laura caught her breath, let it go in a soft "yeah" of approval. Taken off guard, Talon allowed a moment to pass before responding with apparent indifference. "And how many men would like to send you straight to hell for helping put them in prison, Gianini? A cornered man will say anything to take his tormentor down with him."

Paolo's lips twisted in a wolfish smile. "And a guilty man denies blame even more quickly than an innocent man," he responded.

He watched Talon's face redden, his teeth clench. Pity it had taken him so long to remember it, but there was an old Italian saying the priests used to like to quote at him regarding confession and temptation: It's opportunity that makes the thief. Somewhere behind Talon's well-kept mask lay an answer so blatant that even a man like Paolo who didn't believe in instinct could sense it. One more trick and he would have it.

A heavy paneled door with his name on it slid into the periphery of his vision, and he stopped in front of it, thinking hard. Something Acasia had once told him stuck out in his mind: a full-house attitude could beat a pair of aces anyday—unless the other person called your bluff. He just had to hope Talon wouldn't.

"Whatever else he may have done," he said casually, "Abernathy was smart enough to keep detailed records of every person, place, conversation or transaction he handled. Call it insurance." He turned his doorknob and shoved the door inward, watching for Talon's reaction as he did so. "Your name's on a policy," he finished diffidently. Then he stepped through the opening door into his office and stopped dead.

In the wintry light slanting through the bank of windows on the other side of the room, a slender, well-dressed young man stood looking out on the city. At the sound of Paolo's voice, he turned a much younger version of Paolo's face toward the door.

"Hello, Papa," his son said.

"Mauro," Paolo returned, stunned, and, without knowing that he did it, he swung the door shut before either Talon or Laura could enter the office behind him.

Emotion knotted in Paolo's chest, pulsed through his veins in a confusing shimmy of welcome, elation and panic. None of his sons had ever before sought him out, come to him—whether because of their mother's hatred of him and refusal to allow it, or because of his own reticence around them, he didn't know. He'd hoped that as they grew older...but never had he anticipated that it would be Mauro who'd come—first.

He'd thought—perhaps fantasized—that Edouardo, his eldest, his nemesis and therefore, somehow, the child of his heart... But it was Mauro, his middle son, neither the heir apparent nor the pampered youngest, whose Adam's apple bobbed once, nervously, in his throat, whose black eyes anxiously measured, mistrusted, and withheld judgment, waiting for Paolo to act, react. And he couldn't remember how to.

He wanted to hold out his arms, clap his son on the back, hold him at arm's length and exclaim over him, laugh with him, welcome him like the returned prodigal. Except that Mauro wasn't the prodigal in this picture, Paolo thought, he was. Except that none of those moves came naturally to him—especially not when the only thing he could think was *Something's happened; someone's died; he's been sent to bring me the news. Oh, God, Giani...'Douardo...*

He swallowed the taste of fear—it was like gunmetal in his mouth—and asked, "Is everything...everyone... Has anything..."

Mauro shook his head. "No, everyone is fine." His English tangled heavily with his thoroughly Italian but British-tinged accent. "It's nothing, only me. I wanted to come. I had to come. I wanted to—" He paused, searching for what he wanted to say. "I wanted to see you. To—" He hesitated again. "To face you."

Paolo's heart gladdened; he breathed relief, smiling a little. How many times had he prayed for this, never expecting—

A sudden thought occurred to him, stifling elation. "Why didn't you call? Does your mother know where you are?"

Just that quickly, awkwardness passed. As though on cue, the gray sky outside broke and a fragment of wan sunlight strayed into the room.

Mauro grinned and shoved his hands into his pants pockets, swaggering a bit where he stood. Parents everywhere, no matter who they were, what their nationality, what your relationship was with them, could generally be counted on to ask the same questions. "She drove me to the airport and told me to say hello." He dropped his gaze to a point somewhere beyond the tip of his left shoe. "And I thought about calling, but if I'd taken the time, I didn't know if I'd still..." His jaw worked in a motion uncannily like Paolo's. He looked at his father. "If I'd called, I didn't know if I'd have the courage to come. I didn't know..."

He looked at his shoe again and didn't finish, but Paolo heard what he didn't say. *I didn't know if you'd want me.*

Paolo shut his eyes against the sting of emotion and swallowed against the fist that suddenly seemed to wedge tight in his throat. He'd been remiss about many things as a parent, but he'd thought at least he'd made it plain that, no matter what problems he and Maria had with each other, the boys were not part of what he'd had to get away from. That they were each special, each passionately wanted, each loved by his sire without qualm or reservation.

But perhaps during all his absences, his skirmishes with Maria, he'd forgotten to say it out loud, to tell them that no matter what, wherever they were, wherever they went, whatever they needed, whoever they became, he would be there behind them as long as he lived.

Hard to trust a man who, for all his sons could see, had married two women and walked away from both. Walked away from them.

He spread his hands wide at his sides, unsure of how to do this, knowing only that Mauro had to know. "I'm glad you're here," he said simply.

And Mauro, who didn't suffer from the same restraint that had long ago stunted his father's emotions, and who had learned to forgive quickly and completely by observing the toll reticence had wreaked upon his family, launched himself across the room and into Paolo's arms and hugged him.

Paolo was dazed, and it took him a moment to make his arms come up and around Mauro. They moved slowly, but without hesitation, reaching, spanning, closing around.

It was odd to hold this child after so many years, this seventeen-year-old man who was always so reserved in the presence of his brothers, but it was a relief, too. Like a bridge that he'd burned somehow managing to stay connected to the shore by a single strong cable—enough to build on. Willing years of absence and missed hugs away on the strength of an instant, Paolo crushed Mauro to him, knowing it was hardly enough, desperately hoping that what he could offer now would be sufficient to prime the future. He felt Mauro's shoulders shake, pushed him away to find his son laughing.

"That was easier than I thought it would be," Mauro said in Italian.

Paolo grinned. "No, it wasn't," he said honestly, spreading his fingers across the bridge of his nose to wipe away some telltale moisture. "Not by a long shot. Worst moment of my life, stepping into this room, seeing you here, wondering... Well—" He shrugged, cuffed Mauro's face with the flat of his hand. "Doesn't matter. You're here. How long can you—"

"My visa gives me six weeks," Mauro said. He ran his tongue along the inside of his jaw, lifted a shoulder. "After that, I thought maybe, if things worked out, you might want to...you could..." He eyed his toe again, let his plan out in a rush. "Maybe you could spot me a job...help me get into school...let me stay for a while. If it wouldn't be a problem."

"It's no problem," Paolo replied gladly, and with a silent wrench he felt some of the imprisoned places inside him breaking free.

And a child shall lead them, he thought. Only Mauro was no longer quite a child, and not yet a man. He was somewhere in between, beginning to break old ties, forge new—

He turned on the thought to draw Laura forward, to share the moment with her. To make her promises. But for the first time he noticed that Laura was not, and had not been, in the room with them at all. He had, he remembered with a nauseating rush of self-disgust, shut the door in her face, again, cut her out of one of the most important moments in his life and left her standing out in the hall with—

He paled suddenly, felt his gut tighten and twist with foreboding. He'd left Laura out in the hall with Talon. Whom he'd just accused of soliciting bribes from an alleged—albeit white-collar—felon, and perhaps worse.

Like being in Dunne's pocket himself.

The string of obscenities Paolo loosed in his own direction was fluent and explicit. God, he should have seen it before; he should have seen it all along. But Talon, smart cop and astute people reader that he'd always been, had seen it in Paolo from the beginning. Had known that where Laura was concerned Paolo would be blind and deaf to everything but Laura's safety. And Laura's wants, and Laura's needs.

To everything, in fact, but Laura herself.

The threatening phone calls she'd said she received before Gus had disappeared, the man who'd threatened her in her office that night before she'd found Gus's clothes on the beach, the bird beside her telephone...Talon could have engineered all of them.

The sudden weight in Paolo's chest threatened to collapse his lungs. He'd almost put the pieces together at the beginning, but he hadn't taken his suspicions quite far enough—and then he'd been blinded by the very nearness of Laura, his need to assuage her fear. By the ache of memories and the bitterness of emotions that hadn't died, by the feelings that had long been looking for any excuse to find resurrection.

And they had. He would love Laura until the end of time and after, love her not only enough to let her go, but enough to fight to keep her, too. But now he also knew.

It was Talon, all of it. Talon, who wanted something more to retire on than a gold watch, who might only understand the attitudes of middle management, but who was too smart to trust anyone else to carry out a plan that could net him millions.

Dunne's millions.

Damn, Paolo thought savagely, he was an ass, a fool and more for not seeing it before, for slamming the door in her face, for not keeping his arms around her and holding on for all he was worth while he had the chance. Because, if he was right about Talon now—and his margin of doubt was so negligible as to be ludicrous—he might never have the chance to hold Laura again in this life. And in the next only if he was very lucky.

He strode violently toward the door, aware even as he moved, that he was already too late.

"Papa?" Mauro asked, alarmed.

Barely contained, Paolo swung toward his son, hand raised in stricken expression. "Mauro, I'm sorry, I have to go. Understand, I love you and I will be back. We will do what we have to, you and I, but right now, I have just made the biggest mistake of my life, bar none, and if I don't do something to fix it fast, the woman I love could die." Then he spun back toward the door again.

The portal slammed inward before he reached it; he caught it and read the truth on Acasia's guilty face before she spoke it.

"We just got the call," she said without preamble. "Dunne's got Laura."

Chapter 15

"How long?" Paolo snapped.

"Two minutes max. They want you alone on the street in ten." Acasia rubbed her protruding belly. "God, I'm sorry, Paolo. Maybe Jules is right. Maybe I am getting too mellow to work security. I saw Talon head down the hall with her, but I figured—"

Paolo brusquely waved the apology aside. Blame wouldn't bring Laura back, any more than it had returned his sister to the family twenty years ago. Besides, it was more his fault than anyone's that something had happened to Laura, anyway. Because he'd been too shortsighted and distracted to pay proper attention. Not unlike, the destructive little niggle at the back of his mind assured him, the way he'd been too myopic and preoccupied to pay proper attention to what was going on with Lisetta. He shoved the thought away; that was then, this was now—Laura, not Lisetta. Couldn't destroy the present again by living in the past. Had to concentrate. "Demands?"

Acasia shook her head. "Nope, that's it, just you on the street, walking, alone. No wires, no surveillance. Head for St. Paul's. They'll find you."

"Where are Jules and Abernathy?"

"Weight room. It's dry. They'll stay put. For what it's worth, Jules says Abernathy's offered to hit the street in your place. Demands to do it, in fact. Figures he's what Dunne really wants, anyway. Jules cuffed him to the Nautilus machine to make sure he couldn't charge off to play hero. Bit late for him to find his conscience, if you ask me—"

"Not that anyone ever has to," Paolo supplied halfheartedly.

Acasia glared at him, also without enthusiasm. It was an old ritual between them, thrust and parry, feint and jab. They eyed each other across the span of twenty-odd years of uneasy, guilt-ridden acquaintance and all at once knew they'd both outgrown a ritual that had long ago become a relic.

Paolo's jaw tightened. He looked at the wall behind Acasia's head. He and Acasia had been unwilling allies for a long time without particularly liking each other, but it had never really been Casie's fault that Lisetta had died; his problems with Laura had never had anything to do with her—or Julianna—either. "I'll go up and talk to Abernathy, see if there's anything he can tell me that he hasn't already."

Acasia nodded, eyeing the door, understanding what he didn't say. It was the same thing that she, herself, couldn't find words for. They'd hem and haw over something to each other eventually, and that would be enough. All their friendship needed. "I'll come with you. Four ears are better than two."

"Thanks."

Mauro stepped forward. "I don't know what is going on, Papa, but I wish to help. What can I do?"

"Stay here until I come back."

Mauro shook his head firmly. He hadn't crossed an ocean and a wilderness of emotions to be left out of his father's life now. "I will come with you. If you are involved with this woman, what she said—" he lifted his chin at Acasia in another gesture genetically inherited from Paolo "—makes sense. Six ears will be better than four."

For the space of several heartbeats, Paolo stared at his son, ready to argue. Maria would have his hide—and quite rightly, too—for exposing Mauro to this version of America's upper-crust criminal element immediately upon his arrival.

On the other hand, Mauro was barely six months younger than Paolo had been when he'd gone to work for Italy's police force, the same age as Acasia when she'd brought the first of Lisetta's kidnappers to heel, and, truth be told, Paolo had neither the energy nor the time to clash with his offspring over something as trivial as Gus now. He had—he glanced at his watch—under seven minutes to talk to Gus, come up with a plan and get downstairs to find out what Dunne would accept in exchange for Laura.

The fact that he might not accept anything didn't bear thinking about.

He swept a hand at the doorway, capitulating. "Let's go," he said, and followed Mauro out.

Tense and erect, Laura sat in the long white limo, trying to moisten her dry mouth without appearing nervous. Beside her Talon sat, stinking and sweating in his off-the-rack sport coat, a flagrant contrast to the immaculately groomed individual opposite them. Cold, analytical gray eyes considered Laura with approval, flicked disparagingly over the federal agent.

"You should change your suit occasionally, Mr. Talon," William Dunne said as he poured coffee from an insulated silver pot into delicate china cups. "It would make you less offensive." With a pleasant crocodile smile that turned up the corners of his mouth without touching his eyes, he pushed a filled cup on its saucer across the linen-covered table between them and made a polite gesture at the crystal sugar-and-cream set in the center of the cloth. "Please, Ms. Gianini," he said, offering her a pair of silver sugar tongs. "Help yourself."

"No, thank you," Laura said coolly. She reached for the cup, pleased to note that her hand was steady. Behind her ribs, her heart thumped hard, pumping panic with adrenaline through her veins; she felt as if she had a pickax hammering time in her head. Each dull thud seemed to beat inexorably toward the end of her life, but she'd be damned if she let either Dunne or Talon hear that fear in her voice or read it on her face.

By tipping his hand, Talon had virtually ensured her death, she knew. He couldn't let either her or Gus out of this alive now that Paolo had his part in all this figured out; without her or Gus, no matter what Paolo thought he knew, Paolo had no proof. She'd realized that the moment Paolo had voiced his theories, then shut the door, unintentionally—stupidly?—leaving Talon time to stick his gun in her ribs to guarantee her silence while he herded her to the fire door and three flights down the stairs.

So simple. So gallingly, idiotically easy. All the king's horses and all the king's men at her disposal, and she'd walked out of Futures & Securities without a whimper, like some damned docile lamb to the slaughter. Because Talon had assured her that he would feel no compunction whatever over killing Paolo, the boy so obviously his son or the pregnant blonde if Laura even looked at anybody the wrong way. She'd believed him, the same way she'd believed him the night he'd worn the ski mask in her office and told her what he wanted from Gus.

If only she'd put his voice together with the tape in her head sooner, instead of needing this graphic demonstration of how to get four out of two plus two.

Wary, she eyed Talon sideways, watched Dunne across the table, unconcernedly sipping his coffee while he waited for Paolo. He looked like a man comfortable with himself and the life he led; a man in charge of his environment, used to being obeyed because he understood the use of discipline, was ruthless enough to punish what didn't please. A man who'd learned to appreciate and could therefore manipulate a silence.

With trepidation, she wondered if Dunne knew everything Talon had done, or if Talon had his own deadly plan to double-cross him, too. She didn't want to be around if that was the case; he might be willing to gamble with his life for the sake of a few million dollars, but Talon wasn't stupid enough to forget that Dunne would find him replaceable and therefore expendable. Which meant that he'd have plans to save himself at the expense of someone else.

She dropped her eyelashes to her cheeks and leaned back in her seat without relaxing, studying Dunne through slitted lids. There was something entirely too disconcerting about a wealthy man's eyes, a lack of something, an altogether frightening absence of...scruple. Of familiarity.

With a mental start Laura hoped hadn't shown, she rattled her coffee cup back onto its saucer without tasting any of the black liquid inside it. Nausea sent bile churning into her throat, and she swallowed it back.

She knew now why Dunne's name and picture had seemed vaguely familiar to her: Gus had taken her to a charity benefit at the reputed crime baron's home in Southampton once. On introduction to him and his socialite wife, she had assessed William Dunne as wealthy but boorishly chauvinistic and dismissed him as unworthy of note.

One more man she'd underestimated.

God, had she been wrong.

Early-December wind scattered huge drops of freezing rain into Paolo's face, lifted the tails of his overcoat and sent it whipping out behind him when he stepped out of the building. He gathered the wool quickly around himself, buttoned it with fingers made thick and fumbling by the icy air. Inside his head a persistent choirboy's voice chanted in Italian, *Screwed up again, Gianini, when you gonna learn?*

Feeling as if he had a hangover he hadn't enjoyed getting, he stifled the choirboy with some plain street English and crossed the plaza to the sidewalk. In front of him, cars and people rushed along the Manhattan street, turbulent and answerless, but constant and calming. He looked at the teeming street, emptied his mind and breathed.

The most important lesson he'd ever learned in his life was that actually screwing up mattered less than how you handled the aftereffects. Without looking at it, he ran his thumb over the black, quarter-sized-only-thicker bumper beeper in the palm of his left hand. It had a magnetic base that would stick to almost any metal part of a car, made blind surveillance relatively simple for whoever held the receiver, and eased the mind of an operative who might otherwise be forced to go into tricky situations on his—or her—own.

When Acasia had slapped it into his hand on his way out of the office, he'd debated over accepting it, weighing the decided risk to Laura if he was caught with it against the questionable security it might provide. Dunne had not garnered his power by failing to anticipate that a company like Futures & Securities might gamble on the use of an electronic bug, nor by quailing at the prospect of violence.

Business rule of thumb number four, he thought. *When in doubt, don't. Rule five: Show no weakness.*

Once again he felt the flat black surface of the beeper with his thumb. Without a doubt, hardball was Dunne's game; a smart defense was Paolo's.

Glad he remembered how to pray, he palmed the beeper into his right hand and flicked it into a storm drain as he passed. Then, pulling a supple pair of rabbit-lined gloves over his hands, he crossed Church Street and headed toward Broadway, turned right and paced toward Fulton Street and St. Paul's Chapel. He had just passed the entrance to the chapel when the limousine slid to the curb beside him. Two impeccably dressed men in unapologetically European suits stepped out on either side of him, leaving their doors open. At the same time, Talon thrust Laura forward in her seat, making sure Paolo didn't miss seeing her.

"Mr. Dunne sends his regrets that we missed you at the beach this morning," the thug on his left said. "Would you come with us, please."

"Don't," Laura urged promptly, and Talon covered her mouth and jerked her roughly out of sight.

Paolo swallowed, forced himself not to flinch. Not to rush forward, grab Laura and make the alternatives easy for Talon. "I don't do business with underlings."

A figure in the back seat of the limousine leaned forward. Paolo looked into the cool gray eyes of William Dunne. "I can appreciate that, Mr. Gianini. That's the way I work myself." He gestured toward the seat beside him. "Please. We have much to discuss."

He couldn't take his eyes off Laura.

She raised her chin and smiled at him, opened her hand to him on the table, then closed her fingers tightly into her palm, keeping the unspoken intimacy between her and Paolo away from Dunne's and Talon's prying eyes.

Paolo's mouth drew a wry line into his cheek in response. "I'm sorry," he told her quietly. *For everything,* his eyes said. For getting distracted, shutting you out, divorcing you, losing you.

He sank into the plush upholstery next to William Dunne and drank her in while Dunne's minions settled into position near Talon and the limousine pulled away from the curb. She looked wan and guarded, but unharmed. He wanted to reach out and hold her, touch her, run his hands everywhere to make sure, but Talon was wearing a "dare ya" grin and keeping a tight grip on her arm. His other hand remained within grabbing distance of his gun.

Beside him, William Dunne noted the direction of Paolo's attention with every evidence of amusement. The very picture of gracious civility, he poured coffee from the silver pot and offered Paolo a cup. When Paolo made a gesture of refusal, Dunne returned the pot to the small bar in the limo's interior and settled back, sipping, allowing the silence to collect long enough to become menacing before he spoke.

"We were introduced last year in Scarsdale, at the governor's reception, weren't we?"

Without taking his eyes off Laura and Talon, Paolo nodded slightly. Dunne looked pleased. Old acquaintances were almost always more challenging to deal with. They understood his reputation and the stakes. He knew theirs. He'd crush Gianini in the end all the same, but the relationship would be interesting while it lasted.

"I was sure we'd met before. All to the good. You're a fascinating man, Mr. Gianini. You come highly recommended."

"You don't," Paolo said shortly. The unwritten-rule book said don't antagonize and never burn bridges, but he wasn't in the mood for rules—or books, either. Underneath the table, he felt Laura's foot find his, felt something inside him constrict, then swell, savoring the meager contact. The trust and forgiveness. "What I hear about you is 'steer clear.'"

Dunne smiled and inclined his head, as though accepting a compliment. "Excellent advice. Normally."

In silence, Paolo waited for the *why* that was obviously coming. Dunne took his time getting to it. He stroked the fragile china cup and saucer in his hands, eyes half-closed in peaceful contemplation. Paolo wasn't fooled; he'd spent too much time in this arena not to recognize it. Dunne was taking his measure, determining his weak spots, calibrating his own attack.

Hiding impatience, Paolo settled comfortably into his seat and invited Dunne to examine his fill while he himself returned the scrutiny. Like two little boys staring at each other across the breakfast table, wanting to see which of them would blink first. Dunne did the honors, at last, conceding victory with a smile full of charming self-insight. An intelligent, sane and stone-cold-dangerous man, Paolo remembered thinking once. The conclusion didn't change.

"I understand Futures & Securities does...mmm...liaison work from time to time," Dunne said at last. "And that you, yourself, handle particularly—" He hesitated, as though searching for the right word "—particularly delicate cases."

"Cut to the chase, Dunne. We all know why we're here. You hold the cards. Deal. When, where, and how much?"

Dunne made a clicking sound behind his teeth. "Too impatient, Mr. Gianini. First we must negotiate, dicker..." His voice hardened. "Understand each other." He took another sip of his coffee, closed his eyes, savoring the taste. "French roast," he said, opening his eyes. "Excellent flavor. Are you sure you won't try some?"

Paolo stared at him without response, waiting. Underneath the table Laura's foot trembled against his, the strain telling. He rubbed her ankle with the side of his shoe, offering what comfort he could.

Dunne sighed, disappointed. "Really, Mr. Gianini. You're not playing properly."

"It's not a game."

"No, there you're quite wrong," Dunne said, placing his cup on the table. Something barely perceptible seemed to sharpen in his demeanor, as if he were a hunter gathering his muscles under him, ready to spring out of the grass. "It is the ultimate game. A match of skill and cunning where we will each attempt to anticipate and outthink the other. You know it, and I know it. We might as well be honest with each other. Whether you find the challenge amusing—as I do—or not, it's the contest you yourself engage in every day. Our purposes may be different, but the results are the same. We each make money. We each wield power. We understand it."

Paolo's mouth went dry. There was a challenge in Dunne's voice, the demand of one gunslinger to another: ante up, prove yourself, winner take all. In this case, Laura.

He studied Dunne carefully, buying an instant to calm. The other man's eyes were flat and expressionless, but there was a tic in one eyelid, and Paolo thought that underneath the impassive exterior he detected a note of strain. He straightened and sat forward, placed his hands flat on the table. "State your terms, Mr. Dunne."

Dunne pursed his lips. "Mr. Abernathy took some things belonging to me. I'd like them returned."

"Exactly what things are we talking about?"

"Files. A computer ledger. Three million dollars. I want the money in cash, the files, the ledger and Mr. Abernathy returned to me by nine o'clock tomorrow morning."

"Three million is a lot of money. It'll take time to get hold of it."

"Expediency is your forte, Mr. Gianini, is it not?"

Paolo acknowledged the norm with a clipped nod. "The money is in an account in Nassau. If it's not possible to bring it in by nine?"

"I'm afraid Ms. Gianini could suffer a disfiguring accident."

Paolo glanced instinctively at Laura, saw her blanch and repress an involuntary shudder. His knuckles contracted, bunching the tablecloth under his fingers. If anything happened to her, the world wouldn't be big enough to hide Dunne. He made the only decision he could. "Where?"

Dunne smiled and pressed a button in the armrest beside him. Paolo felt the limousine angle sideways and slow; the interview was over. "Winter Cove. It's a private beach five miles due east of Ms. Gianini's home. Mr. Talon will meet you there. You and Mr. Abernathy come alone."

"Nine a.m.," Paolo agreed. "We'll be there."

It was the longest day and night of his life.

Dawn made a spectacular debut, arriving purple and pink, with ropes of slate at the far edge of the ocean, but Paolo didn't see it. Exhausted, he stared out the windows of their bedroom in Laura's house at some undetermined mark in the middle distance and held himself together by his fingernails.

Nothing, not the night he'd spent in emergency with Lisetta before she'd died, nor the forty-eight hours he'd spent with his heart in his mouth when Edouardo had run away after he and Maria had finally told the boys they'd decided to separate, had prepared him for this. Everything he was—heart, soul, spirit and body—ached for want of Laura. He felt numbed, paralyzed, unable to move, to act, to feel.

"I am what I do," he'd told her once by way of apology for coming in late without calling, but he knew now, for the first time since Lisetta's death, that the words were not true. He was not what he did. It was part of him, but his life, his every thought, word and act, was no longer centered on Futures & Securities, he no longer needed the company to free him from guilt so that he could simply exist. He was more than the sum of his business; he was the man who loved Laura Gianini, who needed her as shamelessly as he needed air.

He stared down at the rumpled bed where he and Laura had loved, dozed, then wakened to love again. To simply have her in his bed would never be enough now. He wanted more than that: courtship, commitment, children if she still wanted them, and forever.

He wanted her in his arms, in his life, the way she'd always been in his heart. One way or another, in bitterness or love, conflict or serenity, there was a place inside him that belonged to her alone, always would. She spoke to the best in him, brought out the most tenuous and defenseless aspects of him, the parts of himself he hated. Except, he realized, when he was with her.

When he was with Laura, his life became a constant series of contradictions, things he was aware of but couldn't control: love versus hate, want versus need, give versus take, jealousy, generosity and greed—confusing, conflicting, weakening emotions that clamored simultaneously for his attention. She brought him alive, possessed what he did not: emotional bravery. With her he could be inept, vulnerable, lost, and she would love him anyway. Love him because of his flaws, not in spite of them.

He leaned down, straightened the sheets on the bed. Watched his hands shake.

It did no good to tell himself that neither Dunne nor Talon had anything to gain by hurting Laura before they got what they wanted from Gus. He'd had too much experience with worst-case scenarios to be an optimist about Laura's chances.

He was afraid, not only for her, but for himself if anything happened to her. If she died, so would he. He didn't even want to think about who he'd become without her.

Selfish thought, he knew, but where Laura was concerned, he found himself as greedy as they came.

At the other end of the house, a door slammed, rattling the windows, and he started. Mauro stepped into the room behind him; when he spoke, his voice was hoarse with fatigue tinged with excitement. "They're back," he said in Italian. "The helicopter just landed. They've got the money."

Paolo nodded without turning. "Thanks."

Mauro had stayed with him every step of the nearly eighteen hours that had passed since Paolo's meeting with Dunne; observing, questioning, maintaining the status quo through the long hours of conferences and strategy sessions cum shouting matches with Acasia, Acasia's husband, Cameron Smith—who'd arrived not long after Paolo's return to collect his wife and stayed to lend his not-inconsiderable weight to the banking matters—Julianna and Gus.

Julianna and Acasia were of the opinion that extortionists' demands should never be met, and particularly not all at once. Cameron was of the opinion that one should do whatever one had to when a loved one was at stake, and would Paolo consider allowing him to rent a small but well-trained commando squad from Futures & Securities' nearest rival, Terror Tech, to storm Dunne's castle and get Laura out? Gus was willing to do anything anyone suggested that would allow him to do penance and perhaps die to correct the situation he'd gotten Laura into.

But it was Mauro, whose grandfather owned a bank, who'd diffidently suggested that everyone, including William Dunne, had someone to answer to, be it a board of directors or a house of representatives, and why didn't they take Dunne's mistakes to whoever that was.

Some smart kid he had, huh?

What had Dunne said? *"We'll try to anticipate and outmaneuver each other."*

The plans were in place, the cavalry alerted. And God, Paolo thought, he hoped to hell they had outsmarted Dunne.

* * *

The beach seemed colder than when she'd left it—was it only yesterday?

Laura stared out the tiny window of the tinier room Talon had stuck her in when they'd arrived at Dunne's private hideaway, wistfully eyeing the long stretch of dunes and frozen beach, the empty ocean, wondering if she'd ever again see it through the same eyes that had made her buy her own house down the road. Did the survivor of a train wreck ever again view train travel as a relaxing coast-to-coast adventure? Was the survivor of divorce ever again able to view the prospect of marriage without cynicism?

Interesting question, that. What had made her think about it now?

Paolo.

She moistened the tip of one finger, traced a dissolute design in the frost on the glass. Ice sparkled over everything like frosting, etched prism patterns on the windowpane, turned light into color where there should be none.

"Beautiful," Laura whispered, and by acknowledging the word she felt some measure of peace rise and settle inside her, calming. What were the words to the Navajo prayer she'd read in some Sierra Club book back in high school? *In beauty I walk, with beauty within me, beauty all around me, in beauty I walk...*

Not quite right, but close enough for memory. Close enough to change the quivering, distressed damsel inside her who'd spent the night bargaining with God for her life into the woman who stood here this morning: the woman determined not to let anyone else decide her fate for her.

I am woman, hear me roar, she thought dryly, giving herself a sarcastic mental pat on the head. But she felt stronger for the irony.

She turned to survey her prison by the dusty postdawn light. She'd been able to do little more than stumble her way around it in the dark last night, barking her shins on a multitude of sharp-edged objects as she'd groped about for the old army surplus cot and quilt Talon had told her was in place for her use. She'd spent the night huddled on the edge of the canvas bed, wrapped to her ears in the musty quilt, cold from fear and exhaustion rather than the temperature—which was none too warm, she noted now.

The chamber was rectangular, Spartan—probably a utility

room. She scrubbed a spot clear on the frosty windowpane and peered out the window, trying to collect her bearings. She was on the second floor of the cottage, facing the dunes. Cardboard boxes and rattan patio furniture stored for the winter piled the floor, leaving very little space for her to move. Curious, she opened a box, wondering what a man like William Dunne would store in his summer getaway. Undoubtedly nothing that would make either a good weapon or a lock pick—if she could even figure out how to use one, anyway. Computer codes she could unlock, but doors....

She looked into the box: china, extra glasses, pitchers, plastic cutlery—no metal forks or knives. In the next carton, blankets and linen. In the one after that, jeans, sweaters, designer T-shirts, sweat socks and deck shoes. Nothing spectacular, merely normal things that anyone would store.

Again she eyed the box of clothes, contemplated her feet in the red heels she only wore when she wanted to appear taller and more imposing. Hadn't worked yesterday, that was for sure. Not to mention that her feet were killing her. It was difficult to think clearly when your feet were cold and sore. Her grandfather had often said, if your feet were cold, put on a hat, equating a warm head with warm feet. But in her own experience Laura had found that as long as her feet were comfortable and warm, the rest of her was equal to just about anything.

Without a second thought, she shucked out of her clothes and dug into the box. Moments later she pulled on a blue T-shirt, cream-colored Aran-knit sweater, thick socks, a slightly baggy pair of sage-green duck-weight trousers and slip-on shoes that were a bit too wide but, with a second pair of socks over the first, didn't slop too much.

Fortified by warmth, if not good cheer, Laura rolled her clothes and shoes into a small bundle, folded up the quilt and sat on the cot to take stock of her surroundings with a more calculating eye. According to her watch, it was almost seven, a little over two hours before Dunne had told Talon to meet Paolo.

She pursed her lips and rested her chin in her hand, wondering how Nancy Drew would get herself out of this mess. Rotating her head to unkink the muscles in her neck, she saw the trap door in the ceiling six feet above her head, remembered the various roof levels she'd seen from the too-small-to-fit-through window above the cot. And smiled.

At the beginning of her investment career, she'd learned that the slightest financial setback could make a man desperate and panicky, lead him to make rash decisions that only compounded his problems, rather than alleviated them. Time and again, she'd counseled frightened investors to ride out a momentary loss, advised them that if they couldn't afford to pay, they shouldn't play. Men like Dunne succeeded because they understood that an occasional loss was part of the game, that every venture included risk.

Men like Talon failed, because no matter how smart they were, they panicked too easily, lacking the edge it took to make a reckless, ruthless move count. Sitting beside Talon in Dunne's limo yesterday, Laura had smelled fear on him, but she'd been too frightened herself to look for a way to make use of it.

Today, she was still afraid, but where Talon's mind had apparently ceased to function, hers was at last waking up.

She crossed her fingers and, as silently as she could, moved a rattan chair into the center of the room.

She climbed onto it, reached for the trap door and prayed.

Wind slapped ice-spangled dune grass, whipped white froth on the waves; broken, storm-stripped trees made black etchings against the cold daylight sun.

Standing on the wet-packed sand, silver Haliburton briefcase stuffed with three million dollars in old bills in hand, Paolo scanned the skyline in all directions, looking for some sign of Talon or Dunne's people. Beside him, Gus hefted the case containing his hard drive, shifted the hard copy of the ledger in his other hand.

"'Bout time for 'em to be here, isn't it?" he asked.

Paolo flipped his wrist over, glanced at his watch. "Any time," he agreed, throat tight. Uneasily he looked back in the direction from which they'd come, saw only his Lincoln parked several hundred feet away along the road. Looked at his watch again. It was 9:15. Talon was late; not a good sign.

"Something's wrong," he muttered, then whipped around at the sudden roar of an engine in time to see a sand-colored four-door Jimmy come fish-tailing up the beach toward them. A flashy, late-model sedan followed it.

Twenty yards from them, the two vehicles plowed to a sand-spraying halt. Doors popped open and well-armed men jumped out, fanned across the sand. Misshapen khaki raincoat flapping around him, Talon stepped out from behind the wall of men and walked toward them.

"Where's Laura?" Gus asked.

Paolo gave his head a slight shake, watching Talon. "Don't know. Don't like this. If I say 'Go,' drop everything and run. Got it?"

Gus tipped his head slightly forward, nodding. "Anything you say."

Ten feet in front of them, Talon halted. "Bring the money?"

"Where's Laura?" Paolo responded.

"Waiting for me to come back with the money. Then I turn her loose, call you, you pick her up."

"That wasn't the arrangement, Talon."

"Plans change."

"Not this one," Paolo said tightly. "I don't see Laura here now, you don't get the money or anything else."

Talon made a motion with his hand; the men in back of him came to attention, leveling their guns. "Be smart, Gianini," he started to say, but the sudden flapping of a helicopter rising from behind a dune interrupted him.

Down the strip of wet-packed sand that comprised the December beach, a squad of police cars barreled, lights rolling, sirens whirring. Gaping, Talon swung around. Around him, Dunne's men scattered, looking for escape or cover. The helicopter descended close, fanning sand and water into a muddy mist when the red-haired pilot used it to herd the cowering men together.

"This is the police," a voice blared. "Throw down your weapons and put your hands behind your heads."

Talon grabbed his gun from his shoulder holster, rounded on Paolo. "You did this," he screamed, circling toward him. "She's dead, Gianini, you killed her. You double-crossed me."

"Where is she, Talon?" Paolo shouted, circling with him. "I swear to God, if you hurt her—"

Gus grabbed his arm, pointing. "Look."

Paolo squinted through the stinging sand. Holding her hair out of her face, Laura emerged from a police car, looking disheveled but healthy, and Paolo felt his stomach clutch in relief. She scanned the group, found him, and covered her mouth to catch back her own elation. A plainclothes officer sporting a gold shield caught her and drew her back when she started toward Paolo. Other officers began collecting guns and cuffing Dunne's crew. Talon took advantage of Paolo's momentary distraction with Laura to shove him over and snatch the briefcase full of money, then seize Gus.

Paolo lunged out of the sand too late to stop him. Talon put the gun to Gus's head and, using Gus as a shield, backed toward Paolo's car. "Throw me the keys."

Lawmen snapped to attention, covered him.

"Don't do this," Paolo said. He eased his hand under his coat, brought out his own gun, aimed it. "Let him go, Talon."

"Put it down, Gianini," Talon shouted. "Anybody moves, I'll kill him."

"No prisoners, Talon," Paolo shouted back. "You know how it goes."

Talon cocked his weapon, prepared to use it. Nervous spit flecked the corners of his lips; he licked it away. "Put the gun down real slow and throw me the keys, Gianini," he said hoarsely. "I got nothin' to lose here either way, you know I don't. Come on, do it." The gun trembled against Gus's temple, slipped. Paolo locked his eyes on it, biding the moment. "Do it, Gianini," Talon screamed. "If you don't and I twitch, he's dead."

"Maybe," Paolo said softly, easing back his trigger even as Talon's weapon skidded through the sweat on Gus's face and wavered away, "you won't even twitch," he finished, and fired.

Chapter 16

The beach was dark when he arrived after a long day spent answering questions in the city.

It was over; Dunne hadn't been apprehended yet, but Paolo figured that, one way or another, it was only a matter of time before Dunne turned himself in and begged for protection from his own higher-ups. As Mauro had suggested, they were not terribly tolerant of the mess Dunne had created, and were even now undoubtedly looking for a means to...discipline...the screw-up.

On his own side, the local and federal interrogations into this morning's events had been thorough, but there had never really been any doubt that shooting Talon was justified. There would be a follow-up investigation, of course, but the prosecutor's office was inclined toward leniency, since Paolo had saved the life of one the FBI's longest-term deep-cover agents, Special Agent Angus Abernathy.

Paolo wondered how Laura would accept the revelation that still had him reeling. Eight years Gus had been undercover, amassing a questionable record at the same time that he collected and passed on information on money laundering activities in the guise of a mid-level sleaze. He was good, Paolo had to give him that. He'd never tipped his hand once, not even at the end. He'd stay in protective custody until he could testify against Dunne's organization, then take his retirement from the Bureau in the witness protection program. Hell of a thanks for a job well done.

Still, whether or not Gus was a hero in his government's eyes, Paolo didn't like him. He couldn't. Everything Gus had been since long before Paolo had met him had been a history manufactured by men who held the public trust and who believed the end always justified the means. Except his mother. But nothing, in Paolo's eyes, excused the fact that Gus had used Laura, lied to her, endangered her for the sake of his job, and that was something Paolo could not forgive, even though Laura undoubtedly would. Already had. Even without the truth.

He saw her again as she'd looked this morning, watching the paramedics remove Talon's body from the beach. There had been something in her expression, something chilling and remote—an unrepentant relief, a kind of vengeful gladness, a sense of horrified guilt that she could take even the smallest satisfaction in the death of any man, no matter what he'd done.

But when she'd looked at Gus again, the relief had returned, coupled with a kind of sadness at the sight of the handcuffs his cover demanded he submit to. Only she hadn't known about his cover. She thought Gus's arrest was real. And she'd still lifted her chin and watched him go, offered up a crooked smile when he shrugged an "I-wish-it-could-be-any-other-way" apology at her as the police led him away. Still sketched him a small, two-fingered farewell when he turned around and winked at her when the police ducked him into the back of the patrol car.

Still treated him with unconditional forgiveness.

And Paolo wanted what she'd given Gus for himself.

By sending him a copy of the annulment papers, Maria had offered him forgiveness without words; and she had forgiven herself by suffering that demeaning yearlong scrutiny by the church in its search to discover the simple truth that Maria and he had learned, but never admitted, shortly after their wedding: Marrying each other had been a huge mistake. The kind not easily forgiven by either their families or their faith.

By finding someone to truly love, Maria had finally admitted her part in their mistake and had become stronger, passed her strength to him. Mauro, too, offered forgiveness, sought his own strength by coming to face and forgive his father.

So many things he'd put off thinking about, dealing with—until now, when they'd confronted him all at once.

He'd read many things American to prepare himself to become a citizen, to absorb his adopted heritage, among them the thoughts of the dissenters. Thoreau had said that the mass of men lead lives of quiet desperation, unwilling, unable or afraid to reach out and make the changes necessary to better life around them.

Laura, he knew, had forgiven him long ago, as readily as she'd forgiven Gus. Forgiveness was part of her nature, her gift. All that was left for him to do was to accept forgiveness for himself. Then, maybe, he could begin to find the pathways that would give him and his parents closure, find them a way to forgive Lisetta and let her go in peace.

But first there was Laura.

He drew a deep breath and eyed the door on her porch, the door that one way or another led to his future. He hadn't had two minutes with her since this morning, didn't know for sure that he'd be welcomed the way he wanted to be now, but—

He looked at the bouquet of roses and the bottle of champagne in his hands. Trite, but maybe trite was what they needed at this point in their relationship. Courtship rituals. Mauro had suggested them, and Mauro had been right once today already.

And Paolo hoped.

Awkwardly he juggled the champagne and roses into one arm, stiffened one finger and rang the bell. Waited. Couldn't simply invite himself into her life again, had to let her do it.

He looked at the door again. Still waiting. Listened at the window overlooking the porch. Heard nothing. Got worried and tried the door. It was open.

And Dunne hadn't been apprehended yet.

Guard up, Paolo silently placed the wine and roses on the wooden glider beneath the window, eased the door open and slipped into the house.

Except for a faint glow from the direction of the living room, the house was dark. Ducking to look quickly around the doorways before he passed, Paolo moved toward the light.

Behind its glass grate, a small fire crackled in the fireplace;

in front of it, a wedding-ring quilt was spread on the floor and scattered with overstuffed pillows and deep red rose petals. On the coffee table a bottle of Spumante sat in a bucket of melting ice beside a pair of fluted glasses and a bowl of strawberries. A piece of paper with the single word Beach written on it in Laura's precise hand was propped against the bowl.

At the sight of the invitation, Paolo's lungs constricted with an emotion he was more than ready to throw caution to the winds name. Laura had expected him to come.

She wanted him to come.

Without a backward glance, he opened the glass door to the terrace and took the steps, two at a time, down to the beach.

For the first time in days, the night was clear. Stars hung thick and heavy against the black backdrop, the moon suspended clear and luminous to their fore. The beach glowed frosty and silver in the mist from Paolo's breath.

A hundred yards up the shore, Laura stood silhouetted against the moon, watching the ocean breathe water in and out along the sand. Her hair was loose, blowing about her face; she wore rubber boots, loose jeans rolled up her calves, and the creamy thick sweater that matched the one she'd made for him six years ago. Paolo thought she'd never looked more beautiful.

She turned at the sough of his footsteps through the sand. "'Bout time," she said.

"Past it," he agreed.

For a moment they simply looked at each other, at a loss about what came next. It seemed they had everything in the world to talk about, but nothing to say.

"Look, Laura," Paolo said finally, "about Gus—"

"I know." She nodded. "He called. Apologized. I told him I'd have to think about it. It's somethin', isn't it? Eight years, and I never guessed. Some fool, huh?"

"Softhearted," Paolo responded. "Willingly blind. Able to see something in Gus that he couldn't even see in himself. But no, not a fool."

"Thanks," she whispered.

Paolo shut his eyes and held her whisper tight. "You, too."

Silence took up space between them for an instant, then Laura sighed and reached across the void, filling it.

"I love you, Paolie," she said. "For a long time I didn't want to, but wanting to love you didn't seem to have anything to do with anything. I just did.'' She paused, looked at the constant waves. ''I do.''

Paolo's chest went tight; emotion massed inside him, ready to explode. An all-too-treacherous honesty emerged first. ''I love you, too, Laura, but—''

Laura swung furiously on him. ''God, Paolie, let it lie, can't you? What is it with you? You've always got to start with the 'but', find the qualifier. You're always beyond the hope, ahead of it, to the other possibilities. Why can't you just—''

''What do you want from me, Laura, blood?'' Paolo clenched his fists, let his arms swing wide to encompass the night. ''I can't lie to you now by not saying anything— I've done too much of that. I love you, damn it, I *love* you. It's not enough. I'm not good at love—not good at showing you what I feel, or what I want, or what you mean to me, no matter how deep it goes or how much it tears. I don't have any guarantees that you'll always be able to see it, that it'll always show. I always know how you feel, but what's easy for you is hard for me. I don't want to go through what we did again. I don't want to hurt you. Like they say, the spirit is willing—'' He put a hand to his heart, fierce, passionate. ''But in here, even when I want to, I'm afraid to hope. I don't want to live without you, but... Please, Laura...tell me how to prove it. What do I have to do?''

''*Trust* me, Paolie. I'm not the same insecure little mouse I was seven years ago. I don't need the same guarantees. Just you, Paolie. Only you.''

''Are you sure?''

''Oh, God, Paolo. Why do you want to make everything so hard?'' Laura brought a hand to her mouth, covering painful laughter. ''It's not hard, it's easy. Let it be simple. Am I sure? Find out, damn it. You'll never know until you reach, Paolie. Invite me to stay. Only ask.''

''That's what I came to do,'' Paolo whispered. ''But it's harder to trust the future to a few words than I thought.''

''Try,'' Laura whispered. ''Please.''

He looked across the choppy bay, along the barren winter beach, at the water tumbling across the rocks and the milky lace of flake ice along the shore. ''No man is an island,'' Donne had written, ''no man stands alone.'' But without Laura, Paolo was alone, more singular to himself than he'd ever been; if he didn't change the path he was on now, he would be alone always.

Laura had gotten closer to him than any person ever had or, undoubtedly, ever would. If he walked away from her, let her go, as half of him wanted to, he'd lose his last best hope for the future to unforgivable autonomy and regret. He'd lose Laura.

He swallowed. She couldn't change who he was, or what; only he could do that. He couldn't change her. Didn't want to.

His lungs felt frozen, but there wasn't even any wind to justify his lack of breath. He turned. Laura's sigh dropped like warm silence into the night. He drew courage from the sound.

"Laura," he faltered, "Will you..." And he paused.

Then, across the cold, silvered sand, in immutable hope, he offered her his hand.

Epilogue

Dawn.

Sunshine fisted a hole in the winter clouds, poked through to lighten the sky from the edges of the horizon inward, leaving the clouds to settle behind the light. Beneath the intruding rays, in the center of the room suspended above the beach, the wooden bed frame stood, spartan and firm, the only piece of furniture to clutter the space. Around it, blankets painted the hard wood floor in a riot of color, spilled negligently across naked limbs tangled together in the bed.

Wakened by the light, Paolo jacked himself up on an elbow to survey the room, tipping his head back to see the sky. The view seemed—as it always did these days—impossibly limitless, broad and unending, filled with light and an absence of gray. Because of Laura.

Beside him, Laura sighed in her sleep and turned on her side, snuggling against him. Emotion rushed in at Paolo, and he reached to gather her in, tucking his arm around her, holding her fast and burying his face in her neck: his right, his woman.

His wife.

Again he glanced toward the sky, toward the purpling-gray

tinges of dawn. Down the hall, at the other end of the house, Mauro slept, another link to reconciling his past. An opportunity.

Laura had taken Mauro in immediately, no questions, no hesitation. No jealousy over the time Paolo had needed to spend with his son. He'd been wrong to ever doubt her ability to accommodate and consolidate all the pieces of his life—to fit them into the crazy quilt that was *their* life. If he'd shared his trials, tribulations, his sons with her all those years ago, then maybe...

His arms tightened fiercely around Laura. No, he'd promised himself he wouldn't do this, wouldn't entertain the doubts, the maybes, the what ifs. Now was not the moment to lament lost time, but for making the most of this time, this present, this future. For not screwing up again.

He dipped his head to kiss Laura's neck, smoothed her hair with his cheek. Mauro considered his father a lucky man to have found Laura twice in one lifetime. God knew, Paolo thought, he didn't deserve to be, he'd done everything possible in his life to avoid happiness, but happy he was. And lucky. And grateful. Because Laura was at least twice as stubborn as he was and six times as resilient and ten times as willing to filter out the bad to balance the love.

He had a long way to go to right the wrongs he'd committed in his life, but the prospect no longer daunted him. In March, when spring hinted, he, Laura and Mauro would go to Italy. Giani had agreed to see him and, although Maria wouldn't make promises, she herself had decided to talk to Edouardo about his father, to urge reconciliation and forgiveness. A man without his father's name was still a man, but a man who shunned his father's heart would always be less than he might be. It had taken Paolo twenty years to learn that, but he understood it now. He would act on the lesson by going to Milan to see his own father, his mother, to reconcile where he could, to ask forgiveness where it was needed—to at least open the door to a reconstructed future. To lay his sister and the discomfort of his past to rest...

Laura sighed and stirred in his arms, nuzzled his chest.

...but that was tomorrow.

His heart filled and he smiled and bent to her, found the sleepy pliability of her mouth, reveled in the instant response of her body to the seeking pressure of his. For right now, this instant, Laura lay beside him, her ring was on his finger, his heart lay open in her hands. He'd already gotten back the most impossible joy of all. No matter what wintry waters lay ahead, everything from now seemed possible.

* * * * *

American HEROES
AGAINST ALL ODDS

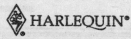

Please address questions and book requests to: Harlequin Reader Service U.S.: 3010 Walden Ave., P.O. Box 1325, Buffalo, NY 14269 CAN.: P.O. Box 609, Fort Erie, Ont. L2A 5X3

PAHGEN

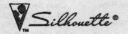

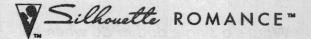